A. G Callant

Saint Mungo's Bells

Or, old Glasgow stories rung out anew

A. G Callant

Saint Mungo's Bells
Or, old Glasgow stories rung out anew

ISBN/EAN: 9783744750523

Printed in Europe, USA, Canada, Australia, Japan

Cover: Foto ©Andreas Hilbeck / pixelio.de

More available books at **www.hansebooks.com**

SAINT MUNGO

OR

OLD GLASGOW

RUNG OUT

BY

A. G. CAL...

FULL-PAGE ILLUSTRATIONS.

———

ILLUSTRATIONS IN THE TEXT.

INTRODUCTION.

A LTHOUGH never· "a penniless lass," Glasgow can boast of "a lang pedigree." Fifty-seven years before the Anglo-Saxon King Edwin set Edinburgh Castle on its rocky site, St Kentigern had founded, in the year 560, the bishopric of Glasgow, and there is reason to believe that the city on the banks of the Clyde was not then in its infancy, for· the patron saint was chief director and prime minister of the kingdom of Strathclyde, and a man not at all likely to bury his talents in a solitude. During the troubled years of Queen Mary, when the University of Edinburgh was just struggling into existence, our Western College was already one hundred and thirty-eight years old. Whilst that of Edinburgh owes its origin to the era of the Reformation, Glasgow can point to a bull of Pope Nicholas V., dated 7th January 1450, for her certificate of birth. Both cities were made royal burghs by the same king—William the Lion (1180).

A Glasgow shopkeeper made the objection to Edinburgh that "there was too much grass in it." While allowing the force of the remark from his purely mercantile point of view, it will be admitted that in the capital on the Clyde the green blades are rather too few and far between to satisfy those whose appetites crave after the beautiful and romantic. The idea of this little book is to cast a few seeds here and there even among the hard paving stones of the city, where, in defiance of ironclad hoof and wheel, they may find a lodg-ment, and in spite of soot and "chemicals" spring up fresh and green to remind the sons and daughters of Glasgow of olden times, and recall voices of the past that it may be well, amidst the din and bustle of the present, sometimes to listen to. Our intention is not to dig and undermine these stony streets of ours for ancient bones and fossil remains. We have no time or capability for unearthing the altogether forgotten. We have simply collected from many sources, and arranged in convenient form, a gathering of interesting facts about Glasgow. We do not pretend to manufacture or cast the bells. Our duty is simply to pull the ropes, and let them tell their story in their own clear, sweet tones, as they were wont to do in the days of long ago. Our book is not a history of Glasgow, but it contains some historic facts that have been overlooked by historians. Many interesting topics we have been compelled to leave untouched through want of space.

"Glasgow for Bells," says the old rhyme, and they have long been famous. In "St Mungo's Bells" will be found a little about them all, from the Bell o' the Brae to Sheriff Bell, not forgetting Henry of the "Comet."

We have gratefully to acknowledge the valuable assistance given by Mr Mathew Shields, who revised much of our MS., and the kindness of Sheriff Rampini and the Rev. G. D. M'Naughton for their contributions on St Kentigern. We have also to thank Mr J. O. Mitchell for the loan of his old hero, "David Dale." And last, but by no means least, Mr John Burroughs, who gave his cordial consent to our bringing his "First Impressions of the Clyde" in "Strange Pastures" again before the notice of his constituents in Glasgow.

Our full-page illustrations have been taken from views that are now very rare. The Trongait and Broomielaw are copied from old prints published by Foulis about 1750. Glasgow from the Green is from an original painting by H. W. Williams, executed about 1795. The Cathedral is from a print of about 1835, and shows the look of the building and its surroundings before the alterations were made. Our smaller illustrations are also of antiquarian interest.

Glasgow, more than most cities, is a place of the present, but she has a past history of which we may all well be proud. Our purpose, as we have said, is to remind the townsfolk of to-day of the stirring events that have happened, and the stirring men who have lived in former times within sound of St Mungo's Bells.

ST MUNGO'S BELLS;

OR,

OLD GLASGOW STORIES RUNG OUT ANEW.

———◦◆◦———

GLASGOW VERY LONG AGO.

THE earliest records of Glasgow are of a maritime order. Down among the alluvial clay of the banks of the Clyde, ancient canoes, or "dug-out" boats, have from time to time been discovered. How long it is since these were deposited it is not easy to say, but very great changes must have taken place on the face of the country since then. Hugh Miller says: "Where the city of Glasgow now stands, three ancient boats—one of which is in the Antiquarian Museum, Edinburgh, and another in the Andersonian Museum—have been dug up since the year 1781; the last not many years ago. One of the number was found a full quarter of a mile from the Clyde, and about twenty-six feet above its level at high water. It reposed, too, not on a laminated silt, such as the river now deposits, but on a pure sea sand." "It therefore appears," says Mr Robert Chambers, in his ingenious work on "Raised Beaches," "that we have scarcely an alternative to the supposition that when these vessels foundered and were deposited where in modern times they have been found, the Firth of Clyde was a sea several miles wide at Glasgow, covering the site of the lower districts of the city, and receiving the waters of the river not lower than Bothwell Bridge." "I may add," continues Hugh Miller, "that the Glasgow boat in the Antiquarian Museum is such a rude canoe—hollowed out of a single trunk—as may be seen in use among such of the Polynesian islands as lie most out of the reach of civilisa-

A

tion, or in the Indian Archipelago, among the rude Alforian
races; and that in another of these boats, the first discovered, there was found a beautifully polished hatchet of
dark green stone—an unequivocal indication that they
belonged to the Stone Period."

The inference drawn generally is that the change of level
of much of the coast-line of Scotland took place within the
human period, and possibly just before historic times.
That it was before the period of the Roman occupation,
there is no room to doubt, from the traces of Roman
remains on the low-lying land.

No one can look on these relics of our ancestors without
being impressed with the amazing development of the art of
shipbuilding, whose home has been so long upon the Clyde.

Tradition survives in a shadowy form connecting Glasgow
with a settlement of Druids in the misty past, many years
before St Mungo was born, telling of sacrifices that were
wont to be offered on the hill where now stands the
Necropolis. The Drygait is said to have been the Druids'
gait, and here is supposed to have been the site of their
dwelling-places. In the Saxon tongue the word *Dry* is the
equivalent for a priest or holy man. In the Celtic it is
Druidh. The tradition will find ready belief, as many will
testify from personal knowledge how accurate is the title.

Tradition also connects the Druids with an old grove
near the church of the Blackfriars.

The Romans of necessity must have been about the
vicinity of Glasgow, for it lies near the track of the Wall of
Antoninus. Like the real gentlemen they were, they left
some coin behind. In Possil Moss, a leather bag containing
about two hundred silver Roman coins was found.

An old Roman road from Carluke is supposed to have
entered Glasgow by Bellshill, Tollcross, East Duke Street,
and the Drygait, crossing the Molendinar Burn, and con-
tinuing by Dobbies' Loan.

About the end of the fourth century the sylvan beauty of
the place, and the crystal purity of the Molendinar and its
overshadowing trees, attracted the notice of the famous St
Ninian, the earliest native Scottish missionary, for here he
built a sacred retreat for himself, sometime before he founded
the church of Whithorn, in Galloway, which is looked upon
as the first Christian Kirk of Scotland.

ST KENTIGERN.

BY SHERIFF RAMPINI.

WHEN the last Roman soldier had left the shores of Britain, the southern portion of the island, with the exception of Wales, fell at once into the hands of the Saxons. It was otherwise with Scotland. For six hundred years afterwards the country was a battlefield on which four contending peoples fought for the supremacy. In the beginning of the seventh century, the first heat of conflict had been so far assuaged that we find the various races settled each within determinate bounds of its own. Four states had been established; but their reciprocal rivalry continued undiminished, and as yet it was hard to say which of the four was destined to be the ultimate victor in the struggle.

The four kingdoms of ancient Alban were situated as follows :—To the north of the Firths of Forth and Clyde, and separated from each other by the great dorsal range of Drumalban, were the kingdoms of the Scots of Dalriada on the west, and of the Picts on the east. To the south of these estuaries lay the kingdoms of the Britons of Strathclyde on the west, and of the Angles of Bernicia on the east. The two modern counties of Kirkcudbright and Wigtown were occupied by a body of Picts, called by Bede, Niduari. From the Welsh and Irish form of the name of this district is derived its present appellation of Galloway.* Each of these separate kingdoms had its own language, its own customs, in short, a distinct individuality of its own; and traces of these characteristics are to be found in the history of the Scottish people long after these four petty principalities had been amalgamated into one.

The most important, the shortest lived, yet perhaps the most interesting of them all was that of the Britons of Strathclyde. On the rocky summit of Alcluith, which, under the appellation of Dumbarton—the fort of the Britons—still preserves its memory, stood the capital of this long-forgotten principality. Its territories extended from the Clyde to the

* Skene's " Celtic Scotland," i. 239.

Derwent, and included not only the five south-western
shires of Dumfries, Ayr, Renfrew, Lanark, and Peebles, but
the modern English counties of Northumberland and West-
moreland. Here, after their expulsion from the province
by the hordes of barbarians who, on the withdrawal of the
Roman troops, took possession of its fertile acres, the
Romanised Britons retreated, carrying with them their
Christianity, and something, at least, of that superficial
culture for which they had bartered their manhood to their
Roman masters. It seems to have been a sort of ethnic
Cave of Adullam to all who possessed the slightest tincture
of Celtic blood. The Welsh, Cornish, and Latin tongues
were all to be heard within its borders. Its population
contained both Cymric and Gael, pagan and Christian, the
disciple of the Druid priest and the proselyte of the Catholic
Church. In this fact, indeed, is to be found the social
interest which attaches to its history. For many a long day
before the various petty chieftainships which had been
established within its territory had been amalgamated into
one state, it had been the arena of a fierce conflict between
paganism and Christianity; but the blood-fray of Arderydd
in 573 had secured the triumph of the faith, and shortly
afterwards we find Rederchen the Liberal seated on the
throne as the first monarch of the Britons of Cumbria or
Strathclyde. This result was due to the exertions of one
man, and that man was St Kentigern, otherwise known as
St Mungo.

He was one of those master-minds which appear in seasons
of great social and political confusion, for the express
purpose, as it seems, of evolving order out of chaos, and of
re-establishing things on a newer and firmer basis. In his
high and inordinate ambition he belonged to that type of
ecclesiastical statesmen of which Wolsey in England,
Richelieu in France, and David Beaton in Scotland are
familiar examples. But as he differed from all of these in
the blameless sanctity of his life, so also he differed from
them in the aim and object of all his ambition. With a
singleness of purpose from which nothing could make him
swerve, he sought to glorify the Church of which he was at
once a ruler and a servant. To this every thought and
act of his life was consecrated. He desired to make the
State subservient to the Church; he laboured with all his

might to exalt the one that it might reflect glory on the other; he transformed an obscure chieftain into a powerful monarch only to hear him acknowledge that it was to the aid of the Church that he owed his kingdom; and if in his own person he aspired to be both priest and king,—the Melchisedek of his day and generation,—this was from no selfish pride, no personal vanity, but of set purpose to show to the world that the Church was subject to no human power, but owned allegiance to Christ or His vicar alone.

Rather above the middle height, of commanding presence, yet with dove-like eyes; clothed all in spotless white, his garments made of the skins of goats, with a coat like a fisherman's bound upon him, and white alb, and a stole over his shoulder; in one hand a pastoral staff of bent wood, in the other, his manual book; sleeping upon a hollowed stone, "celebrating the Lord's night watches with psalms and hymns and spiritual songs," rising before day-light to plunge into the icy waters of the mountain-brook; with low voice and measured words preaching by his silence rather than by his speech,—he stands forth a clear and vigorous personality, even amidst all the myth and marvel and legend and fable with which his biographer, Jocelyn, has invested him. We know, indeed, no more of his life and work than the pious monk of Furness has told us. But this little is sufficient to stamp his impress upon the history of his age.

He was of royal though of illegitimate birth. His mother, the daughter of a "most Pagan king who ruled in the northern part of Britannia," was at an early age converted to Christianity. Betrayed by the son of a neighbouring chieftain, she was—so runs the legend—ordered, in accord-ance with the strict but barbarous law of those days, to expiate her offence by being hurled from the top of Taprain Law. She alighted unhurt at the bottom. But the justice of the people was unsatisfied. Placed in a "very little boat of hides, made after the fashion of the Scotti," she was carried out to sea, and, without oar or sail, left to the fortunes of the elements. The frail skiff drifted across the Firth of Forth to Culross; and there on the desolate shore, by the ashes of a fire which some fishermen had left, her son was born. It chanced that in the neighbourhood, surrounded by a little family of clerics and disciples, there lived a godly

man, whom tradition, without the slightest authority for the
statement, has identified with St Servanus.*   Carried thither
by the shepherds who had found them, the saint received
the young mother and her infant into his dwelling, and here,
after they had been "dipped in the laver of regeneration
and restoration," Taneu and her son continued to reside
until the time arrived for the lad's entrance into the practical
work of the ministry.

Many significant incidents are recorded by his simple
biographer of the boy's early years.   His master's love for
him excited the jealousy of his fellow-scholars; but the
child's innocence and holiness triumphed over all their
machinations.   When they killed the pet redbreast of the
saint and blamed Kentigern for its death, his prayers
restored the bird to life.   When they extinguished the
sacred fire in the church in order to get him into trouble,
his breath brought down fire from heaven upon a little hazel
bough to rekindle it.   His power of working miracles
increased with his years and with his growth in grace.
Many chapters in Jocelyn's life are devoted to his wonder-
working powers, and to the manifestations of divine power
which rewarded the purity and holiness of his life.   Trivial
as they may seem to us now, they are invaluable evidence
to the age in and for which it was written of the surpassing
virtues and excellence of the man of whom they were
recorded.

At length the time came when Kentigern received his
call.   Departing secretly and by night, he journeyed along
the shores of the Firth of Forth till he reached a river
estuary, whose waters divided to let him pass dry-shod.
When he had reached the opposite bank, he turned to look
back. The tide had once more returned to its wonted
channel, and above the bank, supporting his tottering limbs
with a staff, stood his old master, with tears and gestures
entreating him to return to his home.   But Kentigern had
put his hand to the plough, and for him there was no return.
He pointed out to his sorrowing master that between them
a great gulf, both moral and physical, was fixed, which it
was impossible to cross.   The two holy men then mutually
blessed each other and parted, never to look upon each
other's faces again.

---

* Skene's "Celtic Scotland," i. 184.

A journey begun under such circumstances could not fail to be attended with miraculous incidents, but for these we must refer the reader to Jocelyn himself. In process of time he arrived at "Cathures, which is now called Glasgu," and here, elected by the unanimous voice of the Christians of the district to the episcopate, he established his cathedral seat, and "united to himself a famous and God-beloved family of servants of God, who practised continence, and who lived after the fashion of the primitive Church under the apostle, without private property, in holy discipline and Divine service." But evil days were in store for him. His Christian followers were few, whilst paganism was rampant throughout the whole district over which he claimed episcopal authority.

Expelled from his episcopate, he wandered for some time among the mountains of Cumberland. Finally, led by a boar, he selected a site for a monastery at Llanelwy, afterwards called St Asaph's, in the romantic vale of Clwyd, where he continued to reside in peace and quiet until the death of his enemies enabled him to return to his original diocese.

A youth and manhood of local was fitly succeeded by an old age of national usefulness. In their proud and simple dignity the latter years of his life stand out in striking contrast to the florid magnificence of that brave but ductile prince whom his influence had seated on the throne of Strathclyde. Rederchen, despite his Roman descent, was in many respects the true type of the gaudy and reckless barbarian. While the monarch was busied with the enjoyment of the pomp and circumstances of his newly found royalty, the bishop was occupied in engrossing to himself that power which Rederchen seems to have regarded as the only drawback to his kingship. It was indolence, indeed, rather than gratitude, which prompted him to avail himself of the earliest opportunity to divest himself of the cares of government. "Stripping himself of his royal robes, on bended knees and hands joined, he gave his homage to St Kentigern, and handed over to him the dominion and princedom over all his kingdom, and willed that he should be king, and himself the ruler of his country under him as his father, as he knew that formerly the great Emperor Constantine had done to St Silvester. Hence the custom grew up for a long course of years, so long as the Cambrian kingdom lasted in its own proper rank, that the prince was always subject to the bishop." Hence, too, the diocese was always co-extensive with the kingdom,—an important fact, upon which all our knowledge of the extent of the latter is based. The power so strangely placed in Kentigern's hands was not misused. In temporal, as in spiritual affairs, the new kingdom grew apace. It opposed a formidable barrier to Saxon aggression. It sent out missionaries to the Orkneys, to Norway, and to Iceland. It "cleansed from the foulness of idolatry and contagion of heresy the land of the Picts, which is now called Galweithia, with the adjacent parts." It fostered the arts and cherished learning. But though it subsisted until the beginning of the tenth century, and although the descendants of Rederchen's line were to be found among its monarchs for many a long generation, our interest in it as a kingdom dies with the man who gave it birth. When, in extreme old age, and fortified by angelic visions and voices, St Kentigern rested from his labours, our knowledge and our concerns in the state which he founded both alike vanish away.

The following account of St Mungo is from the pen of the Rev. G. D. M'Naughton, B.D., Braco :—

Crossing the Forth, probably near Alloa, passing the night at Kernack (Carnock), he next morning, in a waggon drawn by unbroken oxen, strikes boldly to the south-west. Reaching at last the banks of the Clyde, near where the Molendinar Burn poured into it its as yet pure waters, he determines to settle there, and building a little wooden church he dedicates it to the Holy Trinity.

At first Kentigern did not make much impression upon the rough peasantry of Strathclyde. It was not the first time that the Christian faith had been taught in these regions. More than a century before, St Ninian, from his little church on the Wigtownshire coast as a centre, had done something to make the name of Christ known in the whole country to the south of the Grampians, and some small fragments of his influence still remained. But the mass of the community had long relapsed into heathenism, if indeed it had ever been even nominally Christian. The king, Morken, throned upon the rock of Dumbarton, was bitterly opposed to the new faith. All that Kentigern could do was to sow in patience the seed or Christian instruction, with but little prospect of ever reaping a harvest. After a time this became impossible; so keen was the spirit of opposition aroused, that to save his life he was obliged to leave the scene of his missionary labours on the banks of the Clyde and to seek refuge in Wales.

Here he founded the great monastery of Llanelwy in North Wales, on the banks of the river Clwyd, so called perhaps as reminding him of that fairer stream in the distant north, by the side of which he had sought to dwell, and from which he had been driven. Llanelwy became a large and flourishing institution, containing no less than 965 brothers. These were divided into three classes—the elder monks being engaged in teaching; the younger in learning; while the working brothers performed all the necessary labours both outside and in the monastery. In the chapel divine service was celebrated both day and night, that being the monastic idea of obedience to the apostolic injunction to "pray without ceasing." Kentigern himself, with those brothers whom he thought most suited for the purpose, was accustomed to preach the gospel in all the surrounding districts. In Llanelwy we have a graphic picture of one of those little Christian colonies, by means of which it was that our country was gradually won to Christ. Many years were here spent by St Kentigern, both piously and profitably, St Asaph being one of his disciples, and at last his successor.

For, in the meantime, events were transpiring in the north which were to drag Kentigern from his Welsh exile, and to restore him to the banks of the Clyde. The seed which he had sown in tears had grown up and was beginning to ripen. The Christian party in Strathclyde had been gradually increasing in strength. Matters at last came to a crisis and the arbitrament of the sword. At the great battle of Arthuret, on the Esk, some miles north of Carlisle, in the year 573 A.D., pagan and Christian contended for the mastery. The result was a victory for the cross, and the Christian leader, Rydderch or Roderick, was raised to the throne. A religious revolution had been accomplished in the midst of the political convulsion, and one of the first steps of the new monarch was to recall Kentigern. At first there was a natural hesitation on the part of the saint to quit his

peaceful retreat, and to renew the stormier labours of his
youth.   But this hesitation did not last long.   He is said to
have received an angelic admonition :—"Go back unto
Glasgow," said the heavenly voice, "unto thine own
church, and there thou shalt be for a great nation, and the
Lord will make thee to increase among His people.   Thou
shalt gain unto the Lord a holy nation, and a possession of
a people that cannot be numbered, and from Him thou
shalt receive an everlasting crown."

Accompanied by six hundred brethren, a little Christian
army, he set out for the north.   At Hoddam, in Dumfries-
shire, he was met by King Roderick with a hearty welcome.
There he delivered his first sermon as chief Christian pastor
of the kingdom, criticising the hitherto dominant paganism,
showing that "idols were dumb, the vain inventions of men,
fitter for the fire than for worship, and that the elements
in which they believed as deities were creatures adapted
by the disposition of their Maker to the use, help, and
assistance of men."   From this time onwards, the Church
of the Holy Trinity, beside the Molendinar Burn, became
again the centre of Christian endeavour.   No longer having
the old difficulties to contend with, the preaching of the
gospel was rewarded with some measure of success, and
the heathenism of Strathclyde became more and more
leavened with its power.   Kentigern was the person of
greatest importance in the whole kingdom.   The halo of
miracle once more gathers round his head.   To this time
belong the stories of the queen's missing ring, which, by the
saint's intercessions, was found inside a salmon caught in
the Clyde ; of the ram's head turned into stone, long commemorated in the name of one of the city churches, the
Ramshorn Kirk, which is now St David's.   Much more
interesting is the record of a visit paid by the apostle of
Iona and Pictland to the apostle of Glasgow and Strathclyde.   His outposts by this time were south of the Tay.   A
Gaelic monastery had been founded at Kingarth, in Bute,
and was soon to send an offshoot to Dunblane.   The whole
western coast was Christian.   The two saints, the Gael and
the Briton, might well congratulate each other on what had
been done.   At all events they met, and at parting inter-
changed their pastoral staves in pledge and testimony of
their mutual love in Christ.

In the meantime years were passing over Kentigern's head in the midst of his many labours. His influence was felt over the whole south-west of Scotland. There would, doubtless, be much heathenism left, much pagan ferocity of character, but the milder spirit of the gospel, a higher tone of thought and feeling, had begun to influence human hearts. The whole district, thus for the first time Christianised, has ever since continued to be in some sense Christian.

Kentigern, in spite of his ascetic practices, lived to extreme old age. He passed peacefully away in his bath one January morning in the beginning of the seventh century, and was buried in what is now the crypt of the Cathedral.

The little Church of the Holy Trinity became in the Middle Ages the glorious cathedral of St Mungo. Around it the great city of Glasgow has gradually clustered itself. Other towns have found the reason of their existence in a castle rock, round which they have gathered for protection, but the founder of Glasgow was a preacher, and its first building was a church. St Mungo (for people have taken kindlier to the pet name than to the statelier Kentigern) has always been its patron saint. Tons of wax have been burned in his honour, and his bell was long a precious relic. In the arms of the city we have a condensed record of his legendary history. The fish and the ring are there; the tree, the robin, and the bell; while the whole is surmounted by a figure with a bishop's mitre, a crook in his left hand, and the right hand raised in the attitude of preaching. The motto, "Let Glasgow flourish by the preaching of the Word," even though modern, is not without a truth in it, inasmuch as it was the preaching of Kentigern which laid the foundation of the city's greatness.

The saint's mother has a history of her own. She followed her son to the west, lived in the odour of sanctity, and died a saint, and had a chapel dedicated in her honour, which was entitled to its annual stones of wax from the pious burghers of Glasgow. In Protestant times her very name has been lost; a curious fate has joined together a British princess and an antediluvian patriarch, and a people which has known its Old Testament better than its national history has confounded St Theneu with St Enoch.

THE BELLS SILENT!

FOR five hundred years history is silent as regards Glasgow. There is not the faintest clink of St Mungo's Bells for all that time, but in the contemporary history of the country it is still possible to catch the sound of their echo. These five hundred years saw the British and Christian kingdom of Strathclyde involved in constant warfare, now with the Scots and Picts, and now with the Angles of the East, and now with the Saxons of the South. When at last the Northern hosts had united their strength against the latter, and one king ruled over all Scotland, a breathing space came. The country was not so far back then in civilisation as is generally supposed. There are probably as many savages in Glasgow to-day as there were in all Strathclyde in those days. Nearly the whole of Scotland had been Christianised, chiefly by the efforts of such men as Columba and Kentigern. From the islands of the west, the Culdees, or " Servants of God," had spread the knowledge of the true religion far and wide. Wherever the prefix *Kil* occurs in the names of places, it is believed there was a Culdee station within this period. Kilmarnock, Kilbride, Kilsyth, Killermont, Kilbowie, Kilbirnie, Kilwinning, &c., are instances of names in the neighbourhood of Glasgow. A Culdee settlement was at Manuel, near Linlithgow, named, as many others were, in honour of Emmanuel. What manner of men these Culdees were there is now good documentary evidence to show. One or two points are worthy of notice.   ·

It appears that the Culdees succeeded by hereditary right to their office, and that the property of each was at death divided between his widow and children, or nearest relation. The Culdees cannot therefore be correctly named monks, or their establishments monasteries.

The early Scottish Church resisted the encroachments and errors of Rome. Whilst Wilfrid of Devonshire, under the name of Boniface, was devoting all his energies to the service of the popedom, in connection with the propagation of Christianity in the northern parts of Europe, he was met and opposed by such men as Clemens, Samson, Virgilius, John of Mailros, and others of Scottish descent, who were the boldest protesters against the usurpations of Rome. The first of these especially, both in Scotland and on the Continent, was the determined antagonist of Boniface; and so serious was his opposition, that the latter at length obtained an order from the pope for his deposition from office, and, there is reason to believe, for his perpetual imprisonment. The points the Scots chiefly insisted in opposition to Boniface were :—"(1) That he studied to win men to the subjection of the pope, and not to the obedience of Christ; (2) That he laboured to establish a sovereign authority in the pope's person, as if he only were the successor of the apostles, whereas all bishops are successors as well as he; (3) That he went about the abolishment of priests' marriages, and extolling a single life above measure; and (4) That he caused masses to be said for the dead, erected images in churches, and introduced divers rites unknown to the ancient Church." Boniface, in his letter to the pope, charges Clemens with refusing the authority of the canons and the fathers, with maintaining the right of priests to marry, and with various theological errors.*

At that early period, churches and monasteries were not built of stone, either in Scotland or England. Bishop the Blessed, Abbot of Wearmouth, near the close of the seventh century, is celebrated as the person who first introduced stone buildings into use in England; but even at a period subsequent to this, King Edgar, in the charter he granted to the Abbey of Malmesbury, in 974, says, "All the monasteries of my realm, to the sight are nothing but worm-eaten and rotten timber boards." Bede, speaking of the building of the church at Lindisfarne by Finan, head of the Scottish missionaries, says expressly, that "after the *manner of the Scots*, he made it, not of stone, but of hewn oak, and covered it with reeds." We may rest assured then that the buildings erected by St Kentigern and his followers were mere wooden huts covered with thatch.

Notwithstanding the incorporation of Strathclyde with Scotland, the inhabitants still bore the Welsh name, and were mainly Cymri, till past even the time of David I.

---

* See " Iona," by Rev. W. L. Alexander, D.D., page 118 ; Petrie's " History of the Catholic Church," page 100 ; Spottiswood's " History of the Church of Scotland," page 20.

At the battle of the Standard, in 1138, the "Cumbrenses" and the "Tevidalenses," or Britons of Strathclyde, formed the second division of the heterogeneous army called Scots, which was led to disaster by the Scottish king.   After 1165 the Britons seem to have been wholly merged in the general population.   The absorption of the Cymri and their spoken language points to a large immigration of the Saxon population from Northumbria and other parts of England, who were feeling the pressure of the Norman domination. Professor Veitch mentions two sirnames which at least are purely Cymric,—those of Wallace or *Welsh*, and Kerr or *Caer*.   Others we think might be quoted, but there can be no doubt that the hero of Scotland's freedom and the men who founded Glasgow belonged to the same stock, of which race also came the Covenanters of the west.

The Church was reconstituted during the twelfth century. Before then we have no national documentary evidence of contemporary date; but now land came to be held by feudal charter, important transactions are set forth in formal documents attested by many witnesses, carefully composed chronicles by churchmen make their appearance, and the historian is no longer left to grope in darkness.   The Parish system was established, Diocesan Episcopacy and the Monastic Orders of Rome were introduced chiefly by the help of the sovereign and the Saxon and Norman settlers. The Culdees were suppressed or superseded if they did not cast in their lot with the new system.   The bishopric of Glasgow was founded or restored, and the diocese extended. It was divided into two archdeaconries, and these again into deaneries.   Its cathedral constitution followed the model of Salisbury.   Organs and choirs were introduced in the thirteenth century.   In the early part of the reign of King William, Glasgow had possessed twenty-five churches and their revenues, and several more were added.   The pope deprived the Culdees of their right of electing the bishop. A stout resistance was made, and it was not until 1273 that they were finally robbed of this privilege.

In the twelfth century the diocese of Glasgow was held to comprise the country from England to the northern extremity of Loch Lomond and the Forth.   It included Dumfriesshire, the eastern portion of Galloway, nearly all Roxburghshire, Selkirk, Peebles, Lanark, Ayr, Renfrew, and Dumbarton

shires, and the half of Stirling,—two hundred and forty
parishes in all. By a bull of 1175 all the clergy of the
diocese were commanded to visit Glasgow once a year. It
is not without significance that the diocese of Glasgow was
coextensive with the old kingdom of Strathclyde in the
earlier time, except that the latter extended into the north
of England.

THE CATHEDRAL BUILT.

To return more closely to our subject. As we have stated,
St Mungo's death took place in 601, and for five hundred
years little is known of the church he had founded; but
during the reign of Alexander I., the site of the original
edifice on the banks of the Molendinar was chosen for the
Cathedral of the West. It was erected by David I., the son
of Malcolm Canmore and St Margaret, and in 1115 the
king's chaplain, John Achaius, a man of great learning, was
made bishop.

The building was consecrated on the 7th July 1136. It
was burned down in 1192. A new edifice was consecrated
by Bishop Joceline on 6th July 1197, and it was at this
period that the crypt was built and the tomb erected to the
memory of St Mungo. Bishop Joceline had obtained a
charter from King William the Lion in 1180, constituting
the town of Glasgow into a burgh of barony holding of the
bishop; the charter also conferred the right of holding an
annual eight days' fair in July, so it may be observed that
Glasgow Fair is a very ancient institution. The king endorsed by royal letters the movement to raise funds for the
rebuilding of the cathedral, with an unction and pathos worthy
of church bazaar announcements of to-day. He deplores
"the desolation which had befallen the see of Glasgow—
that church which, though poor and lowly in temporal
estate, is the spiritual mother of many tribes," alluding to
the various tongues and kindred which peopled the west of
Scotland at that time, and paying a tribute to the influence
of St Kentigern, the memory of whose work was still fresh
and green.

SIR WILLIAM WALLACE.

IT is something to remember that Glasgow was fought for by Wallace; this was part of his native Scotland that had to be cleared of the Southern oppressor, and how well he did it we know.

Edward I. had appointed a minion of his own, Anthony Beik, to the see of Glasgow; whilst Earl Percy, as governor of the west of Scotland, made himself at home in the episcopal palace beside the Cathedral.

Wallace with his uncle, Adam Wallace of Riccarton, and the Laird of Auchinleck, and three hundred horsemen, marched by night from Ayr, crossed the Clyde by the horse-ford or by the wooden bridge of Glasgow, and drew up on the ground now occupied by the Briggait. One division of a hundred and forty under Auchinleck made a circuit and approached by the east, whilst Wallace advanced by the High Street.

Tradition says the English numbered one thousand, and when it is borne in mind that the Scottish leader not only excelled in personal daring, but was the foremost military genius of his time, there is no reason to doubt the statement. In all probability the Scots would receive assistance from the townsmen of Glasgow.

The scene of the conflict was near the old College at the Bell o' the Brae in the High Street, where a desperate hand-to-hand conflict took place. Wallace slew Percy with his own broadsword, and Auchinleck coming upon them in the rear, the English fled. Bishop Beik made good his escape. Wallace pursued, and the same day defeated a party of Northumbrians at Bothwell, winning two victories in one day. Two months afterwards, on 11th September 1297, he gained the great triumph of Stirling Bridge.

A PATRIOTIC BISHOP.

BISHOP ROBERT WISHART was elected to the office in 1271, and his name is held in high honour chiefly by reason of the evil reports that were brought against him in his life-

time, for the accuser was none other than our ancient
oppressor Edward I. of England.   He took up his quarters
at the Blackfriars in the Dominican Convent (which stood
on the east side of High Street), in August and September
1301, determined to overawe, in a fortnight, the western
district where the cause of Scottish freedom has for ever
had its home; and he sent a complaint to the pope, accusing
Wishart of not only not excommunicating Robert the Bruce
for slaying Cumin, but for giving him absolution five days
after the deed, and for providing him out of his own ward-
robe with the robe in which he was crowned at Scone.
Longshanks also charges the bishop with going through the
country preaching that it was more meritorious to fight for
the new king than against the infidel Saracens ; and accuses
him of raising money on false pretences, having obtained
timber to make a spire for the Cathedral, and instead of
that, constructing battering-rams and engines of war for
besieging the castle of Kirkintilloch.

Wishart had been appointed one of the Lords of the
Regency upon the death of Alexander III. in 1286, and
protested vigorously against the pretensions of Edward I.
at Norham Castle, maintaining the independence of Scotland against our arch-enemy there.   In 1306 the Bishop unfortunately fell into the hands of the English at Cupar-Fife,
and was kept a prisoner in England for eight years. Bannockburn secured his deliverance, but he had become blind.   He
died in November 1316, and was buried in the Cathedral. His
lifetime had been in the hour of Scotland's darkest trial,
and there was no sturdier patriot than he, as Edward has
testified.

A SEA FIGHT AND ITS CONSEQUENCES.

DURING the reign of David Bruce of Scotland and Edward
III. of England, the two countries were continuously at war.
About the Feast of the Assumption in 1337 two Scottish ships,
whilst on the voyage from France to Scotland, were attacked,
and after a stout resistance were taken, by the English
admiral, John de Ross.   On board were John Lindesay,
Bishop of Glasgow, and with him many noble ladies of
Scotland, men at arms, much armour, £30,000 of money,

B

and a treaty between France and Scotland. The soldiers were all killed or drowned. The lord bishop and part of these noble ladies from very grief refused to eat or drink, and died before the fleet reached English land. They were buried at Wystande in England.

It was William Rae, the bishop who succeeded Lindsay, who built Stockwell Bridge. He died in 1367.

In 1473 Robert Blackadder obtained a bull from Pope Alexander VI. erecting the see of Glasgow into an Archbishopric. Blackadder, who was a favourite of James IV., founded the aisle known by his name in 1490, and made many improvements on the Cathedral. He had a good deal to do with the persecution of the Lollards of Kyle, and died while on a pilgrimage to Jerusalem on 28th July 1508. His successor was James Beaton, the first of the Fife family. He was translated to St Andrews in 1523. Both he and his nephew, the famous Cardinal David Beaton, exercised great influence over the young King James V. During the time of Archbishop Dunbar the two martyrs were burnt in 1539.

THE DOWNFALL OF THE RED DOUGLAS.

DURING the minority of James V. (1527-8), a rebellious army of 12,000 men, under Douglas, Earl of Angus, lay encamped at Glasgow for a short time in the fields north of Ingram Street. It may be remembered that Douglas held the young king under close watch and ward, whilst he himself was suspected of the design of grasping not only the power but the name of royalty, for the Douglas family, as well as the Stewart, could boast of descent from the throne. James made his escape from his tyrant at Falkland, July 1528, and taking refuge in Stirling Castle, proclaimed Douglas a rebel and a traitor. That powerful nobleman assembled his forces in the west, and prepared for attack. Dread of Douglas, more than love for the king, turned the scale, and caused the other chiefs to rally round James in such strength, that Angus was compelled to seek safety in England.

THE MARTYRS OF THE REFORMATION.

AT the great crisis of the Reformation Scotland had but few martyrs, thanks to the good providence of God and the manly courage of her own sons, who soon let the rulers know that they would not endure those scenes which, at that time, were acted freely in so many other countries of Europe. In the sister kingdom of England, during Queen Mary's reign of five years and five months, 284 Protestants were burnt, and a great many more died by imprisonment and maltreatment.

Amidst the morning storm that preceded the glorious day of the Scottish Reformation, two martyrs for the faith laid down their lives in Glasgow. Jerome Russell and John Kennedy, by their noble testimony and unflinching courage, won an imperishable name among the heroes of the Reformation.

Whilst the Romish clergy of St Andrews and Edinburgh had been merciless in their endeavours to crush heresy, and had put its advocates to death in these cities, the adherents of the new faith in the west of Scotland had been more fortunate. Archbishop Dunbar of Glasgow was a humane man, and exceedingly averse to such proceedings. His leniency, however, was so displeasing to the other ecclesiastics, that three of their number were sent from Edinburgh to assist in administering the law of the church. In order to terrify the west country into orthodoxy, it had been decided to bring some victims to the stake. The men devoted to destruction were Jerome Russell, one of the Grey Friars in Glasgow, a man learned for the age in which he lived, and John Kennedy, a young gentleman of Ayr. When brought before the judges, Kennedy, who was only eighteen years of age, discovered some signs of weakness, and would gladly have saved his life by denying the points laid to his charge; but encouraged by Russell, whose faith was of a firmer fibre, Kennedy fell on his knees, and said, "Wonderful, O God, is Thy love and mercy towards me, a miserable wretch! for even now, when I would have denied Thee, and Thy Son the Lord Jesus Christ, Thou by Thine own hand hast pulled me back. Now I defy death; do what you please, I praise God I am ready."

Russell reasoned long and learnedly, but was answered
only with railing and abuse. The Archbishop would have
spared him, but those sent from Edinburgh insisted on his
death.

Whilst the fire was being prepared, Jerome comforted
Kennedy :—" Fear not, brother, for He is more mighty that
is in us, than he who is of the world. The pain which we
shall suffer is short and light, but our joy and consolation
shall never have an end; death cannot destroy us, for it is
destroyed already by Him for whose sake we suffer."
They endured the fire patiently, without any expression of
fear, and their death only accelerated the progress of the
opinions they had avowed.

The scene of the martyrdom was the High Street,
immediately west of the Cathedral, and the date 1539.

BEATON'S FLIGHT.

JAMES BEATON, second of the name, and nephew of the
famous Cardinal, was the last Roman Catholic who occupied
the see of Glasgow. He tried to make a stand against the
Reformers in the palace, and called in the Duke of Chatelherault and Hamilton to his help, but lost heart and hope,
and with such troops as he had he fled from Glasgow to
France, carrying with him " the whole chalices and images
of gold and silver belonging to the Cathedral, and also the
valuable documents."   After acting as ambassador in France
for Queen Mary, Beaton was restored to the temporalities of
the see of Glasgow by James VI. in 1598.   He died in
Paris in 1603, aged eighty-six.

THE BATTLE OF THE BUTTS.

THIS engagement was fought in 1543, and cost Glasgow
more than any battle before or since. It took place about
the site of the barracks in the Gallowgait.

Young Queen Mary being in France, Matthew Stewart,
the Earl of Lennox, took up arms on behalf of the Queen

Dowager against the Regent, James Earl of Hamilton, but the latter entered into a treaty with Cardinal Beaton and the Queen Dowager, and Lennox was left out in the cold. He had arrived from France with brilliant expectations. He was one of the most dashing young gallants of the time, and came of the royal line of Scotland. He had been promised the hand of the Queen Dowager, Mary of Guise, and paid his suit at Holyrood in the orthodox manner of the time. His rival was James Hepburn, Earl of Bothwell, who stood upon an equality with him in many respects, but Lennox beat him at tilts and the strife of arms, and Bothwell retired to his home. In after-years he returned upon the scene as the murderer of Lennox's son and the husband of Queen Mary.

But the Queen Dowager, having brought Hamilton over to her side, now temporised with Lennox, and he found a combination gathering against him. He retired to the west, but 30,000 crowns having reached him at Dumbarton Castle from the King of France, which were sent to promote the cause of the Queen Dowager, Lennox resumed operations. He marched to Leith with 10,000 men, but the other party baffled him, and did not take the field till Lennox, having again returned to Dumbarton, found himself followed in force. His opponents attacked the Bishop's Castle in Glasgow, and, after promising quarter, killed the garrison. " Hamilton hanged sixteen of the defenders at the Cross, and spared the inferiors."

Lennox now found that the French king had deserted him, and he made arrangements for going to England. He was promised a good reception there, but was determined to strike a blow at the Hamiltons before he left. With William Cunningham, Earl of Glencairn, he assembled his forces at Glasgow. The Regent Hamilton tried to occupy the town first, but was too late. Lennox gave him battle on the muir outside, with an army of 800 men, of whom a good many were citizens of Glasgow. Lennox attacked with greater courage than strength, and having taken their brass cannon from the first line, he drove it back upon the second. The battle raged round the Regent, when Robert Boyd of Kilmarnock, with a small party of horsemen, galloped into the thickest of the fight and turned the scale against Lennox and the townsmen. Three hundred were slain, including the two sons of the Earl of Glencairn. The Hamilton party also suffered severely, losing several of their chiefs. Their army had been mainly summoned from beyond the Grampians ; each man had been ordered to have ten days' provisions with him. The inhabitants of Glasgow suffered severely; the city was given up to pillage, and the enemy plundered and destroyed everything they could lay their hands on.

Lennox made his way to England, where he won a handsome wife,—"a princess, in the flower of her age, celebrated for exquisite loveliness,"—Margaret Douglas, the half-sister of James V., the late king of Scotland, and daughter of the Earl of Angus by the sister of Henry VIII., the widow of James IV. Darnley was the son of this marriage. His father returned after being twenty-two years in England. He was appointed Regent of Scotland upon the assassination of the Regent Murray.

THE BISHOP'S CASTLE OR PALACE.

COMPARATIVELY few of those to whom the Royal Infirmary* is a familiar landmark, are aware that it occupies the site of a building which was at once a "place of arms" and the residence of the ecclesiastical ruler of this city and a large portion of the west of Scotland. The castle played a notable part in the most turbulent periods of our history, and it is a pity there is no visible portion of the pile now remaining. It did not share the good fortune of the Cathedral ; and although it cannot be said literally that not one stone stands upon another, its disappearance is as complete as if that fate had befallen it. One very substantial fragment remains, but underground. Underneath the Chronic Surgical House, adjoining the Vicar's Alley, closed up only a few years ago, are extensive remains of the castle walls. They measure about seventy feet long, seventeen and eighteen feet high in some places, and between four and five feet thick, and have been utilised as foundations for that part of the Infirmary. However, if the antiquary cannot

---

* The Royal Infirmary was built in 1792-94.

now gaze upon any part of the castle itself, he may still have the melancholy privilege of viewing a building which is undoubtedly composed in great part of material taken from the ruins of the ancient stronghold. A frowsy edifice in the Gallowgait is all that remains of the once fashionable inn, the Saracen's Head. About the middle of the last century a too liberal town council not only made a free gift of the site of the inn to a certain Mr Robert Tennent, but gave him *carte blanche* among the ruins of the castle. So, we are told by Stuart in his " Views of Glasgow," " the stones with which the inn was built were chiefly taken from the ruins of the Episcopal Palace." The material of which the castle was built was red sandstone.

In " Historical Notices of the Castle of Glasgow" (" Transactions of the Glasgow Archæological Society "), Mr George MacGregor, F.S.A. Scot., has gathered in brief compass nearly all that has been learned about the old edifice.

When the castle was founded is not exactly known. It is referred to in a charter of 1290, and is supposed to have been erected by Bishop William Bondington fifty years before that time.

In 1300 an English garrison held it until Wallace's victory of the Bell o' the Brae.

Bishop John Cameron (1425-1446) built the great tower, which survived until the end of last century. He established legal courts in Glasgow. M'Ure says :—" After Bishop Cameron had built his palace or castle near the High Church, he caused the thirty-two members, parsons, or rectors of the metropolitan church, each to build a manse near the same, and ordained them all to reside here, and to cause curates to officiate in their stead through their respective parishes. This great prelate now being seated in his palace, and the thirty-two parsons having built their manors on the four streets adjacent to the great church, he made a most solemn and magnificent procession and entry to the metropolitan church, twelve persons carrying his large silver crozier and eleven large silver maces before him, accompanied with the thirty-two parsons, the bells of the two steeples ringing, the organs, with the vocal and instrumental music sung by the masters of the sacred music in the cathedral, gorgeously arrayed with costly vestments, and especially when *Te Deum* and mass was to be sung and

celebrated.   And for illustrating the city more magnificently,
he procured a fair from His Majesty, to be held yearly, near
the High Church, the first week of January, commonly
called St Mungo's Fair, but oftener the 20th day of Yuil,
which is a great horse fair, and continues weekly till Skiers-
Thursday, which is very beneficial to the inhabitants in these
streets."

The castle was both palace and stronghold.   Archibald
Beaton (1508-1522) made a high wall round the garden and
built another tower.

In the spring of 1516-17, during the minority of James V.
and Duke of Albany's regency, the castle was attacked by
John Mure of Caldwell, brother-in-law of John Stuart, Earl
of Lennox, who sought to hold it for. the rebel James
Hamilton, Earl of Arran, but it was speedily recaptured by
Albany, who surprised the garrison.   He punished one
French gunner, a deserter, but gave the others favourable
treatment, and made terms with Lennox.

In 1543, during the childhood of Queen Mary, the castle
of Glasgow was again a scene of war, just before the battle
of the Butts (see page 20).   "The Regent James Hamilton, Earl of Arran, beseigit the castle and steppil" for ten
days, and having in vain battered it with his brass cannon,
at last concluded a truce for one day, during which the
garrison were tampered with in a conference, and, upon a
promise of safety, surrendered the castle, but all except one
or two were put to death.

Whilst Mary of Guise was Regent, the castle was gar-
risoned by her French soldiers in 1560.   The Protestant
lords, under Arran, besieged it, and the Frenchmen
surrendered.

After Regent Murray had fallen in the street of Linlithgow, Queen Mary's friends made an unsuccessful attempt to
take the castle in May 1570, but Lennox, the new Regent,
with the help of English troops, dispersed them.   The
following are the particulars :—The Regent Murray was
assassinated in January 1570, and for some months after
the country was torn by strife between the Queen's sup-
porters and the late Regent's party.   Darnley's father, the
Earl of Lennox, who had succeeded to the regency,
received support from Elizabeth, and at the news of the
approach of English troops the Hamiltons retired from

Linlithgow and made a hasty march to Glasgow, intending to destroy the castle lest it should afford a shelter for their enemies. Knowing it was kept by a few young men, and ill supplied with the means of defence, the Hamiltons marched into Glasgow so suddenly, that they cut off the major portion of the garrison from the castle and prevented their entering it. They attacked the castle furiously, but in vain. The garrison was reduced to twenty-four, but received them so sharply that they killed more of the assailants than they themselves numbered, and beat back the rest, with many wounded, while they only lost one killed and had none wounded. The Hamiltons received reinforcements, but learning of the advance of the English they retreated in the evening. The English plundered the estates of the Hamiltons and destroyed the family seat. Lennox gave the castle of Glasgow into the keeping of his adherent Sir John Stuart of Minto, whom he made provost of the city.

In the Register of the Privy Council, date March 20, 1573-4, the castle is described as "ane of the principall keyis of the cuntre." By this time the Reformers were supreme, and the palace was used chiefly as a garrison or council chamber. Archbishop Spottiswoode repaired some of the ruined portions, and resided in it; so did Law and Lindsay; but at the Revolution, 1688, it was abandoned, and soon fell into decay. Late in the seventeenth century it still preserved a stately appearance, but it succumbed to the utilitarian spirit of that time, and was used for building purposes. In 1720 a Glasgow gentleman appealed to the authorities in Edinburgh to prevent its destruction, but without effect; and in 1754 the Saracen's Head Inn was built with its remains. One of the old manses in connection with the Cathedral still stands in Castle Street, an old house with crow-stepped gables.

QUEEN MARY IN GLASGOW.

QUEEN MARY and Lord Darnley spent their honeymoon at Crookston Castle, in the vicinity of Glasgow. In 1565 they led an army of 4000 to the town against an incipient rebellion in which Murray was concerned. The rebels occupied Paisley, but could make no stand against the Queen's forces.

Again, not long after, the young couple brought their troops from Edinburgh to the west in pursuit of Hamilton.

The Queen paid a more memorable visit to Glasgow in 1567, at the time of her reconciliation with her husband, a fortnight before his assassination. She arrived at his sick-bed on January 22nd. The house and garden of the Earl of Lennox, the father of Darnley, was situated about College Street, High Street, and was then in the country; but tradition says the house in which Darnley lodged was in the Limmerfield Wynd, opposite the Bishop's Palace, near the Cathedral. It was a common-looking thatched cottage.

The Queen did not come into the streets of Glasgow on this occasion. She remained a week, returning to Edinburgh with her husband by easy stages, and arrived in the capital on 31st January. The murder of Darnley took place on 9th February 1567.

The "Casket Letters" were alleged to have been sent by Queen Mary whilst in Glasgow at this time. Mr Hossack has clearly shown that they were a collection of clumsy forgeries.

After the disaster of Langside the Queen's party repeatedly occupied Glasgow in considerable force, headed by Argyle and Hamilton.

THE BATTLE OF LANGSIDE.

ONE summer afternoon three hundred years ago, an event took place within sight of Glasgow that has never been forgotten. To this day the mere mention of Langside awakens the sympathy of many a tender heart, as the crowning disaster that befell the unfortunate Queen Mary is brought to mind.

It was on the ground immediately south of the Queen's Park that the battle was fought, and it was from Cathcart Castle, which may be seen rising from a group of trees on the south-east, that Mary witnessed the action (13th May 1568). Her army intended to reach Dumbarton Castle by fording the Clyde at Dalmarnock, but Murray was there before them. They then changed the plan, and marched along the south side of the river from the east, meaning still to avoid battle until the Queen had been placed in security at Dumbarton. But the Regent was quicker, he hurried his troops across Stockwell Bridge at Glasgow, and gaihed the hill of Langside, two miles south-west of the city, and here the engagement took place. It is said the Queen brought 6,000, and the Regent 4,000, men to the field; but the discipline and the skill of the latter were superior. Sir William Kirkaldy of Grange, one of the most stirring soldiers of the age,—and afterwards, when he had learned the falseness of her enemies, the beautiful Queen's last champion, —was on this occasion ranged against her, and to his adroit movement of mounting an infantry trooper behind every horseman, and spurring rapidly to the hill, the coveted position was seized for the Regent. At first Mary's men had the advantage, and stormed the hill successfully; but they could not drive their adversaries from the straggling streets and gardens of the village of Langside, and there the fight raged and swayed for an hour, till at last the Queen's troops gave way and fled. Some three hundred of them were killed, and four hundred were taken prisoners.

At this battle was seen the absurdity of covering men with heavy armour. So overweighted were the warriors at Langside that they could hardly use their weapons, while each was so ensheathed in mail that it was almost impossible to give or receive a serious injury.

Near Cathcart, east of the Queen's Park, is a spot known as Moll's Mire, where tradition says the Queen's horse stuck fast in a bog, and she narrowly escaped capture.

Mary had escaped from Lochleven on 2nd May. The battle was fought on Thursday the 13th; and on Sunday the 16th she arrived at Maryport, in Cumberland, without a change of habit or a shilling in her pocket.

Langside hill commands the best view of the city. It has been extensively built over with villas. Court Knowe, a little height nearly half a mile south-south-east of Langside hill, from where the Queen watched the battle, has been marked with an upright slab. Cathcart Castle, now an ivy-clad ruin near it, is associated with memories of Wallace and Bruce. It was originally the seat of the Earls of Cathcart.*

---

* Haggs Castle, a mile north of Pollokshaws, dates from 1585, was built by Sir John Maxwell, and gave shelter to the persecuted Covenanters.

Murray's men were encamped upon the Burrowfield. After the battle the Regent made a present to the Corporation of Bakers of the ground upon which their *milns* at Partick are built, as a reward for their diligence in preparing bread for the use of his army. The story goes that after the fight Murray assembled the Trades in a large hall in Glasgow, when he thanked them for their assistance at the battle, and concluded by asking if there was anything he could do for them. After a pause Matthew Fawside, Deacon of the Bakers or Baxters, stepped forward and said: "The multures at the mills of the Kelvin are very heavy upon the inhabitants of Glasgow. It would be a great advantage to them if the mills were their property." The Regent at once exclaimed, "Let it be so," and since then the mills have belonged to the Bakers' Incorporation. At that time the mill was styled the Archbishop's Mill, but it was changed to that of Bunhouse. Its situation was the east bank of the Kelvin, adjoining the Old Dumbarton Road. The second or third building was burnt down in February 1885. Its successor belongs to ex-Lord Provost Ure, and has been called The Regent Flour Mills, in memory of the foregoing circumstances.

> "But dark Langside, from Crookston viewed afar,
> Still seems to range in pomp the rebel war;
> Here, when the moon rides dimly through the sky,
> The peasant sees broad dancing standards fly;
> And one bright female form, with sword and crown,
> Still grieves to view the banners beaten down."
> —"THE CLYDE," by JOHN WILSON.

THE SAVING OF THE CATHEDRAL.

BESIDES the fine old Cathedral of Kirkwall, in the Orkneys, Glasgow alone has survived the storm of the Reformation epoch.

In 1560 the Protestant lords sent the following letter:— "To the magistrates of —— burgh,—Our traist friendis, after maist hearty commendacion, we pray ye fail not to pass incontinent to the kirk [of Glasgow, or such other edifice as might require purification], and tak down the haill images thereof, and bring furth to the kirkzyard, and burn thaym openly.

And sicklyke cast down the alteris, and purge the kirk of all kynd of monuments of idolatrye. And this ze fail not to do, as ze will do us singular emplesur, and so committis you to the protection of God.

(Signed)   AR. ARGYLE.
,,   JAMES STUART.
,,   RUTHVEN.

" From Edinburgh, 12th August 1560.

" Fail not, bot ze tak guid heyd that neither the dasks, windocks, nor durris, be ony ways hurt or broken, either glassin wood or iron work."

In spite of this caution, at the outburst of the Reformation, the leaden covering was stripped off the roof. To prevent the destruction of the building, on the 21st August 1574 the provost and council, with the deans of the various crafts and others, met in the Tolbooth, and having respect to the decay and ruin that the High Kirk is come to, "through taking away the lead, sklait, &c., thereof, in the trublus tyme bygane, they all in ane voice consentit to ane taxt and imposition of twa hundredth punds (Scots) for repairing the said kirk and haldying of it watterfast." In 1579 the citizens taxed themselves another sum of six hundred merks for further repair. Before then a great danger threatened the Cathedral. The slip-shod way in which history is written and taught causes many misapprehensions. As an instance, it is commonly supposed that the mob or rabble of Reformers, after pulling down St Andrews Cathedral and other Popish churches, made their way to Glasgow and attempted to destroy St Mungo's Cathedral, but were prevented by the town's tradesfolk. The fact is, it was not until nearly twenty years after the Reformation, and after the mob violence had ceased,* that it was seriously sought to lay hands on Glasgow Cathedral; and the men who wanted to pull it down were no rabble, but the Parliament of Scotland, the fathers and brethren of the General Assembly, the professors of Glasgow University, and the town council of St Mungo's city. But it is all the more to the credit of the tradesmen,—the incorporations of hammermen, weavers, tailors, &c.,—that they made the stand

---

* If the Cathedral was also seriously menaced during the first burst of the Reformation, and saved by the townsfolk then, the circumstances are all the more creditable to them.

they did, and sternly forebade sacrilegious hands being
put on the venerable pile, threatening any who attempted
its destruction with instant death, and terrifying some of the
iconoclasts nearly out of their wits.

In 1579 an act was passed by the Estates, at the desire of
the General Assembly, to demolish churches. Many were
pulled down. Mr Andrew Melville, principal of the College
of Glasgow, was eager to destroy the Cathedral, saying the
material would build three churches. When the crafts rose,
it is said Melville's life was in no small danger from their
violence. The authorities said the building was a monument of idolatry, and the only unruined cathedral in the
kingdom. The provost, Captain Crawford of Jordanhill, ·
gave reluctant consent to the demolition. He said, " I am
for pu'ing doon the auld kirk, but no' till we hae first built
a new ane."

Spottiswoode says:—" In 1579 the magistrates of Glasgow, by the earnest dealing of Mr Andrew Melville and
other ministers, had consented to demolish the Cathedral,
and build with the materials thereof some little churches in
other parts for the ease of the citizens. Divers reasons were
given for it,—such as, the resort of superstitious people to
do their devotion in that place, the huge vastness of the
church, and that the voice of a preacher could not be heard
by the multitudes that convened to sermon. To do this
work a number of quarriers, masons, and other workmen
was conducted, and the day assigned for the beginning.
Intimation being made thereof, and the workmen by sound
of a drum warned to go unto their work, the crafts of the
city in a tumult took arms, swearing, with many oaths, that
he who did cast down the first stone should be buried
under it." To the chagrin of the over-zealous reformers, the
young king at Edinburgh, James VI., then thirteen years
old, approved of the conduct of the craftsmen in saving the
Cathedral, saying, " Too many kirks had been destroyed
already."

It has been argued that because some of the ultra-Presby-
terian historians have not recorded this incident, therefore
Spottiswood's account is not trustworthy ; but any who
reason thus forget how common it is for political speakers
and writers of to-day to avoid any reference to occurrences
of which they or their party have cause to be ashamed.

How often they try to ignore them altogether. The men of long ago had their own share of this kind of human nature. Spottiswood was ordained in 1612, and wrote about what had transpired within his own lifetime. M'Ure says, " and the Town has the constant tradition of it to this day." We see no reason to doubt his story.

A few words regarding Andrew Melville, who is said to have instigated the proceedings, may not be out of place here. Born near Montrose in 1545, he left St Andrews University four years after the Scottish Reformation for Paris. After studying five years there, he was appointed to the chair of humanity in Geneva. He returned to Scotland in 1574, and was almost immediately afterwards appointed principal of the University of Glasgow. As a writer, teacher, and reformer of the Church, Melville displayed the utmost ardour. He bent all his energies to overturn Episcopacy and maintain Presbytery. In 1580 he was appointed Principal of St Mary's College in the University of St Andrews, and there taught the Hebrew, Syriac, Rabbinical, and Chaldee languages. His boldness gave offence to the court, and his scathing denunciations of Episcopacy ultimately cost him five years' imprisonment. In a debate before the Privy Council concerning a Latin copy of verses which Andrew Melville had written in derision of the ceremonies of the Church of England, the old man gave way to indecent violence, seized the Archbishop of Canterbury by the lawn sleeves, which he shook, calling them Romish rags, and charged the prelate as a breaker of the Sabbath, the maintainer of an anti-Christian hierarchy, the persecutor of true preachers, the enemy of reformed churches, and proclaimed himself his mortal enemy to the last drop of his blood. This violence afforded a pretext for committing the hot old Presbyterian divine to the Tower. Relieved in 1611, he was exiled, and became professor of the University of Sedan, where he died in 1622.

A JESUIT MARTYR.

IN 1615 a Jesuit named John Ogilvie was put to death in Glasgow for celebrating the mass, and for affirming that the Pope's authority was higher than the King's. The

following are the circumstances :—During the reign of James
VI., Father Ogilvie, a Jesuit priest, disguised as a soldier,
arrived in Scotland.   He was one of three missionaries,
Campbell and Moffat being the others.   In August 1614
Ogilvie ventured into Glasgow, where Archibald John Spottiswoode held supreme sway both as prelate and magistrate.
Ogilvie succeeded at first in winning converts to his
doctrines; but was betrayed, and on 14th October was
seized by the Archbishop's servants, and after suffering at
the hands of a mob was conveyed to Edinburgh for trial.
Spottiswoode is said to have recommended the torture of the
"boots" as a means of bringing the prisoner to submission,
and of making him divulge the names of his confreres.
This extreme measure was not enforced, but others of a
cruel nature were, and without effect; Ogilvie had a heroic
spirit.   "For eight days and nine whole nights they forced
him to keep awake with styles, pins, needles, and pinchings,
threatening him meanwhile with extraordinary tortures, and
promising great rewards if he confessed," but these proved
all in vain.   Christmas drew nigh, and Spottiswoode having
to return to Glasgow for its celebration, his prisoner was
led back also.   Soon afterwards his death was resolved
upon.   He was tried by a jury, and suffered martyrdom for
his adherence to his faith on 10th March 1615, displaying
great fortitude and a brave forgiving spirit.   The displeasure
generally aroused was so great that other Papists escaped
punishment in consequence.   The mobbing had been done
by Catholics who were led to believe that Ogilvie had
betrayed some of his co-religionists.   It was a benighted
age, a time when the authorities, clerical and secular,
were distinguishing themselves chiefly by torturing and
burning witches.   It is not without significance that it
occurred during the short-lived Episcopacy brought in by
James VI., after the union of the crowns, and that the
King consented to the execution of Ogilvie.

In 1617 James VI. visited Glasgow from England, upon
the only occasion of his coming again to Scotland.

In May 1622 Father George Mortimer was detected in
the house of one Haddow, in Glasgow.   He and Haddow
were apprehended.   The King (James VI.) lost no time in

ordering a court of justice to be held in Glasgow for the trying
of Haddow and his wife for the crime of resetting Jesuits,
certifying that if found guilty they should be banished.
   In September Mortimer still lay a prisoner in Glasgow,
"so heavily deseased, as it is feared he shall hardly escape."
The King ordered that he should be committed to some
ship sailing to a foreign port, death being the penalty if he
returned.

———

THE UNIVERSITY OF GLASGOW.

The University of Glasgow was established in 1450 by
Bishop William Turnbull, who, by request of James II.,
obtained a bull from Pope Nicholas V. for the requisite
authority.   The oldest university—that of Paris—sprung
up about the middle of the twelfth century, and on its model
and that of Bologna most of the succeeding universities were
originally framed.   Scotland, even in the earlier ages, enjoyed the advantage of schools, but it was not until 1411
that the first university—St Andrews—was founded.   Previous to this, it was a custom among the barons and higher
classes to board their sons with the monks for the purposes
of education.   The universities of Oxford and Paris were
greatly resorted to by young Scotchmen.   In 1282 the Baliol
College at Oxford was established for their reception by Devor-
gilla, the daughter of Lord Galloway and wife of John Baliol ;
and in 1326 the Scotch College in Paris University was
endowed by David Murray, Bishop of Murray.   Scotland
was also well represented generally at other colleges, especially at Cambridge and Salamanca.
   The constitution of Glasgow University was modelled on
that of Bologna.   Bishop Wm. Turnbull took a journey to
Rome in 1454 to still further benefit the new institution, and
died there on 3rd September of that year.   At first the
students of Glasgow got the use of a building near the
Cathedral, but in 1459–60 James, first Lord Hamilton, conveyed to the Principal and other regents of the Faculty of
Arts, a tenement in the High Street, with four acres of land
in the Dowhill.   In 1466 an adjacent house was bequeathed
by Mr Thomas Arthurlie.   On the site of these buildings
the old university was built.   The Reformation in 1560
came like a deathblow to the University, which was a Catholic

c

institution.   Queen Mary was the first to endeavour to restore it.   By a charter of 13th July 1563 she provided five
bursaries for poor youths, and granted to the masters the
manse and church of the Friars Predicators, and thirteen
acres of land adjoining.   The Magistrates and Council in
1572 followed so good an example, and made a further en-
dowment.   At this date it appears that the whole of the
members, regents, and students residing within it only
numbered 15 persons.   The whole establishment is described
in Queen Mary's charter as presenting a very mean and
unfinished appearance, and no great improvement was made
till 1630.   In 1577 and 1581 onward steps were made.   In
1662 Charles II. deprived it of the Bishopric of Galloway,
which seriously cut down its revenues.   Liberal bequests
were made to it from time to time by private persons.   In
1610, by Mr Alex. Boyd; in 1617, by Mr Michael Wilson; and
in 1641, by Mr Thomas Hutcheson, one of the founders of
Hutcheson's Hospital, who left £1,000 Scots for rebuilding
the south quarter, and when the sum was paid in 1658 the
addition of the interest raised it to £1,851 Scots.   Robert
and John Fleming left 2,000 merks to help the building, and
Zachary Boyd left 30,000 merks for the same purpose.
After 1693 the Scottish universities began to receive more
liberal treatment.   In 1702 there were 402 students at
Glasgow.   The College buildings stood on the east side of the
High Street on the ground now occupied by the N. B. Railway Station.   They consisted of five quadrangles, and covered
a large space of ground.   The College steeple was 148½ feet
high.   The library was commenced in 1475.   George
Buchanan presented twenty volumes to it.   In 1839 it possessed 40,000 volumes, now it has 100,000.

The Marquis of Montrose give 400 merks to the
University on attaining his majority.   It was paid on 16th
November 1634.

Among the famous men who were educated in Glasgow
University were George Buchanan, Spottiswoode, and
Wodrow, the historians, and in more recent times,
"Christopher North," Hooker the botanist, and Mather,
the Oriental scholar.   Although all traces of the Old
College have been effaced from the ancient stance, no one
can feel otherwise than proud when he thinks of the
magnificent University buildings on Gilmorehill.

The following distinguished men have been Lord Rectors :

Burke, Brougham, Campbell, Peel, Macaulay, and Lytton. James Watt, the inventor of the steam engine, had a workshop and lived within the walls of the University. The College Green is now a network of rails. The Old College Church stood a little distance southward. It was a quaint edifice, with high pitched roof and Tudor spire, and was built in 1699 on the site of the Blackfriars' Convent. The Grayfriars' Monastery stood near the foot of Grayfriars' Wynd. It was founded in 1476, and was destroyed in 1560 by the Duke of Chatelherault, whilst he was engaged besieging the French mercenaries of the Queen Regent in the Bishop's Castle.

SIR GEORGE ELPHINSTONE OF BLYTHSWOOD.

A SECOND battle was fought at the Bell o' the Brae in 1606. It formed a step towards the civic liberty of Glasgow, and is fully related in the Register of the Privy Council. Having been a bishop's burgh, the civic rulers were always appointed by the clergy until the Reformation. Archbishop J. Beaton, before his flight, made over the rights of the burgh to the Duke of Chatelherault, who had championed his cause during the rising storm, but he took nothing to do in the matter. In 1573 the Protestant Archbishop Boyd sought to revive the right which his Romanist predecessors had exercised, but he did not succeed. Next year he made a further attempt, and nominated his own nephew Robert, Lord Boyd, to be provost ; but again he failed, and the right of nomination fell into the hands of the Earls of Lennox. They either acted as provosts themselves, or appointed cadets of their own house to the office. Thus Sir Matthew Stewart of Minto repeatedly held the provostship between 1571 and 1594, quite irrespective of the wishes of the burghers. At last, in the interest of the town, Sir George Elphinstone of Blythswood opposed him, and in 1604 obtained the office of provost for himself. He at once set about procuring that freedom of election for the burgh, which " has been very far impaired this mony years bigane." In 1606 he got the Duke of Lennox to renounce his privilege of electing the magistrates, which renunciation was confirmed by King James VI. The Stewarts of Minto, resenting this curtailment of their power, raised a faction against Sir George Elphinstone, and a very troubled time ensued.

On 23rd July 1606, Sir George was attending the practice
of archery at the butts, and when he was returning " with
his company, who were bot five in number, without ony
kind of armour saving their bows," he was attacked at the
Bell o' the Brae by the adherents of the Stewarts. Sir
George and his friends, one of whom was " John Graham,
the maistor of Montross " (who was afterwards fourth earl,
and father of the great Marquis), defended themselves man-
fully, but had to seek refuge in the Earl of Wigton's dwelling-house, which was furiously besieged by some three
hundred of their opponents. Sir George lodged a complaint
with the Privy Council, who, on 27th August 1606, held that
Sir Matthew Stewart and his companions had committed a
very great insolence and riot, and ordered them to be
" wardit in the burgh of Linlithgow till His Majesty's will
be made known concerning them."

In 1607 the solitary peel of Elphinstone Tower was built
in the Gorbals by the Elphinstones, on obtaining the supe-
riority of the barony of the Gorbals in that year. It was
the home of Sir George, and was long a prominent object in
the main street, being the last bit of baronial architecture in
Glasgow.

The father of Sir George Elphinstone bought the lands of
Gorbals from Bishop Boyd. His son, the hero of the foregoing, was a burgess, and received the honour of knighthood
from James VI., and was made a Lord of the Session and
Gentleman of the Bedchamber. Charles I. made him Lord
Justice-Clerk, which office he held till his death in 1634.
" He got the Gorbals erected into a burgh of barony and
royalty, yet," says M'Ure, " he died so poor that his corpse
was arrested by his creditors, and his friends buried him
privately in his own chapel adjoining his house." His son,
by a daughter * of Lord Boyd, got nothing, everything being
seized by creditors. He died and left no children.

Lord Robert Douglas, Viscount of Belhaven, having
bought the barony of Gorbals from Sir George's creditors,
made additions to the tower and chapel, "and affixed his
name to the front piece thereof." He was succeeded by his
nephew, Sir Robert Douglas of Blackerston, who was one of
those sent to plead with Montrose after the battle of Kilsyth.
He sold the barony of Gorbals to the town of Glasgow.

* See " Boyhood of Montrose," p. 39.

THE MARQUIS OF MONTROSE.

THE good folks of Glasgow were thrown into a state of terror when the news of the rout of Kilsyth reached them, and when they heard that the victorious cavalier host was approaching their gates.

Montrose encamped near the town, and sent a message to the inhabitants. It contained a wholesale order for bonnets, shoes, and the sinews of war; but as it was unaccompanied by a remittance they were otherwise than elated at its large proportions. The magistrates had espoused the cause of the Covenanters, but circumstances being changed, Provost Bell and his colleagues (according to one account) sent a deputation to Kilsyth, to congratulate the Marquis on his victory, and invite him to spend a few days with his troops in Glasgow. Another authority says their message was only to plead him to abate his demands. No doubt the ambassadors would put as pleasant a face as they could on their business. They succeeded in getting the "quantities" reduced. Montrose came to the town, and was fêted for two days. He left his army on Bothwell Muir, twelve miles from the city, thereby showing some solicitude for the well-being of the inhabitants, among whom he had spent some of his boyhood's years. He borrowed from them £4,166. 13s. 4d. for carrying on war on the King's behalf.

Some of the magistrates were afterwards brought to book by the Covenanting powers for having on this occasion wished success to Montrose. David Leslie, after his victory of Philiphaugh, took possession of Glasgow, and borrowed £1,666. 13s. 4d. from the community, grimly remarking that this money was for the purpose of paying the interest of the sum lent to Montrose.

Three Royalist prisoners whom he brought were executed at Glasgow :—Sir William Rollock on the 28th October, and Sir Philip Nesbit and Alexander Ogilvy of Inverquharty on the 19th October. David Dickson, Professor of Divinity in Glasgow, and son of a Glasgow merchant, is reported to have said regarding the executions,—"The wark gangs bonnily on."

A yet more dreaded and unbidden guest than either

Montrose or Leslie arrived in the city soon after,—that was
the plague. Verily it was a time of visitation. Famine
succeeded the plague, and fire followed the famine. A
great conflagration destroyed the Saltmarket, Trongate, and
High Street in 1652, the wood fronts of the houses offering
no resistance to the flames.

THE BOYHOOD OF MONTROSE.

MUGDOCK AND STRATHBLANE.

WE have mentioned that Montrose spent some of his boyhood's years in Glasgow.   The family house of the Grahams
was at Mugdock, Strathblane, some eight miles from the
city.   In Mr J. Guthrie Smith's book on "The Parish of
Strathblane" much interesting information is given.

The Grahams of Montrose had lands in Strathblane about
1225–70. A charter of confirmation to David of Graham
by Alexander III., dated 27th December 1253, shows that
he had received one grant of lands in "Strathblathane"
from Maldoven, Earl of Lennox, and a second from Malcolm,
this Earl's son, who died in 1248. A third acquisition of
lands by the family was in the time of the fourth Earl of
Lennox, between 1270 and 1292. Their seat Mugdock
Castle was built prior to 1372. In 1458 James II. created
Mugdock into a barony in favour of Patrick, Lord of the
Graham. The old Strathblane family were often at the
front. Sir Patrick was slain at the battle of Dunbar, in
1296, fighting against the English. His brother Sir John
the Graham, the friend of Wallace, two years after fell at
Falkirk in the same righteous cause ; Sir David, a successor,
was taken prisoner at Durham, along with King David II.,
in 1346 ; William, first Earl of Montrose, fell at Flodden in
1513 ; Robert his grandson fell at Pinkie in 1547 ; but John
the third Earl, and his son John, the father of the great
Marquis, lived out of the tumult. James the fifth Earl was
the great Marquis, and one of the most gallant of Scotsmen.

The young lord was born in 1612, and when twelve years
of age was settled in Glagow with a private tutor, two pages,
and a valet, with the intention of preparing him for the

University of Glasgow, and at the same time keeping him under the eye of his father, who was then living at Mugdock. He was an only son, but had five sisters. Whilst in Glasgow he lived in a house belonging to Sir George Elphinstone of Blythswood, called in a receipt granted for the rent by Agnes Boyd, the wife of this knight, part of "our great ludgin situat in the citie of Glasgu, near the towne heid thereof." The house in the Drygait, which was afterwards called "Montrose's Lodging," and which was formerly the manse of the prebendary of Eaglesham, had not by this time been bought by the family.

The accounts of James Duncan, "burgess of Glasgow, factor of Mugdock," and those of the Earl's factors at Montrose and Kincardine, are interesting, and throw some light upon this Earl's life, and the earlier part of that of his distinguished son. The following entries occur :—

Item, given the 12 of March 1625 to Patrick Lytstone
   for ane dusone goiff balls to my Lord . . iij. lib.
Item, to the ministers man that brocht books to my
   Lord at command . . . . vj. sh.
Item, for iiij. unce of tobacco to my Lord be the way
   cuming to Montross from Kincardin, at vij. sh.
   vj. d. the unce . . . . . xxx. sh.
Item, given the 14th of Apryle for iij. ells ane quarter
   ell round linning claith to my Lord his black
   breiks . . . . . . xxiiij. sh. vj. d.
Item, for twa dusone tobacco pypes the said day . viij. sh.
Item, that day for ane pig full of ink to my Lord . vij. sh.
Item, for ane pair of shone to Lord James the 26
   Oct. 1623 . . . . . xxvi. sh. viij. d.
Item, for shone to the bairne Beatrix . . xl. sh.
Item, for twa pair of schoone to the Lord James twa
   naigis . . . . . . xviij. sh.

The "Lord James" was the future great Marquis, and the "bairne Beatrix" was Lady Beatrix Graham, afterwards Lady Maderty.

After his father died in 1626, the Marquis went for three years to St Andrews University. When only sixteen he married Magdalene Carnegie, youngest daughter of David, Lord Carnegie; she died in 1633, leaving two sons. Montrose went to France for three years, where he improved his education, and held a commission in the French Guards. During the first Covenanting episode Montrose took the popular side against Charles I., signed the Covenant, and was one of the leaders of the "blue bonnets" at the Tweed in 1648, and afterwards at Newburn ; but becoming alarmed at the course of events he went over to the king's side.   He was arrested, and imprisoned in Edinburgh, and his house " herried " in 1641 by order of the Committee of Estates ; but it was only partially destroyed, for on being released the Earl returned to Mugdock, and lived there in retirement till 1644, when he made the memorable rising for the King. He had been created a Marquis by Charles in 1643.

Once more Mugdock Castle was " herried," by the Buchanans in 1644.   In the following year Montrose or his friends took ample revenge, and brought the laird of Buchanan to poverty.   Argyle at the death of the Marquis got Mugdock, but at the Restoration was sent to the right-about in favour of Montrose's son, in 1655.

The ruins of the old castle occupy a commanding position. Built before 1372, it was at one time surrounded on three sides by Mugdock loch.   Its successor, the house of 1655, was removed, and a new mansion built in 1874.

It is not a little curious to learn from the same volume that a certain John Graham of Dugaldston, Mugdock, became a tailor and bailie of Glasgow.   He flourished in the city during the years immediately before 1720, and may have been the veritable Bailie Graham of whose caustic tongue Bailie Nicol Jarvie stood in wholesome dread.

THE COVENANTERS.

DURING the long struggle for civil and religious liberty the townsfolk of Glasgow were devoted in their attachment to the Covenanting cause, and their city became a kind of capital of the Covenanters.

At the beginning of the troubles there was great in-dignation at some of the clergy for their declension to Episcopalian ways and practices.

At that period, about 1637, the gentler sex were particu-larly unceremonious towards turncoat ministers.   Baillie gives an account of the treatment Mr William Annan, the prelatic minister of Ayr, met with from the women of Glas-gow :—" At the outgoing of the church, about thirty or forty of our honestest women, in one voyce, before the bishope and magistrats, did fall in rayling, cursing, scolding, with clamours, on Mr William Annan ; some two of the meanest were taken to the Tolbooth. All the day over, up and down the streets where he went, he got threats of sundry in words and looks ; but after supper, when need-lesslie he will go to visit the bishope, he is no sooner on the causey at nine o'clock on a week night, with three or four ministers with him, but some hundreds of inraged women of all qualities are about him, with neaves and staves and peats, but no stones ; they beat him sore; his cloak, ruff, hatt, were rent ; however, upon his cries, and candles set out from many windows, he escaped all bloody wounds ; yet he was in great danger, even of killing."

The National Covenant was signed in March 1638, and on 21st November of the same year the General Assembly of the Kirk of Scotland was held in Glasgow in the Cathe-dral or High Church, with Alexander Henderson as Moderator. The Marquis of Hamilton attended as Lord Commissioner for the King, and dissolved the Assembly ; but disregarding him, they declared Episcopacy abolished, and removed the bishops, excommunicating eight of them. At the close of the meeting the 133rd Psalm was sung.

The bold position of the Assembly required strong sup-port. It was endorsed by the Scottish Parliament. A numerous host of well-trained veterans was brought home from the Continent, and with their help Alexander Leslie led a serviceable army of blue bonnets to Duns Law (3rd June 1639), effectually checkmating the King.

The Water Port of Glasgow was built about this time by the Covenanting townsmen, as a means of defence against any attack of the Royalists.

The restoration of Charles II. (1660) brought trouble to the Presbyterians. Donald Cargill, the minister of the Barony, spoke his mind pretty freely on the occasion ; and although soon driven from his church, he continued in the city, exercising great influence for the cause of the Covenant. In England the Act of Uniformity was passed in August 1662, by which two thousand clergymen, refusing to submit to Episcopacy, had been ejected from their parishes and ex-posed to innumerable hardships. On the 1st of October of the same year, Middleton and his council met at Glasgow, and passed a similar act for Scotland, requiring all clergymen

admitted since 1649 to submit before the 1st November to
be re-admitted to their parishes by their patrons and re-
ordained by the bishops, removing from their livings all who
should refuse obedience.   This atrocious act was known as
the Act of Glasgow, and was said to have been passed when
all the councillors except one were drunk.   Three hundred
ministers were evicted for refusing to conform to it, and this
was the cause of the conventicles or out-of-door preachings
of the Covenanters.

Middleton, the King's commissioner, was a most unfit
person for such a position.   He was a soldier of considerable experience of defeat, being the General Middleton that
Montrose encountered and overthrew at the Bridge of Dee.
He had shared in Hamilton's disastrous campaign against
Cromwell, and had been finally defeated by the Protector's
men on 26th July 1654 at Loch Garry.   He soon showed
such evidence of his unfitness for dealing with the people,
that he gave way to Sharpe and Lauderdale; and was sent to
be Governor of Tangiers, where he lost his life by falling
down a staircase whilst intoxicated.

Matthew Paton, shoemaker, of Newmilns, a Covenanter
taken at Pentland, was executed in the city on 19th December 1666.   During the same year many others were hanged
in Glasgow for being Covenanters.

In 1674 the city was fined £100 for allowing a Presbyterian minister to preach within its bounds ; and in the same
year, guards were placed at the gates to prevent any of the
inhabitants going out to conventicles in the country.

In 1677 a bond was made out by the Government, which
the people of Glasgow were ordered to subscribe.   It contained a complete renunciation of Presbyterianism.   A great
many refused to sign it.   In consequence of their non-com-
pliance, the Highland Host, an army of uncivilised Celts,
were brought to the city.   They arrived on 26th June 1678,
and plundered the townsfolk right and left.   They lived at
free quarters for five days.   It is said that half of them
brought spades and sacks, which were intended to be used
in plundering the citizens.   These gentry next transferred
their attentions to Ayrshire, in which county their booty is
said to have amounted to over £137,499 Scots.   They paid
a second visit to the city, but made an ignominious departure, for the students and other youths barred the bridge,

the river being high, and as the Highlanders approached, laden with their loot, they were made to relinquish it, and to leave the town by the West Port in parties of forty. Two thousand men in all are said to have been thus intercepted.

During the great fire of 1677 the Tolbooth was in danger, but the magistrates refused to let out the prisoners, the most of whom seem to have been Covenanters. The "well affected" of the townspeople got long ladders and set them free. Kerr, the laird of Kersland, escaped among the rest. He had been a prisoner for eight years, and had experience of durance vile in some half-a-dozen prisons. He took to the persecuted wanderers, and died in Utrecht in 1680.

On 29th May 1679 a band of Covenanters came to Rutherglen, and defied the authority of King and Parliament (see page 171). Two days after, Drumclog was fought and won. Claverhouse's horsemen galloped out through the streets of Glasgow at such a pace that one of them rode over and killed a child; their appearance after their discomfiture was greeted with grim satisfaction by the townsfolk. Claverhouse's watchword at Drumclog was "No quarter," and had he succeeded a fearful butchery would have stained the brown moor. Had some of the Covenanters got their own way, every Royalist prisoner would have been put to death.

A few days after Drumclog the Covenanters made an assault upon Glasgow, to which Claverhouse had fled. A small body of Royal troops, under that leader and Lord Ross, prepared for defence. The insurgents, whose numbers were now considerable, entered the town in two columns, one approaching by the Gallowgait, the other by the College and Wyndhead. The King's troops had made barricades at the Cross, Town-house, and Tolbooth, and received them with such a withering fire from behind these barriers and from windows of houses, that the Covenanters were completely beaten off. Eight were killed and a great many wounded.

Tradition says Claverhouse would not permit the citizens to remove the bodies of the slain, and they lay in the streets until the Covenanters, having received further reinforcements, again menaced the city, when the Royalists evacuated it, retreating upon Kilsyth. A week or two after (on

22nd June 1679) the battle of Bothwell Bridge extinguished the hopes of the rebels.*

The Duke of York (afterwards James II.) visited Glasgow on 3rd October 1681. Provost Bell took him to his house in the Briggait, and the duke was made a burgess; but before leaving the town a protest against the persecutions was thrust into his hand, which rather disturbed his equilibrium. The provost received the honour of knighthood on account of the duke's visit.

In 1683 Lady Mure of Caldwell, widow of the laird of Caldwell, with her eldest daughter, was cast into prison on suspicion of holding a conventicle in her house in the Saltmarket. Her husband having been implicated in the Pentland rising, had escaped to Holland, where he died some years after. The widow had returned to Scotland, but her estate, house, and furniture having been conferred on Dalziel of Binns for his services at the battle of Pentland, she settled in a very humble way in Glasgow. On the 22nd May 1683, with her daughter Jean, aged twenty, she was carried to Blackness Castle, where they were kept close prisoners. At the end of six months the daughter was liberated in consequence of her health breaking down, but Lady Mure was confined for more than three years.

Patrick Walker,† in his "Life and Death of Mr Daniel Cargill," brings a startling accusation against the famous Walter Gibson, one of the founders of the commercial prosperity of Glasgow. Alluding to two of his youthful associates, he relates that they were taken prisoners in December 1684. "Meldrum, that wicked persecutor, apprehended

---

* Claverhouse occasionally found time for other recreations in the west than chasing and killing Covenanters. At Paisley, on 10th June 1684, he was married to Lady Jane Cochrane, granddaughter of the Earl of Dundonald. She had a moderate dowry; and as she came of a Whig family, the match created surprise and amusement among the Cavaliers. Claverhouse was summoned in haste from the very marriage altar to suppress a rumoured rising of Covenanters in Stirlingshire. He fell at Killiecrankie (27th July 1689), and his only child died three months after. The widow married again, and had another child. Both were accidentally killed in 1695, by the fall of a house, in Holland.

† Patrick Walker was a Covenanter in his youth, and when eighteen years of age had a hand in shooting a trooper, who was chasing some of the wanderers. He is admiringly referred to in the "Heart of Midlothian" by David Deans.

them and carried them to Glasgow. Walter Gibson, merchant there, got a gift of them and other twenty-eight, who starved and poisoned them with little and bad victuals above all that ever I heard of that carried our banished to foreign lands; few of them in that ship lived any time in Carolina. . . . Merchants, such as Gibson in Glasgow and Malloch in Edinburgh, Pitlochie, a laird in Fife, and many others, got gifts of them (the Covenanters), who transported them to Carolina, New Jersey, Jamaica, and Barbadoes, to be their slaves; but none of them made their plack a bawbee with trading in such wares."

An order of the Privy Council, dated 27th May 1684, quoted by Wodrow, permits penitent Covenanters to be transported in "the ship belonging to Walter Gibson, merchant in Glasgow," to the plantations. His brother, James Gibson, was captain of this ship, and seems to have treated his prisoners with extreme rigour. He is accused of kidnapping some unaccused persons, in defiance of all law. A record of persecutions endured by a worthy Glasgow townsman, Mr William Nevin, during these troublous times has been preserved. He was arrested in 1679 on suspicion of having been at Bothwell Bridge, for which charge no evidence could be found; but he had attended a conventicle at Williamswood, near Glasgow, and, along with some others, he was sentenced to be banished to America. No ship being ready, they were allowed to escape at Gravesend, and return to Scotland again. In 1684 he was arrested at midnight in Glasgow, accused of having been at one of Mr Renwick's conventicles. After a year's confinement in Edinburgh, he was taken to Dunnottar Castle, where he suffered great hardship, and was ultimately sent to America (September 1685). After the Revolution he was on his way home to Scotland, when the vessel was captured by the French. Mr Nevin died in Glasgow after all.

Wodrow says, "On 19th March 1684 five worthy and good men were executed at the Cross of Glasgow, upon as slender a probation as was ever sustained in any case." They were accused of "being at Ayrsmoss and Bothwell Brig," and were tried before special commissioners in Glasgow. They were executed two days after sentence, and were buried in the High Churchyard of Glasgow, beside other sufferers. James Nisbet was a relative of one of these men, called John Richmond, of Knowe, and intimate with the others. He attended the funeral, and being observed by his own cousin-german, Lieutenant Nisbet, was apprehended. He refused to renounce the covenants and to own the King's authority, as he expressed, in so far as he had made the works of reformation and covenants treason. After he was condemned he wrote, "I am come here to lay down my life for the testimony of Jesus, for asserting Him to be king and head of His own house, and for no matter of fact they have against me." He was hanged at the Howgate Head, near Glasgow, in the midst of a great crowd.

THE MARTYRS' STONE.

The Martyrs' Fountain was erected twenty-five years ago in Castle Street. The old martyrs' stone is now lying in a field on Garngad Hill It has an incription, "Repaired 1793." Both it and the modern monument commemorate the same names; the aforesaid James Nisbet, of Highside, Ayrshire, who suffered in Glasgow on June 11, 1683; and

James Lawson and Alexander Wood, who were shot at Pol-
madie for refusing to pray for the King, on July 29, 1684.
The unfortunate Earl of Argyle, when his rising had
proved abortive, was captured near Paisley, and was brought
a prisoner to Glasgow Tolbooth. He was executed in Edinburgh on 30th June 1685. But the game was at last played
out. At the outbreak of the great Revolution, five hundred
sturdy Covenanters assembled in Glasgow, to testify their
attachment to the Protestant cause, and their determination
to uphold their rights and liberties. They marched to Edinburgh, under command of the Earl of Argyle and Lord
Newbattle, and soon scared Claverhouse out of the capital.
The newly formed regiment won undying fame by the
heroic defence of Dunkeld against the Highland Jacobites
(21st August 1689), and since then the 26th Cameronians
have proved their prowess on scores of hard-fought battlefields.

At the Revolution the Papists and Episcopalians were, of
course, sent to the wall. Some rabbling took place when
the Episcopalian clergy, and those who had become such at
the bidding of the King, were expelled from their pulpits. The
provost of Glasgow, Walter Gibson, and his brother, distinguished themselves in rather an unseemly way. They tried
to stem the rising tide of Presbyterianism, and with a band
of hired ruffians attempted, with the incumbent, to force an
entrance into the High Church. A company of forty women
who were at the door resisted their entrance, when a pitched
battle ensued. Thirty-two women were wounded, and died
in consequence. The Covenanting party came to the rescue,
and there was a terrible mêlée in the churchyard, when
sticks and stones were freely used.

OLIVER CROMWELL.

CITIES are in the custom of conferring upon illustrious
strangers who may come within their precincts the
" freedom of the city," but Glasgow has had the experience
once or twice of receiving visitors who took "the freedom of the city" upon themselves without undergoing the
ceremony. Foremost of these, and with a firmer foot than

even old Longshanks', heavy and bloodstained as his was, comes Oliver Cromwell, and no more interesting notices of Glasgow are extant than the picturesque accounts furnished by those who bore him company. After having been baffled for months and nearly driven to his wits' end by the adroit generalship of David Leslie, Cromwell had at last, and in one brief hour at Dunbar, swept the Scottish Royalists before him like chaff (September 3, 1650), and now Scotland lay at his feet.

"On Friday afternoon, October 24, 1650," says one, "we reached Glasgow. That morning my lord, at a rendezvous, gave a special charge to all the regiments of the army to carry themselves civilly and do no wrong to any. The town of Glasgow, though not so big and rich, yet to all seems a much sweeter and more delightful place than Edinburgh."*

It is said the Presbyterians had prepared a little treat for Oliver. They filled the vault of the Bishop's Castle with gunpowder, intending to blow him up as he entered. The Ironsides at least got the hint of such kindly intentions, and the Protector, instead of arriving by the head of the High Street, entered by the Cowcaddens and Cow Loan (Queen Street). The Marquis of Argyle had made a hasty retreat two days before. Cromwell took up his quarters in the Salt-market, in a house known as Silvercraigs Land. It belonged to Campbell of Silvercraigs (of the Blythswood family), and stood on the east side of the street opposite the Briggait.† On the Sabbath following Cromwell went in state to the Cathedral or High Church, where Zachary Boyd, the minister of the Barony, who occupied the pulpit, opened his mind so freely upon him, that Captain Thurlow, the general's secretary, wanted to pistol him where he stood. Oliver forbade that mode of argument, saying, "No, no; we will manage him in another way." The Reverend Zachary was invited to dinner, and by that means and a prayer of three hours' duration, was won over to a more satisfactory state of mind. They kept him out of bed until three in the morning.

Carlyle, in his "Life and Letters," gives the following

---

* Salmon and trout abounded in the Clyde at that period.
† After having done service as a weaving factory, it became a furniture warehouse, and has now entirely disappeared. Its site is occupied by the Corporation Model Buildings.

particulars:—"After the defeat at Dunbar, Strachan and Kerr fled to the west, and gathered five thousand west country Covenanters at Dumfries, whilst Leslie with the covenanted young King occupies Stirling. 'While Ker and Strachan are busy at Dumfries,' says Baillie, 'Cromwell, with the whole body of his army and cannons, comes peaceably by way of Kilsyth to Glasgow. It is Friday evening, October 18, 1650. The minister and magistrates all flee away.' The people were much afraid till they saw how they were treated. He endeavoured to effect an understanding with Kerr. But they decided in any case, on the whole, to fight against Cromwell. They feared that it will not be good to fight under the Covenanted King for the cause of Christ and Scotland. Not a very hopeful enterprise. Cromwell hears that Kerr is on the march to Edinburgh to try to relieve Edinburgh Castle. O. C. leaves Glasgow on Monday thitherward, pressing news, some false alarm of movements about Stirling, having arrived by express from the east. Some foolish tumult in Glasgow was quelled by the intervention of Cromwell's soldiers."

A few months later Cromwell paid a second visit to Glasgow. The position of affairs is not much changed. Leslie is still in force in the north; Inverkeithing has not been fought yet. Cromwell has been suffering from ague. "O. C. arrives at Hamilton on Friday night late, and sees Glasgow again on Saturday, 19th April 1651. On Sunday forenoon he came unexpectedly to the High Inner Kirk, where he heard Mr Robert Ramsay preach a very pertinent sermon to his (Cromwell's) case." "My Lord General sent to them to give us a friendly Christian meeting, to discourse of those things which they rail against us for; that so, if possible, all misunderstandings between us might be taken away, which accordingly they gave us on Wednesday last. There was no bitterness nor passion on either side; all was with moderation and tenderness. My Lord General and Major-General Lambert, for the most part, maintained the discourse; and, on their part, Mr James Guthery and Mr Patrick Gillespie."

Of the Rev. Hugh Binning, who at the age of nineteen had been elected to the chair of philosophy in Glasgow, it is said, "The eloquence, fervour, and great theological attainments he displayed in the famous dispute which Oliver

Cromwell caused to be held at Glasgow in April 1651, between his own Independent clergy and the Scottish Presbyterians, astonished even the Protector himself. Finding that
Binning had completely nonplussed his opponents, Cromwell
asked the name of 'that learned and bold young man.' On
being told it was Mr Hugh Binning, he replied, in the true
spirit of Alexander with the Gorgian knot, ' He hath bound
well indeed, but (putting his hand on his sword) this will
loose all again.'" Binning died of consumption in 1653,
aged twenty-six. His monument may be seen in the vesti-
bule of Govan Parish Church.

"The army quitted Glasgow, after some ten days, rather
hastily, Wednesday, 30th April."

Gramaghee was a Highland epithet for Cromwell. The
word signifies one that holds fast as in a vice.

DONALD CARGILL,

THE COVENANTING MINISTER OF THE BARONY.

ONE of the four central prominent preachers around whom
traditions of the Covenanters are clustered was the minister
of the Barony parish of Glasgow. Cameron, Cargill, Peden,
and Renwick uttered no uncertain sound at that crisis of
Scotland's history. Whilst Peden barely escaped a bloody
death, the other three were called upon to lay down their
lives for the cause,—Cargill and Renwick on the scaffold,
and Cameron on the battle-field. Donald Cargill had no
other charge than the Barony; and by his brave unflinching
testimony during the darkest hour, not only served his own
day and generation, but it is to him and such as he that
his fellow-citizens of Glasgow and of Scotland owe their civil
and religious liberty.

Cargill was born about 1610, of a respected family in the
parish of Rattray. Schooled at Aberdeen and St Andrews
College, he was called to be minister of the Barony parish of
Glasgow. Upon the 26th May following, the day appointed
to commemorate the Restoration (1660), an unusual crowd
came expecting to hear a sermon in honour of the King.
Instead of that, upon his entering the pulpit, Mr Cargill

repudiated any such idea, and denounced the King for his evil life and treacherous disposition, saying it was a black day for Scotland when such a king came to reign over her. For this outspoken zeal he was constrained to seek safety in concealment, finding shelter in private houses, and often sleeping among the broom near the city. He never lost a chance of private preaching, and became a great vexation to the Government. Middleton made great efforts to arrest him in 1662, but he escaped. The Council banished him to the north of the Tay, but this had no effect; he remained about Glasgow, preaching at the conventicles in the immediate vicinity. In October 1665 a public search was made for him in Glasgow, but being warned, he rode boldly past one body of soldiers before he was recognised, and afterwards made good use of his horse's speed. After several wonderful escapes, he was at last apprehended, and made to stand before the Council on 11th January 1669, when he bore faithful testimony. Through the interposition of some persons of quality, his wife's relations, and others, he was dismissed. Ten years after he was at Bothwell Brig, and was wounded and taken prisoner, but to his own surprise the soldiers let him go. A day or two after he was pursued, from his own chamber in Glasgow, out of the town, and again he walked boldly past a troop of horsemen. Next Sunday he preached at Langside. Early in 1680 he went to the shores of the Forth, where he continued till the scuffle at Queensferry, when his friend Haughhead was killed and he himself wounded. He continued to preach as before, every time he got an opportunity. Richard Cameron and Cargill then joined company, and went about preaching together, until the former was surprised and killed at Airsmoss. Cargill made his way northward, and, in no ways dismayed, in September following, at a numerous gathering in the Torwood, Stirlingshire, he formally pronounced sentence of excommunication against some of the most violent persecutors of the day. Cameron and Cargill together had drawn up the Sanquhar Declaration, which was published at the Market Cross of Sanquhar, 22nd June 1680, and in consequence of which the Government offered three thousand merks for the arrest of Mr Cargill, but after the act of the Torwood the amount was increased to five thousand merks. He was looked upon as the arch-enemy of the Government, and indeed was the only prominent leader left of the Covenanters.

Marion Hervey, a servant girl of Borrowstouness, aged twenty, was executed in Edinburgh in 1681, for hearing Cargill, and for assisting him to escape at South Queensferry. Isabella Allison suffered with her; she belonged to Perth, and was apprehended for having heard Donald Cargill, and for refusing the test. Still nothing would silence or terrify him. The old veteran of seventy-one preached at Maybole and other places, in spite of the prize of five thousand merks set on his head. At last he was seized by a farmer, and given up to the Government. "His captors hasted from Lanark to Glasgow, sixteen miles, fearing a rescue; when they came near the city, they turned Mr Cargill on the horse and led him in backward, which made many to weep to see their old minister in that position. While waiting at the Tolbooth till the magistrates came to receive them, one John Nisbet, the Archbishop's factor, said to Mr Cargill in ridicule, three times over, 'Will you give us one word more?' alluding to an expression he used sometimes in preaching, to whom Cargill said with regret, 'Mock not, lest your bands be made strong; the day is coming when you shall not have one word to say, though you would.' This also came quickly to pass, for not many days after Nisbet fell suddenly ill, and for three days his tongue swelled, and though he was most earnest to speak, yet he could not, and died in great torment and terror. From Glasgow they were taken to Edinburgh, and (15th July) were brought before the Council. Chancellor Rothes (being one of those he had excommunicated at Torwood) raged against him, threatening him with torture and a violent death. To whom he said, 'My Lord Rothes, forbear to threaten me, for die what death I will, your eyes shall not see it.' Which accordingly came to pass, for Rothes died the morning of that day in the afternoon of which Mr Cargill was executed."

Mr Cargill was hanged at the Cross of Edinburgh on 27th July, along with Walter Smith and another Covenanter named Brig. When on the scaffold the old man sang part of Psalm cxviii. When going up the ladder he said, "The Lord knows I go on this ladder with less fear or perturbation of mind than I have sometimes entered the pulpit to preach." He was interrupted with the beating of drums, and could only finish three verses,—16 to 18,—which he used often to quote during life :—

> " The right hand of the mighty Lord
> Exalted is on high ;
> The right hand of the mighty Lord
> Doth ever valiantly.

> " I shall not die, but live, and shall
> The works of God discover.
> The Lord hath me chastised sore,
> But not to death giv'n over."

With an immovable fidelity to conscience, Donald Cargill had a tender sensitive nature, and, with his own death full in view, gave himself to comfort his fellow-sufferers. In a letter to one of them before execution he says, " Farewell, dearest friend, never to see one another any more 'till at the right hand of Christ. Fear not, and the God of mercies grant a full gale and a fair entry into His kingdom, which may carry sweetly and swiftly over the bar, that you find not the rub of death." He spent many hours in prayer, and met his death upon his knees, with his hands raised in the attitude of devotion. It was when the youth James Renwick saw Cargill executed, that he resolved to take up the cause. We know how nobly he sustained it.

In the year of the Revolution it was found that there were not fewer than eighty societies of Covenanters, numbering seven thousand members, banded together to fight the battle of freedom to the end. So Scotland, as well as Israel, can produce her seven thousand who had never bowed the knee to Baal, even in her darkest hour.

> " There's nae Cov'nant noo, lassie,
> There's nae Cov'nant noo ;
> The Solemn League and Covenant
> Are a' broken through.
> But the Martyr's grave will rise, lassie,
> Aboon the warrior's cairn ;
> An' the Martyrs soun' will sleep, lassie,
> Aneath the waving fern."

—ROBERT ALLAN.

"BASS JOHN" AND THE QUAKERS.

AMONG other citizens who were cruelly persecuted for being Covenanters was John Spreull, merchant. He was seized and subjected to the torture of the boots, but refused to give any information about Mr Cargill, or about the pretended plot against the Duke of York. He was fined £500 sterling, and then sent to the Bass Rock, where he was imprisoned for six years, being relieved at last unconditionally.

In 1691 two Quakers—Christopher Story and Thomas Blaire—came on a tour to Scotland. Upon arriving at Glasgow, in March, they were very badly treated—mobbed, stoned, and spat upon by the rabble—by men, women, and children, and it is not a little surprising to find that their chief persecutor was a certain Mr John Sprewel, tobacco merchant. He haled them before a magistrate, and wanted to have them examined as to their religious opinions; but the bailie would not entertain the charge made against the inoffensive men, and dismissed them, admonishing Sprewel to see to their protection. This he certainly did not do, but suffered the crowd to treat them most shamefully. There is little room to doubt that this persecutor Sprewel and " Bass John " were one and the same man. He showed as little toleration for the meek and long-suffering Quakers, as the Privy Council for our truculent Covenanting forefathers.

ARCHBISHOP LEIGHTON.

" A purer, humbler, holier spirit than Leighton never tabernacled in Scottish clay."—FLINT.

THE name of Robert Leighton, the most eminent of all who have occupied St Mungo's see, will not soon be forgotten. Born in 1611, he was educated at the University of Edinburgh, and took his degree of M.A. in 1631. After residing on the Continent, chiefly at Douay, for about ten years, he returned to Scotland, and became parish minister of Newbattle. In 1652 he was chosen principal of Edin-

burgh University. Leighton's father had been most merci-
lessly treated by Laud for opposing Episcopacy, but after
the accession of Charles II., when it was again attempted to
force it upon Scotland, Leighton accepted, though with
reluctance, a bishopric, in the hope of moderating the
violent dissensions of the time, choosing that of Dunblane,
as being the smallest and poorest in revenue. The despot-
ism of Sharpe and Lauderdale deeply grieved him; and in
1665, and again in 1669, he went to London to beseech the
King to check the oppressive measures of these men, saying
he would not consent to the planting of the Christian religion itself in such a way, much less a form of Church
government. Charles promised amendment, but nothing
was done. On the resignation of Bishop Burnet, Leighton
was made Archbishop of Glasgow, only accepting the dignity
on condition that a measure should be passed for embracing
the Presbyterians; but as Sharpe and his colleagues were
allowed to treat the Covenanters with the same tyranny as
before, Leighton resigned his see in 1673. After spending
ten years in Sussex with his sister, he died in London, 1st
February 1684. He was celebrated for his learning, integrity, disinterestedness, and gentleness. Although his
bishopric only yielded him £200 and his archbishopric
£400 a year, he founded exhibitions in the Colleges of
Edinburgh and Glasgow.

OLDEN TIMES IN GLASGOW.

ANENT SABBATH PROFANATION, ETC.

AFTER the Reformation a number of curious local regulations were enforced in Glasgow. Our ancestors must have
felt the Presbyterianism of these olden times rather too
much undiluted to be comfortable. The ministers ruled
their flocks, lambs as well as black sheep, with a rod of iron,
and meddled in all kinds of affairs, no doubt for the good of
the people. In 1582 the booth (shop) doors of traffickers
were ordered to be "steiked" on Wednesdays and Fridays
during the hours of preaching, under a penalty of twenty
pounds Scots. The fleshers were censured for killing in the

time of the week-day sermons. Inquisitorial conduct was
carried into private life,—for it was ordered that no gatherings or banquets were to take place at baptisms or marriages ;
the dinner or supper was to cost only 1s. 6d. Scots, or 1½d.
sterling, and married persons were to find caution to that
effect.

From about 1574 to 1600 the gates of the city used to be
locked on Sundays, not only to exclude Highland vagrants,
but to keep the inhabitants from wandering out to see plays
at Rutherglen.   Officials, rejoicing in the name of "Bum-
beadles," had the task of arresting any persons walking about
during the hours of kirk service, and of compelling them to
go to the kirk.   Too often these worthies came off second
best in their endeavours thus to evangelise the Philistines.
But very lax ideas of the solemnity and sanctity of the Sabbath must still have prevailed, for, according to Cleland,
"On the 7th May 1594, the Presbytery of Glasgow pro-
hibited the playing of bagpipes on Sunday from sun-rising to
its going down, and practising other pastimes after canonical
hours, under pain of censure."

Until 1773 John Anderson, the town herd, was wont to
blow his horn every morning in the High Street as the signal
for the townsfolk to turn out their cows.   His musical march
was made along the Trongait and up Cow Loan, or Queen
Street, which was then a veritable slough of despond, to the
town's pastures at Cowcaddens, from whence he returned in
the evening, sounding his horn as he came.   This worthy
always sported his figure in kilts.   His horn is still carefully
preserved. ·

Of Glasgow in the olden times, Daniel Defoe, writing in
1727, says :—"The four principal streets are the fairest for
breadth and the finest built I have ever seen.   The lower
storeys for the most part stand on vast square Doric
columns, with arches which open into the shops,—adding to
the strength as well as the beauty of the buildings.   In a
word, 'tis one of the cleanest, most beautiful, and best built
cities in Great Britain."

These four streets were the High Street, Gallowgait, Saltmarket, and Trongait.

Although the walls of the city are often spoken of in old
documents, it is doubtful if there ever was any continuous
rampart or wall round Glasgow.   Each street, however, was

terminated by a port. Some of them remaining in the year 1690 are described as of solid oak, with big iron nails.

Westward from the Cross was St Thenaw's gait, spanned by the West Port. The name of the inner port was about 1550 changed to the Trongait. The part of the street beyond the port continued to be known as St Thenaw's gait or St Enoch's gait, but beyond Queen Street it was called the Dumbarton Road. It did not get its new name of Argyle Street until the West Port was taken down in 1750. St Mungo's gait was at the north side of the town. The Nether Barass Yett terminated what is now Saltmarket Street, which was formerly known as the Waulkergait.

A gate was built again at the foot of Stockwell Street, about 1639, by the Covenanters, as a defence against Charles I., and called the Water Port. Another port was at the west end of the Briggait; whilst at the junction of Bell's Wynd and Candleriggs stood a very handsome gate, which was only taken down about 1735.

The Clyde was deeper long ago, and is said to have been navigable for ships of light draught as far as the burgh of Rutherglen, but about the beginning of the present century it had certainly become filled up with mud. There is no authentic authority for the supposed shipping trade of Rutherglen. M'Ure in his history is quite supposititious. The ship on the Rutherglen seal is probably the *navis antiqua* of heraldry, and only signifies that the town is on a river more or less navigable. There may have been some sort of flat-bottomed barges for carrying coals to Glasgow, but that would be all.

Even in 1566 the river was fordable by carts and carriages twelve miles below Glasgow.

A hundred years later Thomas Tucker, one of Cromwell's servants, who was appointed to arrange the customs and excise in Scotland, reports of Glasgow and the Clyde, November 1656 :—" The situation of this toune in a plentiful land, and the mercantile genius of the people, are strong signs of her increase and growth, were she not checked and kept under by the shallowness of her river, every day increasing and filling up, soe that noe vessels of any burden can come nearer up than fourteen miles, where they must unlade and send up their timber and Norway trade in rafts or floates ; and all other comodityes by three or foure tonnes of goods at a time, in small cobbles or boates, in three, foure, five, and none above six tonnes about. There are twelve vessells belonging to the merchants of this port, viz., three of 150 tonnes each, one of 140, two of 100, one of 50, three of 30, one of 15, and one of 12; none of which come up to the toune."

In 1755, at Glasgow, the Clyde was only fifteen inches deep at low water; now it is fifteen feet deep at low water, and twenty-six feet deep at high water.

THE RISE AND PROGRESS OF TRADE AND MANUFACTURES.

THE earliest branch of commerce was the export of cured salmon. Large numbers were sent to France, and various kinds of French goods taken in exchange.

In the year 1667 a whale-fishing company was formed, and a soap manufactory established. It may be well to call attention to the latter statement, because some have supposed that St Mungo founded the business in question. In 1669 sugar-refining, tanning, and rope-making were commenced in Glasgow, also the manufacture of plaids and coarse cloths. The soap and candle works were in the Candleriggs, and the sugar works in the vicinity of Stockwell Street. The foreign trade of Glasgow seems to have been commenced in earnest about 1687, by John Anderson of Dowhill, and by Walter Gibson, who was the projector of the first quay at the Broomielaw.

During Queen Mary's reign, in 1556, the royal burghs were taxed, when Glasgow appears only to be the eleventh town, in point of wealth, in Scotland. The figures are as follows:—Edinburgh, £2,650; Dundee, £1,265; Aberdeen, £945; Perth, £742; St Andrews, £300; Montrose, £270; Cupar, £270; Ayr, £236; Glasgow, £202; Haddington, £147.

In 1695 the city stands second in wealth among the towns of Scotland. The assessments were:—Edinburgh, £3,880; Glasgow, £1,800; Aberdeen, £726; Dundee, £560.

The improvement in the position of Glasgow had been

brought about by the growth of the trade in raw and refined sugar, by herring fishing, &c. The only soap manufactories in Scotland were to be found in Glasgow at that time. Early in the seventeenth century St Mungo's city made a good start in the race for trade and wealth. Says Dr J. Hill Burton :—" Glasgow was the only place where there was the same kind of visible progress in the early half of the century as the rest of the country developed in the latter half. . . . The Union revived the shipping trade, which had been paralysed by the Navigation Act; but it was not till 1716 that the first honest vessel in the West India trade crossed the Atlantic from the western capital. In 1735 Glasgow possessed 67 vessels, with a tonnage of 5,600. Of these 47 were foreign traders, the greater portion of them crossing the Atlantic. This, small as it may seem, constituted nearly half the shipping of Scotland, the aggregate tonnage of which is believed not to have exceeded 12,342, while that of England was estimated at 476,941." *

THE FOUR YOUNG MEN.

We have all heard of "the four young men who made Glasgow," and their names deserve to be recorded here. John Glassford of Dugaldston, born 1715, died 1783; Archibald Spiers of Elderslie, born 1714, died 1782; William Cunningham of Lainshaws ; and James Ritchie of Busbie. These four, by their enterprise and energy, not only wrested from English rivals a great English but a great Continental trade. By them the importance of Glasgow as a mercantile centre was firmly established. They were all clever pushing men, and at the start did not possess £10,000 among them, but going into the Virginia tobacco trade they made large fortunes, and all bought estates.

John Glassford of Dugaldston was a native of Paisley, and became one of the most extensive foreign merchants and shipowners of his time. He owned a fleet of twenty-five ships and all their cargoes, turned over half-a-million a year, and imported enormous quantities of tobacco. Glass-

* " In 1851 the tonnage of Scotland was 536,266, while that of England was 2,803,052. If the earlier numbers can be depended on, in 1735 the Scottish shipping slightly exceeded a fortieth of the English, in 1851 it had become nearly a fifth."—KNOX's " British Empire," xxxvi.

In 1885 the tonnage of the vessels registered at the port of Glasgow was 1,018,476 tons.

ford Street was called after him; and his house, the Shaw-field Mansion, was pulled down in 1792 to allow the street to be opened.

William Cunningham made a great hit in buying up stocks of tobacco just before the outbreak of the war. His house is now part of the Royal Exchange. James Ritchie also had a mansion in Queen Street. Archibald Spiers made extensive purchases of land in Renfrewshire, and founded a county family. He was successful not only in making money, but in keeping it. But he had to part with it all one day, for in December 1782, just as his grand new mansion of Elderslie on the Clyde was finished, he caught a fatal chill in visiting a damp basement which a river spate had invaded, and died on the 10th. Elderslie has hardly known its laird as its master. The family have now abandoned it, and it has become a letting house, one of the last occupants was James Morton of the City Bank.

In 1772 the total British imports of tobacco were 90,000 hogsheads, and Glasgow accounted for 49,000, most of which was exported to France.

The American Revolution brought about the ruin of the tobacco trade in 1775.

Sugar next came to the front.

In 1763 James Watt set himself to work at the problem of the steam-engine in Glasgow, and in 1769 his invention was patented. In all the features of the engine he did not leave much for successors to discover.

During the close of last century the rise of Glasgow and local industries is almost as marvellous as the rapidity with which they extended. In 1780 James Monteith set up a web of pure cotton, the first ever woven in Scotland. In 1783 David Dale firmly fixed the trade here by founding the New Lanark mills. Again, in 1783, Archibald Shettle-ston, of Calton, invented the flying shuttle. In 1792 Scott and Stevenson put up at Springfield the first steam-engine in a Scotch cotton-mill. Again, in 1792, William Kelly, of New Lanark, introduced the mechanically moved spinning-jenny. In 1793 the power-loom was brought into practical use in Glasgow. In 1795 Archibald Buchanan, of James Finlay & Company, introduced lighter spinning machinery, worked for the first time by women. A few years later James Finlay & Company, with their works at Catrine,

Deanston, and Ballindalloch, employing 2,500 workers, and equipped with the best appliances for spinning, weaving, bleaching, and finishing, stood at the very head of the cotton trade. In 1770 William Stirling founded the calico printing firm of William Stirling & Sons, and at his death, seven years later, he left a business that astonished his day and generation. In the same year, 1777, Cooksons, of New-castle, in company with Provost Patrick Colquhoun, opened at " Verreville " the first crystal manufactory in Scotland. Again, in 1777, George Macintosh opened in Ark Lane his " secret work " for making cudbear. In 1780 David Fleming & Company started card making. In 1783 David Dale and George Mackintosh founded Barrowfield, the first turkey-red work in Great Britain. In 1786 William Menzies opened in Gorbals the first licensed distillery in Glasgow ; —there were only three before it in Scotland, and it would have been no loss if there had never been one at all ; that industry has left its trail of desolation and suffering. In 1789 Thomas Edington founded the Clyde Ironworks. In 1794 David Fleming & Company began the making of files. In 1796 Charles Macintosh (of waterproof fame) founded Hurlet, the first alum-work in Scotland.

Dr Smiles mentions, that towards the end of the seven-teenth century a Protestant refugee from France succeeded in establishing a paper-mill in Glasgow,—the first in that part of Scotland. The Huguenot who erected it had escaped from France accompanied only by his little daughter. For some time after his arrival in Glasgow he maintained himself by picking up rags in the streets, but by dint of thrift, dili-gence, and intelligence, he eventually contrived to accumu-late means sufficient to enable him to start his paper-mill, and thus to lay the foundation of an important branch of Scottish industry.

POPULATION, ETC.—At the time of the Reformation the population of Glasgow was estimated at about 15,000 ; in 1688 the figures given are 11,948 ; in 1751, about 20,000 ; in 1801, 83,769 ; in 1811, 116,460 ; in 1821, 147,043 ; in 1831, 201,416 ; and in 1841, 283,134.

Edinburgh contained in 1801, 82,560 ; in 1811, 102,987; and in 1821, 138,235 inhabitants. Glasgow increased her population from the time of the Union, tenfold within a lifetime.

THE SHAWFIELD RIOT.

IN 1706 there were some disturbances at Glasgow anent
the Union. Jacobite influence, and a sermon by the Rev.
Mr Clark of the Tron Kirk, were blamed for raising the
excitement. A man named Finlay, who had been a sergeant
in Dumbarton's regiment, and who had served abroad in
Flanders, aspired to the command of a large army of patriots,
but the numbers were not forthcoming, and the insurrec-
tion collapsed. The provost had to hide for his life at one
period of the disturbance.

A more serious riot broke out in 1725, on 23rd June, the day
when the extension of the Malt Tax to Scotland was to take
effect. Duncan Campbell of Shawfield, M.P. for Glasgow,
had voted for the obnoxious measure, and was suspected of
having given the Government information on the habits and
statistics of Scotland necessary for the preparation of the tax,
as well as having exposed a system of evasion of duties in
the Scottish tobacco trade. Mr Campbell was not in town
at the time, but a furious mob beset his house, the famous
Shawfield Mansion (see page 64), shouting, "Down with
Walpole and up with Seaforth!"

The magistrates did not deal with sufficient firmness at
first, and the military were not authorised to interfere until
the riot had assumed serious proportions. The house was
pillaged, and greatly damaged. The wine cellar happened
to be very well stocked. During the endeavour to quell the
disturbance nine of the mob were shot and seventeen
wounded, whilst nineteen persons were arrested. A strong
party of soldiers arrived under General Wade, and the provost—John Aird—and magistrates were themselves apprehended, accused of having favoured and encouraged the
mob, and of laxness in dealing with the riot. On 17th July
a strong military guard escorted them to Edinburgh Castle.
They were afterwards confined in the Tolbooth. A sympa-
thising company of fifty Glasgow shopkeepers followed them
to the capital, for the refusal of the Lord Advocate to accept
bail was considered harsh, if not illegal. Three days later
their bail was accepted. Of the nineteen rioters imprisoned,
some were whipped through the streets of Glasgow, some
banished, and others liberated. Captain Bushel was next

tried for the murder of nine inhabitants. Although convicted and condemned, he was not only pardoned, but soon after promoted. This leniency was remembered twelve years afterwards, and was a great cause of the Porteous Mob in Edinburgh, 7th September 1736.

Mr Campbell recovered, by authority of Parliament, £6,400 from the community for damages done to his property; with the expenses the amount reached £9,000. Shawfield Mansion became afterwards the property and residence of Mr John Glassford (see page 59), and was taken down for the purpose of opening Glassford Street. It had been built in 1711. With the money which Mr Campbell received for compensation he paid for his purchase of the island of Islay.

PRINCE CHARLIE.

CHRISTMAS of 1745 was a time of unusual anxiety to the citizens of Glasgow. Prince Charlie and his gallant army, on their retreat to the north, came to the town, and of all places Glasgow had most reason to dread their appearance, for no town had shown more marked hostility to them, or given such cause of offence.

At the previous outbreak of the Jacobites in 1715 the city had raised 600 men, who were sent to Stirling, where Glasgow maintained them during the emergency. The townsmen also fortified their city, making a ditch twelve feet wide and six feet deep.

At the present crisis (1745) Government had left Glasgow entirely unprotected. A small body of troops had been removed on 12th August, and although the citizens raised a body of 1,200 volunteers, the Government was unable to supply them with arms until Charles had left Scotland. Whilst in Edinburgh he had extorted £5,500 from Glasgow; but on the 30th of October the townsfolk showed their spirit by celebrating the King's birthday, with ringing of bells and public festivity.

The Glasgow Regiment of Volunteers was under the command of the Earls of Home and Glencairn. The Jacobites having departed to England, they were marched to Stirling, to prevent reinforcements from the Highlands reaching them. Now, upon Prince Charles's threatened return, the city was in a worse state than ever.*

On his retreat from Carlisle, Prince Charles travelled by way of Annan, Dumfries, Drumlanrig, Douglas-Castle, and Hamilton. He lodged in the palace of the Duke of Hamilton, and spent a day hunting through the parks there, shooting two pheasants, two partridges, and a deer.

As the Jacobite army approached Glasgow, it was with great difficulty they were prevented from sacking and burning the village of Lesmahagow, for the following provocation. The brave young Kinlochmoidart, whilst on his way back from the Highlands, where he had been sent to try to raise Macleod and MacDonald of Sleat, passed through Lesmahagow, where he was recognised by a student of divinity named Linning. This officious probationer gathered a mob of the people, and succeeded in arresting the Jacobite and his attendant. Kinlochmoidart was conveyed to Edinburgh, and was afterwards executed at Carlisle, whilst his captor was rewarded by the Government giving him the appointment to the pulpit of his native parish.

Never in the course of the rebellion had Prince Charles's army been in such straits, and they now presented a very tattered worn-out appearance. On their way towards Glasgow they stripped such natives as they met of their shoes and other articles of dress, and a good many private acts of plunder were committed; but the conduct of the army as a whole was exemplary. The first troops came on Christmas Day 1745, and the Prince arrived next morning. He fixed his headquarters at the Shawfield Mansion. In order to magnify the appearance of his army, he marched his men in through the front gate and out by the back garden, when they retired to the Back Cow Loan (Ingram Street), and appeared again as if they had newly arrived by Queen Street and the

---

* " Lord Mahon says—'How strange the contrast between Manchester and Glasgow! The most commercial town in England, the most friendly—the most commercial town in Scotland, the most adverse—to the Stewarts;' but it was not by the commercial, or more properly speaking, manufacturing element that the partiality to the Stewarts was caused in Manchester, but by its retention of what Glasgow never had to any noticeable amount,—a resident landed gentry, or local aristocracy, disconnected with business."—J. H. BURTON.

Trongait. But this manœuvre was observed by the acute citizens, who, recognising the botanical badges and the tartans of the various clans as they reappeared again and again, laughed them to scorn.

The contempt of the townsmen for the Highlanders was so provoking that they wanted to sack the city, and it is said the proposal was only defeated by Lochiel threatening to withdraw his clan if such violence was permitted.

The friends of Government made a careful estimate of Prince Charles' forces at Glasgow as 3,600 foot and 500 horse, the latter all worn out, and 60 of them carrying sick men. Of the infantry 600 had no arms, or seemed unable to use them.

The Shawfield Mansion, where the Prince had taken up his abode, was a very fine house, and the best in the city. Built by Mr Campbell, M.P., of Shawfield, it was in 1745 the property of Colonel William M'Dowall of Castle Semple. Its position was a little way north of the line of the Trongait. (When Glassford Street was made the house had to be pulled down.)

During the eight days Prince Charles lived here, his table was spread in a small dining-room, where he was attended by his officers and waited upon by a few Jacobite ladies.

The Prince sent for Provost Buchanan, and demanded the names of those who had subscribed for raising troops against him, threatening to hang the provost if he refused to tell; but Buchanan would name no person but himself, and professed his willingness to "come awa and be hanged" in such a cause. He was forced to pay a fine of £500. Clothing for the troops and stores were demanded to the extent of more than £10,000 sterling, which the citizens were compelled to pay under the threat of military execution. "Charles," says Home, "required the magistrates of Glasgow to furnish his army with 1,200 shirts, 6,000 short coats, 6,000 pairs of shoes, 6,000 pairs of stockings, and 6,000 bonnets, the value of which, added to the £5,500 paid on the 27th September, amounted to £10,000." Paisley was made to pay £500; and other adjacent places were also looked after by the Highlanders, and compelled to contribute.

Charles admired the beauty and regularity of the streets of Glasgow, but remarked with bitterness that nowhere had

E

he found so few friends. During the week only sixty recruits came in, whilst many of his men deserted for a time in order to visit their homes. Although of the people of Glasgow a goodly proportion were of Highland birth or extraction, they nearly all hailed from Protestant counties, such as Argyle, which had no leaning towards the cause of the Stewarts.

Business was at a standstill during the occupation of the Highlanders. They made three parades through the city, each time proclaiming their leader Regent, at the Cross.

"But," says Alexander Smith, "with all his beauty and his misfortunes, his appearance in Glasgow created little enthusiasm. He scarcely gained a recruit; only a few ladies donned in his honour white breastknots and ribbons.* He . levied a heavy contribution on the inhabitants. A prince at the head of an army in want of brogues, and who insisted on being provided with shoeleather *gratis*, was hardly calculated to excite the admiration of prudent Glasgow burgesses."

Whilst the Prince was riding through the Saltmarket one day a pistol was snapped at him. Another act of violence is recorded:—A Highlander stopped a joiner going home from his work one night, and required him to deliver his shoes. They had silver buckles, and he refused. The Celt stooped down to take them off, when the joiner in a fit of rage dealt him a blow on the head that stretched him lifeless on the ground.

A review of the rebel troops was held on the 2nd of January. After getting their new outfits, they were marched by the Saltmarket to the Green, where the parade was held on the south-west triangular corner near the river known as the Flesher's Haugh. A thorn-tree at its northern boundary, under which he stood whilst reviewing his men, was long called Prince Charles's tree. Next day the Jacobites left the city.

It was remarked by some of the observing townsmen that there was a shadow of sadness on the face of the Prince, as if he realised that his enterprise was doomed to fail. But the women folk of the west were quite taken by the dashing appearance of the gallant young Prince. The personal

---

* *See* page 166, "Prince Charlie and a Camlachie Beauty."

bravery of Charles has been called in question by some of his enemies; but when it is remembered that his mother was the granddaughter of John Sobieski, the heroic King of Poland, the statement of his own followers as to his eagerness to face the foe, will be thought more credible than any doubts of the Hanoverians.

"At Glasgow," says Chambers, "Charles learned with some accuracy how much, or rather how little, was the support France was giving him. The supplies in amount remind us of those given to a man perishing of famine by a comrade, who dropped into his mouth, from time to time, a small shell-fish, affording nutriment enough to keep the sufferer from dying, but not sufficient to restore him to the power of active exertion."

The Highlanders evacuated Glasgow on the 3rd of January, and reached Bannockburn on the following day. The order for clothing was supplied within the week's time, but as all was not quite ready, two hostages were carried off, Mr Archibald Coats and Bailie George Carmichael. Charles also took a printing-press, type, and three printers.

The Glasgow Volunteers, as we have already said, had been engaged garrisoning Stirling Castle, preventing northern Jacobites passing southwards at the fords of the Forth. Amongst others who were doing similar duty, was a body of volunteers furnished by the congregations which had recently seceded from the Kirk of Scotland, and who were afterwards known as the Associate Synod, of whom our modern U.P.'s are the descendants. They made themselves very conspicuous, carrying banners on which was painted, "For religion, the covenants, king, kingdoms." Upon receiving the news of the rebels' return to Scotland, these all, with Price's and Ligonier's foot, and Hamilton and Gardiner's dragoons, marched from Stirling to Edinburgh.

In the march from Glasgow, Prince Charles slept the first night at the mansion of Kilsyth, which belonged to a forfeited estate, and was now in the possession of Mr Campbell of Shawfield. Next evening he was a welcome guest at Bannockburn House, the residence of Sir Hugh Paterson, one of the most zealous of his friends (and the uncle of Clementina Walkinshaw). As the Jacobites approached Stirling, the Rev. Ebenezer Erskine tried to inspire the remaining garrison of the castle to make a stand against them, but they thought it safer to surrender. Professor Anderson, the founder of the Andersonian College, was also there, and very anxious to experiment upon them with some new gunnery he had invented.

On the 17th January the battle of Falkirk was fought, when all the royalist regiments ran away, except those on the extreme flank, viz., the 4th or Barrels, of which Wolf was Major, Ligonier's, and the Glasgow Militia. These bravely stood their ground, and repulsed the rebels. Their part of the line was not attacked in the first rush of the battle, and they were able to pour destructive side volleys upon the Highlanders as they followed the flying royalists, whilst a ravine prevented the rebels from getting at them with the sword.

A great rejoicing was held in Glasgow after the battle of Culloden, — music, bell-ringing, and bonfires in every street. The Glasgow regiment was back in the town at the time, and there was a general drinking of healths all round.

In 1749 Parliament granted £10,000 to the magistrates of Glasgow to reimburse them for the money that Prince Charles had mulcted them of. It was through the exertions of Provost Andrew Cochrane and a few patriotic Scotch members of Parliament that the vote was passed.

The " Cochrane Correspondence " gives an account of a post-chaise journey from Glasgow to London in 1748, by Provost Cochrane and Bailie George Murdoch, a deputation from the Town Council " to apply to His Majesty and Parliament for reimbursing the sums extorted from the town upon account of the town's loyalty by the rebels during the late unnatural rebellion." A previous deputation had failed, and Cochrane and Murdoch were kept dancing attendance at St James's for six months before they extorted from English gratitude an ungracious recognition of Scotch loyalty.

The expense weighed heavy on the good provost's spirit —£472. 11s. 8½d. as per detailed account rendered to the Council.

As this account shows, the deputation travelled in a

chaise bought for the occasion, price £28. 2s. 6d. (the 2s. 6d. apparently being a modest tip to "the makers' servant"). The journey from Edinburgh to London took eleven days, and the "post hire" cost £21, besides "hostlers, riders, horns, &c., £2. 2s.," and adding another day, and £2 for hire and driver between Glasgow and Edinburgh *via* Whitburn, the whole journey took twelve days, and cost £25. 2s., exclusive of all personal expenses.

GEORGE WHITEFIELD.

VISITS TO GLASGOW.

GEORGE WHITEFIELD visited the city in September 1741, and preached some ten or twelve times upon the first occasion of his coming to Scotland. He was then in his twenty-ninth year. The presbyteries gave him rather a chilly reception, but he found his way at once to the hearts of the people. He says of Glasgow, "The congregations were large, and so also were the contributions for the orphans in Georgia."

The famous religious revival at Cambuslang took place about the time of his second visit to the north in the following year. One out-of-door meeting was kept up until half-past one in the morning, the people refusing to go away. It was held on a hill-side during a cold February night, and there was an immense gathering. At this season Whitefield became acquainted with Colonel Gardiner. Only three years later that gallant soldier met his death, and Glasgow had soon very different guests to entertain in the shape of Prince Charlie and his Highlanders.

In 1748 Whitefield was again in Scotland, and found immense audiences in Glasgow. A motion had been made in the Synod of Glasgow and Ayr to prohibit him from preaching in any of the seceding churches, but the statements of his opponents were disproved, the motion was out-voted, and he was permitted to occupy any of their pulpits. Writing to Lady Huntingdon, he informs her, that the Seceders were very angry with him for not preaching up the Scotch Covenant; "but, blessed be God," he adds, "I preach up the covenant of grace."

He arrived from Belfast in July 1752 at Glasgow once again, where "many thousands attended to listen." The people seemed never weary, and he was followed more than ever. "To see them," he said, "bringing their Bibles, and turning to every reference, is very encouraging." Numbers left their distant homes in the country at three or four o'clock in the morning to hear him preach. Next year, in July, he preached five times in one day in Glasgow, and at the last discourse nearly twenty thousand were present. Other visits followed in 1756, 1757, 1758. Nowhere did he feel the parting with his friends so keenly as in Edinburgh and Glasgow. During another itinerancy in 1760, a young lady, Miss Hunter, offered him all her money and lands, £7,000, which he generously refused. Upon his declining it for himself, she pressed him to take it for the benefit of his orphan-house in Georgia, but he absolutely refused the gift. He was again in Glasgow in 1763.

THOMAS MUIR,

THE PIONEER OF REFORM IN SCOTLAND.

SCOTTISH Radicalism is said to have originated as early as 1745. The Duke of Cumberland had hardly quitted our shores when a strong reactionary feeling set in against the Government, owing to the harsh treatment of the Jacobites, and above all to the cruelties of the Duke. The Hanoverian line of kings was never much loved by the people of Scotland. It would have been strange if they had. The immorality of the court was only equalled by the stolid indifference and opposition of the kings to the desires of the people for parliamentary and other reform.

Political gatherings were forbidden, and for twenty-five years before 1795 there had not been a meeting in Edinburgh at which politics formed the theme of discourse. Fox had many admirers in the north, and his birthday was celebrated by a dinner in the Scottish capital. But only fearless and independent Whigs dared to attend, because Government spies were deputed to take the names of those who were there. Some of the guests would ask the spies to hold up their lanterns to make certain that they knew them, and laugh them to scorn.

In 1793 there were 20 Parliamentary members returned by Scotch counties, with no more than 100 voters; 10 members were returned by Scotch counties with no more than 250 voters; 15 members returned by 15 Scotch burghs with no more than 125 voters. The number of county voters in Scotland at this time was 2,624; and the largest constituency was Ayrshire, with a voting strength of 220. In the general election of 1790 there was no contest in twenty Scotch counties. The Dundases manipulated them, and got their Tory friends returned. The total number of burgh electors in Scotland in 1790 was 1,289. The counties of Bute, Clackmannan, and Nairn had an alternate election with Caithness, Kinross, and Cromarty. In England matters were even worse. In Edinburgh, which had a population considerably over 100,000, thirty-three persons had the appointment of a member of Parliament in their hands. Buteshire had only one voter, and this individual, with great solemnity, convened a meeting, took the chair, proposed and seconded a motion that he was a fit and proper person to represent the county, and then declared himself unanimously elected. A Catholic was not allowed to own a horse of greater value than £5, and if it were worth more a Protestant could demand it for £5. If a combination of workmen met to talk over schemes for their improvement, they were liable to severe punishment. It was for demanding reforms to such a state of matters, that men were sent by the Tory Government to the hulks to herd with felons.

One night, in the autumn of 1792, knots of working men had assembled in front of the Star Inn, at the head of Glassford Street, and were eagerly discussing the successes and failures of the French Republic. A turbulent spirit was brooding over Europe. Revolution was in the air, and blazing fiercely in the lands of the Bourbons. In no city was the development of the drama watched with greater interest than Glasgow. At that time, as now, it was a purely commercial centre, and the bulk of the population of 66,500 was working men and women. There was no outlook of hope in Scotland in the direction of reform. But some of the seeds from which the new Republic sprang were wafted to England, and had found their way north, where they took firm root. In these days news travelled slowly. The gathering in front of the "Star," after hearing the latest intelligence from Paris from a gentleman who had arrived by the coach, entered the inn, and proceeded to form themselves into a Reform Association. Amongst them were spies of the Tory Government. When the audience had settled down and a chairman had been appointed, a young man of medium height, broad shouldered and robust, entered and took his seat beside him. The hearty cheers which greeted him showed that he was known and popular. Take a good look at him in the feeble and flickering light diffused from the tallow candles with which the room is illuminated. He was the pioneer of the reform movement that triumphed in 1832; his name is Thomas Muir, the first and most distinguished of Scotland's political heroes. A firmly set head, fine forehead, keen blue eyes, a small mouth indicative of strong will - power, aquiline nose, with finely chiselled features,—such is the man who is destined to make his mark on the age.

Thomas Muir was born in Glasgow, on the 24th August 1765; and being an only son, his parents gave him a first-class education in the Universities of Glasgow and Edinburgh. In 1787 he was admitted a member of the Faculty of Advocates, and his talents and energy secured for him a brilliant though brief legal career. At an early age he took up the cause of reform, and soon his clear commanding voice rang out at many a gathering of the people, speaking of hope for the oppressed.

With the threats of prosecution hanging over them, the meeting in the Star Inn proceeded to form a society called "The Friends of the Constitution and of the People;" each member had to sign a declaration, expressing his loyalty to the crown, and that he was of good moral character. Branches were formed in nearly every town in Scotland, and within a month the membership exceeded five thousand. In December a British Convention was held in Edinburgh, when two hundred delegates were present. It attracted European attention. Dundas and his myrmidons endeavoured to crush the movement. The delegates from England were seized, and upon 2nd January 1793 Muir was arrested. He was liberated on bail, and proceeded to Paris, where he arrived in time to witness the execution of Louis XVI. and the horrors of that terrible epoch. Six months after, upon arriving in Scotland he was cast into Stranraer jail, and upon the 30th August he stood at the bar before the High Court at Edinburgh charged with sedition.

Muir's defence was an admission that on the great question concerning equal representation of the people in Parliament he had exerted every effort to procure reform, and a denial of disseminating seditious literature. The Crown failed on every count to establish the charges. The trial was national in interest, and evoked extraordinary excitement. The court was crowded with the *elite* of Edina, and thousands could not obtain admission. The Lord Justice-Clerk was the notorious Braxfield. The jury was packed,—the judges having the nomination of the jurors in their own hands. Muir conducted his own defence, although the Hon. Henry Erskine offered to appear for him. In his address to the jury, Muir made a name that is imperishable while the English language is spoken, and proved himself one of the most brilliant orators that ever adorned the Scottish bar. In the dim candle-lit court he addressed the jury from ten o'clock at night till one in the morning, and moving rapidly to and fro in the dock, he concluded with a peroration of singular beauty and pathos :—" I may," he said, "be condemned to languish in the recesses of a dungeon; I may be doomed to ascend the scaffold. Nothing can deprive me, however, of the recollection of the past ; nothing can destroy my inward peace of mind arising from the remembrance of having discharged my duty."

During the utterance of these words the silence of death pervaded the court ; but as soon as he was finished, a wild hysterical shout of triumph rose from those in the gallery and in the corridors, such as had never been heard within the walls of the court before. "Clear the court," shouted Braxfield; but again the applause, mingled with sobs, broke the silence. Braxfield said that the indecent applause given the prisoner convinced him that a spirit of discontent still lurked in the minds of the people, and that it would be dangerous to allow Muir to remain in the country. The court adjourned at two o'clock in the morning, and met on

the same day at twelve, and the jury returned a verdict of
"Guilty."   Braxfield sentenced Muir to fourteen years'
transportation "beyond seas."   When sentence was passed
many of the audience were moved to tears.   Muir rose once
more, and in a clear ringing voice said,—"Were I to be led
this moment to the scaffold, I should feel the same calm-
ness which I now do.   My mind tells me that I have acted
agreeably to my conscience ; and that I have engaged in a
good, just, and a glorious cause, which sooner or later must
and will prevail, and by a timely reform save this country
from destruction."   He was then removed from the bar.

From Leith to London Muir was conveyed, and thence,
along with Margarot, Skirving, Palmer, and Gerald, in a
convict ship to Botany Bay.   His subsequent adventures
rival those of *Robinson Crusoe.*   One day when working as a
convict he was addressed by a sailor in significant tones :
"Fear not, you shall soon be free."   The American Government actually fitted out a vessel, the "Otter," to try to effect
his escape.   She came to Sydney without awakening suspicion, and a chance occurred of getting Muir safely on
board, when they immediately set sail, 11th February 1796.
But after four months at sea, the "Otter" was unfortunately
wrecked on some sunken rocks off the west coast of South
America.   Of the crew only Thomas Muir and two sailors
escaped, on a raft, to the shore.   They were at once seized
by savages, and looked for immediate death.   Our hero
was separated from the others, and never learned what was
their fate.   He was kindly treated, and after three weeks
succeeded in making his escape.   He walked four thousand
miles along the west coast of South America, in constant
danger from the natives, and at last reached the Spanish
settlement of Panama, destitute and in rags, with injured
bleeding feet.   His knowledge of Spanish enabled him to
procure an escort across the Isthmus of Darien.   He next
made his way to Vera Cruz, in Mexico, buoyed up by the
hope of getting a ship to the United States, but was dis-
appointed.   He was taken ill, and by his own wish conveyed to the Havannah.   Learning by some means about
his past career, the Spanish authorities apprehended him as
a man whose opinions were dangerous.   He was confined
in a loathsome dungeon in Havannah for four weeks, where
he contracted a horrible disease.   At last he was shipped

for Spain as a prisoner, and was made to do the work of a
common sailor during the voyage.   The vessel was attacked
by the British under Sir John Jervis, near Cadiz, and a
fierce struggle ensued, Muir behaving with singular courage.
The Spaniards were worsted, and their vessel was boarded
by the men of the "Irresistible." After the action they were
clearing the decks, and were in the act of throwing Muir
overboard, supposing him to be dead, when he uttered a
groan, and a book fell from his breast.   A British officer
lifted it, and was astonished to find an English Bible, with
the inscription—"To Thomas Muir from his afflicted and
affectionate mother." It was her parting gift upon his
banishment.   The officer had been a schoolfellow of her
unfortunate son, who was now desperately wounded; he had
lost an eye, and was terribly hurt.   His friend nursed him
like a brother, got him quietly landed at Cadiz, and treated
in an hospital there.   After partial recovery he went on to
France, where every one received him like the hero he was.
The Government made him a free citizen, and he reached
Paris on 4th February.   But his course was run ; he never
got over the injuries he had received in the fight.   He died
soon after.

On the monument in the Calton Cemetery, Edinburgh,
which was erected in 1844 to the Martyrs of Reform, the
first name inscribed is that of Thomas Muir.

THE RADICAL RISING OF 1820.

FROM 1812 till 1822 Castlereagh and Sidmouth were the
Home and Foreign Secretaries, and more tyrannical and
despotic men never held office.   The latter was instrumental
in getting fourteen reformers hung at York in 1813 ; eight
at Lancaster and three at Nottingham in 1817 ; and Wilson,
Baird, and Hardie in Scotland in 1820 ; and the banishment
of scores of others.

These were unhappy days for the lower orders.   Between
the same period, 1812 to 1820, 15,000 souls were evicted
from the straths of Sutherlandshire, and from the Western
Isles as well shiploads of the Highlanders were taken and

sent to Canada. The Radicals of the country looked upon Glasgow as their capital and headquarters, and it was resolved to make a demonstration or rising there on Monday the 1st of April. No secret was made of the date, and the Government concentrated what troops they had accordingly. Their treacherous spies went about the country spreading insurrectionary ideas and circulating the grossest falsehoods, professing to come from the Radical leaders, encouraging the people to rise and make a bold stand. It was said that Cathkin Braes was to be the first camp of the rebels, and Radicals from all quarters were to gather there. Glasgow was in a state of great excitement. On the Saturday and Sunday before the Monday of the rising, things came to fever heat. During Saturday night, a treasonable address summoning the people to arms was posted all over the town. It is said to have been concocted and circulated at the bidding of the Tory Government by some of their wretched tools. Many of the ministers referred to the document that Sabbath. Dr Chalmers, in St John's, prayed that the country might be saved from the horrors of civil war. On Monday 5000 soldiers arrived in Glasgow. Work was at a standstill; crowds of weavers, cotton-spinners, machine-makers, and colliers paraded the streets. Numerous arrests were made; and many houses, chiefly in Calton, were searched for arms. Government offered a reward of £500 for information that would lead to the arrest of the authors of the address. This of course was a mere blind. Even if it had been the work of the Reformers, in itself it was a harmless production, for being founded or copied from what was their published opinions and policy, it declared that all private and public property must be protected, and only demanded just rights for the people,—"Equality of rights, not of property," &c. The object of the Government seemed to be to precipitate a rising. On Tuesday, at the instance of a spy named Lees, a man called Shields went to Strathaven to James Wilson, the leader of the Radicals there, telling him to muster his men the following morning and march to Cathkin Braes, where they would meet several thousands of insurgents. Other two spies—Turner and King—went on similar errands to Carron and Condorret by Bonnymuir. The story they told was that the blow had been already struck in England. The treacherous address, and these diabolical lies, were the direct causes of the battle of Bonnymuir and the execution of Wilson, Baird, and Hardie.

For twenty-five years, when Radicalism was a crime, the house of James Wilson, the Strathaven stocking-weaver, had been a rendezvous of the Reformers. His correspondence with Thomas Muir in 1792 shows him to have been fairly well educated, and to have a clear sense of the wrongs under which the people suffered. Though sixty years old, his enthusiasm for the cause had not cooled.

It is doubtful whether it was owing to genuine Radical counsels, or merely the result of the treacherous messages of their enemies, that the Strathaven men had been meeting under cover of night, and secretly drilling, in view of a contemplated struggle. On Tuesday, April 2, the evening before the Glasgow Fast, as we have already said, one of Richmond's emissaries arrived at Strathaven, saying he had been sent by the Radicals in Glasgow to tell them to come next day to Cathkin Braes ; several thousands of Reformers would gather, and, under some Jacobite general who had arrived from France, would face the king's troops. Another messenger soon after came, stating that the fighting had commenced, and told of warfare in the High Street of Glasgow. The Strathaven men believed these stories, and immediately set about procuring firearms. Early next morning they gathered. There were seventeen who met in Wilson's house, one of whom—Mr John Caldwell—still survives. Stevenson threatened to shoot a farmer if he did not hand over his gun. On reaching Kilbride they learned that they had been tricked. They immediately dispersed ; the guns were hid, and few of them were ever discovered. Stevenson stuck to the flag. Wilson arrived at the house of Mrs Hunter, shivering and wet to the skin, for a violent thunder and rain storm had burst upon them. Mrs Hunter has survived to extreme old age, and told the story of her unfortunate friend only the other day to a contributor of the *North British Mail*. On returning to his house in Strathaven, Wilson was arrested on a charge of high treason, tried in Glasgow, and found guilty, on 30th August 1820, and, in presence of 20,000 persons, was hanged and then beheaded at the Cross of Glasgow.

Stevenson escaped from Greenock to Liverpool and thence to Australia, carrying the flag with him.

A monument has been erected over the grave of Wilson in Strathaven kirkyard, which has become the shrine of enthusiastic Radicals from all quarters. " The principles for which he forfeited his life were those which banished Muir and the other pioneers. They have long since been conceded, and the murder of Wilson is one of the darkest blots in the history of the Tory party."

It is noteworthy that men like Edward Irving and Thomas Carlyle sympathised warmly with the Reformers.*

THE BATTLE OF BONNYMUIR.

"On Wednesday, 5th April 1820, a party of about fifty Radicals, chiefly from Glasgow, and supposed to be on their way to Carron, gave battle to the military. They stopt one of the Stirlingshire Yeomanry who was going to join his troop at Falkirk, and made him turn. Lieutenant Hodgson of the 10th Hussars, and Lieutenant Davidson of the Stirlingshire Yeomanry, immediately rode from Kilsyth with a party of each corps in pursuit of the men, whom they overtook near Bonnybridge. On observing them the Radicals cheered and advanced to a wall, over which they commenced firing. Some shots were then fired by the soldiers in return, and after some time the cavalry got through an opening in the wall and attacked the party, who resisted till overpowered by the troops. Nineteen prisoners were taken and lodged in Stirling Castle. Lieutenant Hodgson received a pike wound through the right hand, and a sergeant of the 10th Hussars was severely wounded by a shot in the side and by a pike. Three horses were also wounded. Four of the Radicals were wounded ; five muskets, two pistols, eighteen pikes, and about one hundred rounds of ball cartridges, were taken. One of the prisoners was so seriously wounded that he was left in the house of a farmer, from which he was forcibly carried by his friends in the evening. The result of this attempt seems to have awakened the Reformers to a sense of the hopelessness of their cause. The weavers and others about Glasgow and

* The information regarding Thomas Muir and the 1820 troubles has been gathered from the *Scots Magazine*, from " An Examination of the Trials for Sedition in Scotland," by Lord Cockburn, and from an interesting series of papers on the early reformers which appeared in the *North British Mail* in August and September 1887.

Paisley showed a disposition to return to their work, and in a few days tranquillity seemed to be restored. On Saturday there was an outbreak at Greenock, where five prisoners were released. In the disturbances there five men were killed and a great many hurt."—*Scots Magazine.*

The Bonnymuir prisoners were tried at Stirling on 13th July. - Twenty-two were found guilty and sentenced to death, but all were pardoned except two,—John Baird, weaver, Condorret, aged thirty-one years, and Andrew Hardie, weaver, Glasgow, aged twenty-seven. Both were unmarried men, and had been in the army. They were hanged and beheaded at Stirling.

JAMES WATT.

"A heart to resolve, a head to contrive, and a hand to execute."
—GIBBON.

ABOUT the middle of last century (1752) a tall strapping lad began his apprenticeship in Glasgow. Before hé left the city (1768) he had learned far more than any living man could have taught him. He had acquired a knowledge that was to revolutionise the world.

James Watt was born at Greenock, on 19th January 1736. His father was the Town Treasurer, a bailie, and a merchant in good circumstances. Being a delicate boy, James was educated mostly at home. In 1750, to amuse himself, he made an electrical machine. He studied natural philosophy. Chemistry was a favourite subject, and he also read works on surgery and medicine. At sixteen he was apprenticed to an instrument maker in Glasgow. From the age of fourteen he had been much in the city, at the house of his uncle, Mr Muirhead. He spent one summer on the banks of Loch Lomond. On 18th June 1754, when eighteen years of age, he returned to Glasgow, and remained nearly a year, living with the Muirheads. It was his Aunt Muirhead who scolded him for trifling with the tea-urn, little knowing to what purpose his "trifling" was coming. In 1755 his mother, Agnes Muirhead, died, aged fifty-two. In June the same year Watt went to London, to acquire further knowledge of his trade. He rode all the way, and spent twelve days on the journey. Whilst in London he was afraid to walk

abroad in the evening, lest he might be seized and sent to
India or the American plantations.   After a year the state
of his health compelled him to return to the north.

Some astronomical instruments had been brought home
from Jamaica by Mr Macfarlane, who died, bequeathing
them to the University of Glasgow.   They were somewhat
spoilt by the sea air, and James Watt being accidentally in
the town, having just arrived from London, got £5 to clean
them and put them in good order.   This was the beginning
of his connection with the University authorities.   Watt
purposed to begin business in the city, but owing to his
not being a burgess he met with opposition from the cor-
porations of arts and trades.   The University, however,
allowed him to open a shop within the precincts of
the College, where he established himself as a mathematical instrument maker.   This was about 1757, and six
years passed before he commenced his attack upon the
steam-engine.   Professor John Anderson, the founder of
the Andersonian College, gave him a small model of Newcome's engine to repair.   This invention of Newcome,
which has often been called a steam-engine, was not a
steam-engine at all, but was worked by means of atmospheric
pressure.   Watt became so absorbed in this subject that he
left the College (1763) and retired to a private room near
the Broomielaw (now James Watt Street), where, with a
single assistant, he commenced those experiments that have
had such tremendous results.   In 1762 his brother John
was drowned at sea in one of his father's ships whilst on
a voyage to America.   He was twenty-four years of age,
and three years younger than James.   In the summer of
1765 Watt married his cousin, Miss Miller, a Glasgow
young lady.   She being the daughter of a free burgess,
he was at liberty to trade in the city.   He opened a
mathematical instrument shop in the Saltmarket, but continued his experiments on the steam-engine.   He afterwards added land surveying and civil engineering to his
occupations, and was engaged more particularly in planning
and surveying canals.   For this work he invented a new
micronometer, and a machine for drawing in perspective.
One biographer says his shop or house was situated about
King Street, adding, " his dwelling-place was enlightened
by his wife, who made sunshine in that shady place."

Dr Samuel Smiles says:—" Of James Watt, the laborious, patient, never-tiring mathematical instrument maker, many men in his time knew far more than he, but none laboured so assiduously to turn all he did know to useful practical account. He cultivated carefully that habit of active attention on which all the higher working qualities of the mind mainly depend. Even when a boy Watt found science in his toys. The quadrants lying about his father's carpenter's shop led him to the study of optics and astronomy; his ill health induced him to pry into the secrets of physiology; and his solitary walks through the country attracted him to the study of botany and history. While carrying on the business of a mathematical instrument maker he received an order to build an organ; and though without an ear for music, he undertook the study of harmonies, and successfully constructed the instrument. And in like manner, when the little model of Newcome's steam-engine belonging to the University of Glasgow was placed in his hands to repair, he forthwith set himself to learn all that was then known about heat, evaporation, and condensation, at the same time plodding his way in mechanics and the science of construction,—the results of which he at length embodied in his condensing steam-engine." Long after he was consulted about the best mode of carrying water in pipes under the Clyde, along the uneven bed of the river. When turning his attention one day at table to a lobster, from the model of its shell he invented an iron tube, which, when laid down, was found effectually to answer the purpose. It was whilst taking a walk in Glasgow Green one Sunday afternoon, when near the Arns Well, that the idea of the double-condenser suddenly occurred to Mr Watt's mind, and the great problem was happily solved. In 1768 he joined Mr John Roebuck, and on 5th January 1769 the engine was patented. In 1773, whilst surveying a line of canal between Fort-William and Inverness, since made by Telford, and called the Caledonian Canal, Watt received the news of his wife's death. In 1774 he removed from Scotland to Soho, near Birmingham, where he entered into partnership with Matthew Boulton in the business of constructing steam-engines, which they carried to the height of perfection. The new partner threw such mercantile enterprise into the undertaking that a fortune was realised. £47,000 had been spent before the patentees derived any returns. Watt retired in 1800, by which time the steam-engine was at work throughout the United Kingdom. He invented the copying-press, a steam-drying press, and also made improvements in bleaching. Mr Watt had married Miss Anne Macgregor, another Glasgow lady, in 1776, and the handsome fortune he had earned enabled him to spend the evening of life with ease and comfort in the bosom of his family. It is related that when past seventy he imagined that his faculties were on the decline, and accordingly determined to put them to the test by undertaking some new study. He chose the Anglo-Saxon language, and soon proved that his fears were groundless by the easy way he mastered it. Mr Watt was engaged for thirty years upon the condensing engine before he brought it to perfection. He declined to take up the task of adapting steam to marine or other locomotion, but left other men to prosecute that great subject.

During the time he lived inside the College Watt made several organs, guitars, flutes, and violins. The organ alluded to by Dr Smiles became long afterwards a disturber of the peace. It was introduced for the service in St Andrew's Parish Church by the Rev. Dr Ritchie about 1812, and such an innovation in a Presbyterian kirk raised a great hullaballoo in the city. James Watt used to attend St Andrew's at an earlier period. And regarding the incident of the lobster shell, the Water Company had come to Watt for advice. The difficulty was in laying pipes to bring pure spring water across the Clyde to the Water Company's engine at Dalmarnock, the channel of the river being uneven and liable to movement. Mr Watt solved the trouble by constructing a long and pliable, or rather articulated, suction-pipe, with joints formed on the principle of those in a lobster's tail. The pipe was two feet in diameter, and one thousand feet in length. A piece of plate, valued at one hundred guineas, was presented to Mr Watt by the company. He died, aged eighty-three, on 25th August 1819, at Heath-field, near Soho. A statue was erected to his memory in Glasgow University. His widow lived to extreme old age in 1832.

Matthew Boulton used to say—" We deal in what kings love—power."

ADAM SMITH.

ADAM SMITH came from his Fifeshire home in 1737, entering the University of Glasgow when only fourteen years of age. Here he remained for three years, when he removed to Oxford, with the idea of eventually taking orders in the English Church, but that intention was very soon abandoned. At Glasgow his chief studies were mathematics and natural philosophy; during the seven years that he remained at Oxford his education was of a wider scope. Having given evidence of his ability in Edinburgh, the logic chair of Glasgow University was conferred upon him in 1751, and next year he became Professor of Moral Philosophy, which honoured office he held in Glasgow for thirteen years. As a public teacher he greatly excelled. He trusted almost entirely to *extempore* elocution; and while his manner was not graceful, it was plain and unaffected, and as he warmed with his subject, the listeners were charmed by the richness and beauty of his discourse, and the clearness of his reasoning. In 1763 he resigned his professorship, in order to take a prolonged tour on the continent of Europe, as companion to the Duke of Buccleuch. Ten years of comparative seclusion in his native town of Kirkcaldy ensued, where he produced "The Wealth of Nations." In 1762 he had received from the University of Glasgow the degree of LL.D.; and in 1788 the students elected him Rector, an honour which he appreciated very highly.

DAVID DALE;

AN OLD GLASGOW WORTHY.

DAVID DALE is pretty much forgotten now-a-days. Few of us could tell how Dale Street, Bridgeton, and Dale Street, Tradeston, came by their names. The more shame to us! We have had no citizen better deserving to be remembered. David Dale's mercantile services put him on a level with the four young Virginians, the recognised founders of our mercantile importance. But his mercantile services, great and varied as they were, were only part of his astonishing activities. The work he put through his hands of one kind and another shows what can be done with method and through-put, an easy temper, and a good digestion. For the end of last century and the beginning of this, it is impossible to look into our history—mercantile, manufacturing, financial, municipal, benevolent, religious—without coming on David Dale at every turn. Even distant country ministers had heard how in other parishes David Dale of Glasgow had been in those cruel times like a good providence, and sighed that he might be the *Deus ex machinâ* for their poor people too.

Originally a herd boy at Stewarton, and afterwards a weaver at Paisley, Hamilton, and Cambuslang, David Dale came here as a young man, and became a dealer in linen yarn, tramping the country, and buying in pickles from farmers' wives. From this small beginning he developed a large trade in importing yarns from the Low Countries. He was at the same time an inkle manufacturer as Campbell, Dale, & Co.; and a manufacturer of printing cloth as Dale, Campbell, Reid, & Dale. Further, he was the father of the cotton trade in Glasgow,—we may say of Scotland. His works at New Lanark, founded, with Arkwright's co-operation, in 1783, were the first of any importance in Scotland, and, with 1,334 hands, were at one time the largest in Great Britain.* He was also a partner in the original mills at Blantyre and at Catrine (each the nucleus of a great work), and in those persistently unlucky works at Stanley. He was one of the benevolent copartnery (George Mackintosh, William Gillespie, George Dempster of Dunnichen, and others) that built Spinningdale on the Dornoch Firth; and across the island, in the parish of Kilmore, near where Oban now stands, he had a small cotton work of his own. And

---

* Mr Dale sold the mills at New Lanark to an English company, one of whom was the famous Robert Owen, who married his daughter. He undertook the management, and tried to introduce a new social era among the workers, for he was a noted apostle of Socialism. The fame of the new system spread far and wide. The Czar Nicholas and about 20,000 visitors came in one year to see New Lanark under Mr Owen's *regime*. Frequent disagreements arose between Mr Owen and his partners as to the customs and education of the little colony, and he retired in 1829. The works are still carried on, but without any of Owen's eccentricities.—A. G. C.

cotton was only one of his trades. In company with Robert
Tennent and David Todd he was deep in a disastrous
attempt at coal-mining in Barrowfield (the grave of more
than one Glasgow fortune) ; and in 1783, besides founding
New Lanark, he (in company with George Mackintosh)
founded Barrowfield, the first Turkey-red work in Great
Britain, and he opened a branch of the Royal Bank, the
first permanent establishment in Glasgow of any of the great
Scotch banks. All this, somehow, left him plenty of time
for other work. In that same 1783 (a lively year even for
him) he took an active part in forming the Chamber of
Commerce,—he was one of its first directors, and was twice
chosen its chairman ; he was in the Town Council, and was
twice chosen a magistrate ; and he was always ready to lend
a hand to the public interest. But after all the business of
his life was philanthropy and religion. To make men
happier and better, he gave his money (as it was said)
by shols fu', and time and trouble with as little stint.*
His givings were ceaseless, and sometimes could not
be hid. In the terrible years between 1782 and 1799,
when meal rose to 21s. 4d. a boll, he chartered ships
and imported great quantities of grain, to be sold cheap to
the poor people. He always tried to make business yield
something better than profit. The Dornoch and the Oban
factories were opened expressly as a means of giving work to
the starving Highlanders ; and at New Lanark, long before
such things were the fashion, he set himself to provide his
workpeople with good houses, good sanitation, and good
schooling, intellectual, moral, and religious. Outside of
these connections of his own he was a friend to every good
cause. He was a warm supporter of missions ; he visited
Bridewell to preach to the prisoners ; he helped to found
here the earliest auxiliary of the Bible Society, and to his
death acted as the Society's treasurer for Glasgow and the
West of Scotland. Originally a member of the Church of
Scotland, he became a founder of the "Old Scotch Independents ;" he travelled all about to counsel and comfort
their scattered congregations ; to his own congregation in
Greyfriars' Wynd he had at his death acted for thirty-seven

* He once said :—"I gave my money to God in handfuls, and He
gave it back to me in shovelfuls."—A. G. C.

years as pastor, preaching regularly on Sundays, and occasionally on other days ; and, to help his pulpit work, he had taught himself to read the Scriptures in the original Hebrew and Greek. Withal he was a genial, humorous man ; he was given to hospitality, and he would sing an old Scotch song with such feeling as to bring tears to the eyes. Strange to say David Dale had in his day to suffer public insult. His taking on him the work of the Christian ministry fired the latent sacerdotalism of Scotchmen ; he was denounced as a Nadab or Abihu, he was hooted and pelted on his way to his Sunday labours, and his little chapel was attacked by the crowd. But none of these things moved him ; he lived down the scathe and the scorn. When he rested from his labours on the 17th March 1806 all the town mourned, and he was laid in the Ramshorn Kirkyard with a great following of gentle and simple. He lies below a plain stone let into the east wall, bearing on it—

THIS BURYING-GROUND
IS THE PROPERTY
OF DAVID DALE,
MERCHANT IN GLASGOW.
1780.

By his wife, Ann Campbell, he left five daughters, of whom the eldest was married to the well-known Robert Owen. His portrait is preserved for us in Kay's " Morning Walk " (reproduced in Stuart), and his places of business and of residence are still to the fore. He occupied as offices and warehouse the two southmost blocks on the east side of St Andrew's Square (two slabs on the verge of the pavement mark where the sentry-boxes stood before the bank, and the tenement pierced by an arched pen was afterwards occupied by one of the many benevolent schemes of a citizen who, like David Dale, manages to combine a laborious business with much public, charitable, and Christian work). His house stands at the south-west corner of Charlotte Street ; and his country house, Rosebank, near Cambuslang, is still there, though the roses now-a-days are few and far between.*

* The foregoing sketch of David Dale is from the pen of Mr J. O. Mitchell, Glasgow.

SIR JOHN MOORE.

This distinguished military commander was born in the Trongait, Glasgow, on 13th November 1761. His grand-father, the Rev. Charles Moore, was an Episcopal clergyman in Stirling, and hailed from County Armagh, his forefather having fought for William III. Sir John's father, Dr John Moore, was a physician, and man of literary pursuits, the author of "Zelucco," &c. He was an early appreciative friend of Robert Burns, and it was to him the poet wrote an account of his own life-story (August 1787). On his mother's side our hero came of an old Glasgow family, the Andersons of Dowhill, Gallowgait, and Anderston (see pages 147 and 176). His great-grandfather was Provost Anderson, and an earlier ancestor was the chief man among the trades when they saved the Cathedral. Sir John was schooled on the Continent and at the High School of Glasgow, and chose the military profession when a mere boy. Whilst his father was abroad with the Duke of Hamilton, he obtained an ensigncy in the 51st foot at the early age of fifteen, and soon saw active service. In July 1779 he was at Penobscot, Boston, and distinguished himself by holding a position with a few soldiers against the Americans, when every one else had retreated. When he had attained the rank of captain, he entered Parliament as representative of four Scottish burghs, through the influence of the Duke of Hamilton, and was a supporter of Pitt till 1787, when active service again called him to the field. He became major of the 51st in 1788, and displayed great ability in the organising and training of troops. In 1790 he was made lieutenant-colonel, and led his regiment through much hard service in Corsica. In 1794, when General Dundas had decided that the Martello tower was too strong to be stormed, Colonel Moore expressed a contrary opinion, and ultimately led a storming party right into it. This redoubt was the first of the class, and gave the name to the kind of fortification of which many were soon after built. Side by side with Moore during part of this Corsican campaign was a body of seamen, led by Captain Nelson, who afterwards rose to such eminence. They were close together in action when Nelson lost an eye through a ricochet shot throwing up dust in his face. Moore was wounded (10th July 1794) at the attack on the Mozello fort at the siege of Calvi. In 1796 he acted as brigadier-general to Sir Ralph Abercrombie in the West Indies, and was appointed governor of St Lucie, in the capture of which he had a principal share. Next year he returned home, and was employed in Ireland during the rebellion, attaining the rank of major-general about this time. He went on the expedition to Holland in 1799, where he did all that military prudence could accomplish to repair the mistakes of an incompetent commander, and where he was again wounded severely. Soon after he was in the thick of the fighting in Egypt, and at the battle of Alexandria he received two more wounds. For his skill and valour in that campaign he was rewarded with the Order of the Bath. He was next sent on a military and diplomatic mission to the Court of Sweden, and successfully displayed equal dexterity and firmness. In 1808 he was appointed Commander of the British Army in Spain. The Spanish forces failed to keep the field, and Bounaparte concentrated all his forces, numbering 100,000 men, against Moore, who, with a small force, without supplies or reinforcements, fought his way through the Peninsula, defeating the French on every occasion that he could tempt them to come to close quarters ; but, unable to hold his position for fear of being surrounded and cut off, he made the memorable and arduous retreat to the coast followed by Soult, who attacked him at Corunna, January 16, 1809, where in the moment of victory Sir John was fatally struck by a cannon ball. His death caused a great sensation throughout the country. The House of Commons ordered a monument to be erected for him in St Paul's Cathedral, and Glasgow, his native city, also erected one to his memory; but the ode by the Rev. Charles Wolfe, " The Burial of Sir John Moore," has done more than these to keep his name before successive generations of his countrymen.

THOMAS CAMPBELL.

OF none of her gifted sons has Glasgow more cause to be proud than of Thomas Campbell. Born on 27th July 1777, in the High Street, in a house long since demolished, he spent the first twenty years of his life in our midst. His family had been settled for generations at Kirnan, near Inverary. His father, Alexander Campbell, went in early life to Virginia, and established a mercantile connection. There he fell in with a fellow Scotsman, Daniel Campbell, who returned with him to Glasgow and became his partner, whose sister Mary he married in the Cathedral on 12th January 1756. The outbreak of the American Revolutionary war in 1775 was the ruin of the business. Thomas was born two years later, and his father was a poor man all his life after. If the morning of the poet's life was not altogether overshadowed by black clouds, it was at least early toned down to very sober grey, owing to the straitened circumstances of his family. He had to endure what so many thousands of his townsmen since then have experienced, the chilling and depressing anxieties of genteel poverty. Being the youngest of eleven children, and the son of their old age, Thomas was the favourite child of his parents. His mother was a woman of decided character and ability. She was passionately fond of music, particularly sacred music, and sang many Scotch songs with taste and effect. At eight years of age our hero was sent to the grammar school, at eleven he began to compose verses. At thirteen he entered the University, where the first year he carried off three prizes. Latin and Greek were his favourite studies, but he soon after proved his excellence in logic, &c. His verses on the queen of France appeared in a Glasgow newspaper when he was fifteen. He walked to Edinburgh, and was present at the trial and condemnation of Gerald for sedition, and was shocked at the iniquity of the proceedings. In politics he was always a Whig. When sixteen, the failure of a lawsuit straitened more than ever the circumstances of his father, who was now eighty-five, and had to support a large family chiefly by small mercantile annuities. Thomas got the situation of tutor to a family in Mull. On his way thither he saved a boy from drowning. After crossing to Mull, he walked in one day thirty miles, the whole length of the island, to his destination. After spending five months in Mull, he returned to Glasgow, and engaged in private teaching. In 1796 his University career came to a close ; and after residing at Downie, near the Crinan Canal, for a short period, he made his way to Edinburgh, where happily his abilities were soon appreciated, and his poems were brought before an admiring public. His life subsequently was on the whole successful, most of it being spent in London. His father died in 1801, aged ninety-one, and his mother in 1812.

In 1826 Campbell was elected Lord Rector of Glasgow University, and he delivered his inaugural address early in the following year. Ardently attached to his native city and the place of his education, where he was now so honoured, he carried his feeling of gratification almost to weakness. But his temperament excited by the recall of early sensations rendered this very excusable. He dined with the Senatus Academicus in the room where he had never been but once in his life, and that was when a youth on a charge of breaking windows in the College Church. He spent two months in the city, and so popular was he with the students that they elected him Lord Rector three times in succession. His death took place on the Continent in 1844, and he was buried in Westminster Abbey.

As a poet Thomas Campbell's position stands upon an unshaken basis. No other, of modern times, has been so much quoted. He never wrote a line of which any one could be ashamed. In his verses may be found only the purest and noblest sentiments.

LORD CLYDE.

THIS distinguished soldier was born within sound of St Mungo's bells, on 20th October 1792. His grandfather was out for Prince Charlie in the " forty-five;" and his property in Islay being forfeited in consequence, he settled in Glasgow. Colin's father, John Macliver, was a carpenter by trade, and married Agnes Campbell, in Glasgow, on 29th January 1782. Colin was the eldest of their children, of whom there were two sons and two daughters. He attended the High School, and a writing school in Wilson Street. When ten years of age he was removed to Gosport by his uncle, Colonel John Campbell, who thenceforth took charge of him. When fifteen and a half years old he got a commission in the 9th regiment of foot (May 1808). At the Horse Guards his name was entered by mistake as Colin Campbell by the Duke of York, with the remark " Another of the clan!" and from that day Colin, for professional reasons, assumed his mother's name, Campbell. Two or three months later the boy ensign landed in Spain, and in August took part in the battle of Vimiera. That winter he shared in Sir John Moore's campaign and in the memorable retreat. In this terrible operation, conducted in the dead of night, young Campbell bore his share.* His regiment lost an officer and one hundred and forty-eight men, who died on the road or fell into the enemy's hands through exhaustion. For some time before reaching Corunna, Colin had to march with bare feet, the soles of his boots being completely worn away. After the victory of Corunna (16th January 1809), the Ninth furnished the fatigue-party which dug the grave on the ramparts for Sir John Moore, the enemy's guns opening a heavy fire whilst the burial-service was being read.

Colin Campbell subsequently took part in other Peninsular campaigns, and twice distinguished himself by conspicuous bravery. In 1813 he led the forlorn hope at the siege of San Sebastian, and was severely wounded. In 1814 he took part in the expedition to the United States. After seeing much service he attained to the rank of colonel in 1842. During these past years he did much important work in training and educating soldiers. Sir John Moore had introduced at Shorncliffe a system of discipline and organisation in which the officers and men of each company were brought very close together, and the feeling of *esprit de corps* was firmly established in the British army in consequence. Sir Colin followed up the same plan, and strove to have it said of his men, as was said of his townsman's during the Peninsular war, that no regiment stood the test like those which Sir John Moore had trained. In 1842 Colonel Campbell was at the attack on Chusan in China, and again received honourable mention in the *Gazette*. He served in the Punjab, commanding the left at the battle of Chillianwallah. He next commanded, with unwavering success, against the hill tribes in the Peshawar district. His later career is fresh

* A veteran countryman, Sir Roderick Murchison, underwent the same trying ordeal when a boy. He was also present as an ensign at Vimiera.

in our memory.   In 1854 he was appointed to the command
of the Highland brigade in the Crimea, and led his three
kilted regiments—the 42nd, the 79th, and the 93rd—up the
heights of Alma.   At Balaclava with the last named corps,—
the Sutherland Highlanders, "the long thin red line tipped
with steel,"—whom he did not even form into square, he beat
back the Russian cavalry who were swooping down upon
the port with its shipping and stores.

He received distinguished honours.   On his return from
the Crimea he was presented with a sword in Glasgow, and
a banquet was held in the City Hall.   Fifty years had come
and gone since he left his native city.   In 1857, at the outbreak of the Indian Mutiny, Sir Colin was appointed to the
chief command, and proved his capacity for the great work.
Next year he was created a peer of the realm, with the title
of Baron Clyde, and an annuity of £2,000.   It was his own
choice that he was called after his native river.   He arrived
from India in 1860.   Saving on himself, Lord Clyde was
always most open-hearted and generous.   He never married,
but provided handsomely for his relatives.   His father had
died at Portobello, in 1859, leaving one daughter, who had
always been Sir Colin's special care.   It is said his fondness
for Scotch poetry was a characteristic that seemed to grow
with him with his advancing age, and his affection for his
old sister, Miss Campbell, was very touchingly shown.   She
closed his eyes at Chatham, where he died on 14th August
1868, aged seventy-one.   He had risen by his own bravery
and ability to be the foremost soldier of his country, and was
buried in Westminster.   The most notable characteristic of
his generalship was the care he took of his soldiers' lives.
He was always successful, and all the victories he won were
taken at a minimum cost of his soldiers.

THOMAS CHALMERS;

A GLASGOW CITY MISSIONARY.

DR CHALMERS was elected minister of the Tron Church on
25th November 1814.   His coming to Glasgow was hailed
with delight by the Evangelicals, for Moderatism had long

held undisputed possession of all the best churches in the Kirk of Scotland. The call was accepted, one reason for deciding to leave Kilmany being that Chalmers calculated on finding in the city more stimulus to exertion and study, and "a warm Christian society to revive the deadness and barrenness of his own soul." The induction took place on 21st July 1815, a few weeks after the battle of Waterloo. The new minister, who was now in his thirty-fifth year, came with the intention of visiting every family in his parish. As it contained 10,000 souls, he had his work before him. But he used to call on as many as two hundred and thirty people in their own homes in a day, and then finish up by preaching to an audience of eighty or a hundred in one of the houses at night. He established efficient Sabbath schools through the district. He had great faculty for organising, and exerted himself to relieve the clergy of the city, himself included, from many unnecessary red-tape parochial duties, so that more time could be devoted to practical religious purposes. Whilst carrying on active aggressive home-mission work, in a manner out of sight, the Tron Church was thronged every Sabbath, for it was realised that a preacher and orator of the highest order had appeared. His "Astronomical Discourses," delivered on week days at this period, were printed, and the sale rivalled that of some of Scott's novels, with which they ran a neck-and-neck race. Next year he preached in London, and the multitudes who went to hear him included the most notable men of the day. Canning was moved to tears. "The tartan," said he, "beats us all." Scotland was proud to know that one whose accent at once proclaimed his nationality, was recognised as a man of matchless eloquence by the greatest statesmen and preachers of the time. On 21st February 1816 the University of Glasgow conferred the degree of D.D. upon him.

Chalmers had an extraordinary power of abstraction ; while he was moving about at wayside inns, or spending an hour or two in a friend's house, he could withdraw into himself at any moment and engage in severe composition. He never burned the midnight oil, but rose early, studying from six till nine, even in the winter mornings.

With the view to elevating the uncared-for masses he pleaded for more churches, and at his urgent solicitude the magistrates built St John's, in the Gallowgait, in 1819, and offered the incumbency to himself.   He accepted the appointment, though there was as yet no congregation, and the district was mainly working-class; but the church was filled at once, and the Doctor had here full liberty and scope to carry out his idea of parochial oversight, as he had not had in the Tron.   Whilst the city was relieved of all responsibility and expense, day schools on a large scale were established, and the poor were provided for, entirely by voluntary generosity, administered under the most careful supervision.   (See also " Edward Irving.")

But labours such as his were beyond human strength, and after a few years' incessant toil he began to feel his health giving way under the strain.   But he was anxious to obtain more leisure for pursuing intellectual studies, so when in January 1823 he received the offer of the chair of moral philosophy in St Andrews University he at once accepted.   He departed from Glasgow amid the regrets of multitudes who knew the noble work he had done, and who felt that the city would be permanently the better of his having lived among them.   Not a few complained in a rueful way of his withdrawal from the pulpit; it was a great blow which Glasgow sustained when he was removed from the peculiar work which he had been doing there, but wherever he went he carried the fire with him, and although in Fife his audiences were fewer, they were more select.   In St Andrews, and afterwards in Edinburgh, he was dealing with the men who were to be the future ministers of Scotland; and in acting as he did, preferring the professorial to the ministerial life, his influence told through his students upon a whole generation of his countrymen.

EDWARD IRVING.

In October 1819 Edward Irving entered on the real work of his life, amidst the wynds and closes of Glasgow, as assistant to Dr Chalmers in the overgrown parish of St John's.   It was a noble enterprise, to reclaim to habits of decency and devoutness that semi-paganised population of weavers and labourers and factory hands, sunk through

long neglect into sullen recklessness, or soured into suspicion and dislike of all above them.   Into this labour
Irving threw all his energies; visiting from house to house,
preaching at times in the open street, praying by the bedside of the sick and dying; entering into all their house-
hold cares and sorrows, talking with the weaver at his loom,
and the cobbler at his last; able to do little by means of
silver or gold, but giving them such as he had, the sympathies
of a large and loving nature, and gaining that trust and
affection which money cannot buy. He never entered into the
meanest attic in the Gallowgait without the greeting, " Peace
be to this house."   On the heads of the children he laid his
hands, giving each the benediction, " The Lord bless thee,
and keep thee."   Everywhere he carried about with him a
solemn atmosphere, a consciousness of the dignity, the
sacredness of his calling, which indeed no Christian minister
should ever lose, but which in him had something more
deeply interfused,—a tincture of the antique and the liturgic;
the spirit of George Herbert of Bemerton breathing the
unwholesome atmosphere of Glasgow wynds.   He preached
regularly in St John's, but not, on the whole, with much
more acceptance than in the bygone Kirkcaldy days; still
he attracted round him a circle of congenial minds, who
relished his originality, and found a charm in his discourses,
but on the mass of the people it was the everyday influence
of his character, as he went in and out amongst them, that
bound all hearts to him like a magnetic spell.   Nothing
could transcend his own admiration for Chalmers, who was
then in the full maturity of his powers.

"Glasgow was at this period in a very disturbed and
troublous condition.   Want of work and want of food had
wrought their natural social effect upon the industrious
classes; and the eyes of the hungry weavers and cotton-
spinners were turned with spasmodic anxiety to those wild
political quack remedies, the inefficacy of which no amount
of experience will ever make clear to people in similar circumstances.   The entire country was in a very dangerous
mood. . . . The discontent was drawing towards its climax
when Irving came to Glasgow."   This Glasgow parish had
come to singular fortune at that moment, in getting two
such men to labour in it.

The following story is worth recalling :—" A certain shoe-

maker, radical and infidel, was among the numbers of those
under Irving's care; a home workman of course, always
present, silent, with his back turned upon his visitors, and
refusing any communication except a sullen *humph* of
implied criticism, while his trembling wife made her de-
precating curtsey in the foreground. . . . Approaching the
bench one day, Irving took up a piece of patent leather,
then a recent invention, and remarked upon it in somewhat
skilled terms. The shoemaker went on with redoubled
industry at his work; but at last, roused and exasperated
by the speech and pretence of knowledge, demanded, in
great contempt, 'What do *ye* ken about leather?' This
was just the chance his assailant wanted; though a minister
and a scholar he was a tanner's son, and could discourse
learnedly upon that material. Gradually interested and
mollified, the craftsman slackened work, and finally forgot
his caution, and suspended his exertions altogether. The
upshot was, that the infidel shoemaker was transformed into
a regular church-goer. His excuse at first was, 'He's a
sensible man, *yon;* he kens about leather?'"

Irving's person and personality were strongly marked. In
height six feet two, and proportionably powerfully built,
every feature seemed to be impressed with the characters
of unconquerable courage and high intellect. The head
cast in the best Scottish mould, with a profusion of long
black curly hair, his forehead broad, deep, and expansive;
thick black projecting eyebrows, overhanging very dark
deepset and penetrating eyes. Such was Edward Irving,
and he had come of a good stock, for the Annandale youth
could look up to French Huguenot as well as to Scottish
Covenanting ancestors.

In his Glasgow lodgings, the same longing began to stir
Irving that had come over him before, the desire to go forth
as an evangelist to the heathen, when the call came to him
summoning him to an obscure little chapel in London. In
a few months all the great metropolis was ringing with the
fame of the Scottish preacher. . . .

We cannot enlarge on the brightness and the sadness of his
after-career, but for the last act of that life-tragedy, the old
scene has again to be introduced.

His wife had hastened to Edinburgh at his summons,
and found him—weak and suffering as he was—bent on

accomplishing his journey to Glasgow, whither he said the Lord had called him ; and there once more, in the closing days of October 1834, he found himself amidst the old familiar streets where his ministry began. To all who saw him he was a dying man ; but by this time it had become an article in the creed of the new community he had founded, that sickness and infirmity were temptations of the enemy,— that if faith were but strong enough, they might be set at defiance ; and he looked forward out of the mists that crept and thickened around him, into a certainty of more strenuous and faithful toil in his Master's service. Once or twice he was able, with a faltering broken voice, to exhort the brotherhood of Glasgow, in the room where they assembled, and this closed his career of service. Weary and worn with the fever that had so long consumed him, he lay down at last. He expired at midnight, 8th December 1834. Apparently at the end he realised the truth, for the last words he uttered were, "If I die, I die unto the Lord ; living or dying I am the Lord's."

We cannot wonder that the tidings of the premature departure of one who had filled so large a space in the eye of his generation should have produced a deep sensation of sympathy and regret. He was only forty-two. Around the grave all the strifes and agitations of the last few years were hushed into sacred stillness, and those who had been forced to stand aloof and mourn the aberrations of his later career, could only remember how good and how great Edward Irving was. Men of all ranks and of all Churches —and chiefly of that Church of which it had been so long his pride to call himself faithful son and loyal servant— mingled as sincere mourners in the funeral train which bore him to his resting-place in the crypt of Glasgow Cathedral.*

DR RALPH WARDLAW.

RALPH WARDLAW, D.D., was born at Dalkeith (December 22, 1779), but spent his life in Glasgow. His father removed there when Ralph was six months old, and became a merchant of the city, attaining the honour of being a bailie at a time when such an honour was a tolerably

---

* *See* "Life of Edward Irving," by Mrs Oliphant, and sketch in *Good Words* of recent date.

certain index both of personal character and social standing. He resided in Charlotte Street. After being schooled in Glasgow Ralph devoted himself to the ministry, and studied under Dr Lawson of Selkirk, but embracing Independent views in the opening days of the century he became one of the first preachers in that body. A chapel was built for him in North Albion Street, Glasgow, where his services were greatly appreciated. He took a good share of itinerating work, visiting both the north and south of Scotland. Of his early congregation a considerable proportion were weavers from Bridgeton. At that time weaving and weavers were in their palmy days. Bridgeton was then separated from Glasgow, and the Independents residing in the village, constrained by a feeling then running strong against their principles, kept much by themselves. On Sabbath mornings they were accustomed to meet to " go up " in company to Albion Street, and in the same manner to return. Their departure caused quite a sensation in their quiet neighbourhood, and as they passed might be heard the remark, " There goes Wardlaw's brigade."

Before his first chapel was ready he busied himself compiling a hymn-book for the use of his congregation. A second edition published a few years after contains 493 hymns, of which eleven are by Wardlaw himself, who possessed the poetic faculty. They are not only among the best hymns in the selection, but they are among the best which the English language possesses. In 1811 Wardlaw became Professor of Theology in the Glasgow Academy in connection with the Independent Church. In after-years Dr Livingstone was one of his students. In 1818 the degree of D.D. was conferred upon him by Yale College. In 1819 his new church, seated for 1,600 hearers, was opened in West George Street. It now forms part of the North British Railway Company's offices at Queen Street Station. Its Grecian front was considered to be almost sinfully fanciful, and gravely objected to by some of the Independents of that day.

A rather unlucky site had been chosen for the building. It was an old filled-up quarry, and in order to get a foundation on the solid rock it was necessary to dig out all the loose material. Among other debris was the remains of a Presbyterian church that had been pulled down and thrown in there. One day the minister of this church, an eminent clergyman and a great friend of Dr Wardlaw, asked him how the new church was getting on. The Doctor explained that the difficulty was in finding a foundation. "Ay, Dr Wardlaw, I doubt it's not easy to get a foundation for Independency in Scotland," was the jocular rejoinder. "Not till we get quit of all your Presbyterian rubbish," the Doctor readily responded.

Wardlaw threw himself into the anti-slavery movement · (1830–33) with great ardour. His views alienated many friends, and he became the special object of wrath of the West Indian party, who were of some importance in Glasgow.

Wardlaw's commanding genius and eloquence brought him into the front rank in any cause which he espoused. As a controversialist he seems to have specially excelled. Baptists and Unitarians engaged his energies. When the Voluntary question had been brought to the front by others, he was drawn to express his views on civil establishments, and his eloquent expositions of what he believed to be the truth in regard to the matter were of such weight, that he was looked up to as the leading champion of dissent in Scotland.

In 1838 Dr Chalmers made a crusade to London to deliver lectures in defence of church establishments, and these created such an effect, owing to the fame and eloquence of the lecturer, that the London dissenting churches united in asking Dr Wardlaw to come and reply. He accordingly delivered a series of lectures there in April next year, which conclusively turned the tables on his friend and countryman, who had adopted somewhat peculiar grounds of defence. . The lectures were published.

Dr Wardlaw died on 17th December 1853, aged seventy-four, and was buried in the Necropolis.

Trinity Congregational Church, of which Dr William Pulsford and Rev. John Hunter have been pastors, was originally a split from Dr Wardlaw's church, in which his assistant, Mr Porter, played a conspicuous part. Dr Alexander Raleigh succeeded Wardlaw in 1855, and the Railway Company having bought West George Street Chapel, the new church in Elgin Place was opened next year. Raleigh was followed successively by the Revs. Henry Batchelor and Albert Goodrich.

Dr Wardlaw's first church may still be seen on the west side of North Albion Street, near the Mitchell Library. It has had many vicissitudes; was the scene of the labours of Campbell of Row, after he had been expelled from the Church of Scotland; and is now some sort of tallow store. There was much difficulty in getting a foundation, for it had to be built on hundreds of long stakes driven through mud. Curious to say, North Portland Street, not far off, proved a quarry of splendid freestone.

REV. ALEX. RALEIGH, D.D.

DR WARDLAW was succeeded in 1855 by the Rev. Alexander Raleigh, for whom the new place of worship in Elgin Place was opened in August 1856, West George Street Church having been acquired by the Railway Company. With such a preacher as Raleigh, we need hardly say the church was filled; his stay was all too short. He lost a child when in Glasgow; and the climate not agreeing with him, he accepted a call to London, where he took and kept a foremost place until his death. He preached his last sermon to his congregation in Glasgow on 12th December 1858. In February 1865 the degree of Doctor of Divinity was conferred upon him by the University of Glasgow.

CAMPBELL OF ROW.

THE Rev. John M'Leod Campbell was one who largely influenced his day and generation, and was closely connected with Glasgow. He is chiefly remembered as being the victim or hero of the Row heresy case. Born in Argyleshire in 1800, he studied at Glasgow University from 1811 to 1820. Among his most intimate associates were Edward Irving, F. Maurice, Thomas Erskine of Linlathen, and his own cousin, Dr Norman Macleod. Mr Campbell became parish minister of Row, on the Gareloch, but as his teaching was not considered orthodox, the Church of Scotland tried him for heresy. The libel was that he had taught the doctrine of "universal atonement and pardon through the death of Christ," and also the doctrine that "assurance is of the issue of faith and necessary to salvation." He was deposed by 119 votes to 6 (May 24, 1830). Before the vote was taken, his father, Dr Campbell, ended his speech thus:—"Moderator, I am not afraid for my son ; though his brethren cast him out, the Master whom he serves will not forsake him ; and while I live, I will never be ashamed to be the father of so holy and blameless a son." After the deposition he preached a great deal. In 1832 he settled in Glasgow, where a congregation rallied round him, occupying at various times the Lyceum, Dr Wardlaw's vacated church* in North Albion Street, and a church in Blackfriars Street. It was hoped by the Irvingites that he would cast in his lot with the Catholic Apostolic Church, but although much attached to Edward Irving he could not see his way to such a change. In 1835 he discontinued preaching through fail-ing health. From 1851 he published various theological books, and during these years he resided much in Glasgow, chiefly in Partick. He lived to see a gradual but marked change in religious thought, which he had greatly helped to produce. Although he had been so unjustly and ungener-ously treated, no bitterness ever seemed to possess his soul. He died on 27th February 1872. Norman Macleod said of him, "He was the best man without exception I have ever known."

———

DR NORMAN MACLEOD.

NORMAN MACLEOD was born at Campbeltown on 3rd June 1812, and studied in Glasgow both at school and college. In 1837 he was appointed to Loudon, in Ayrshire. In 1851 he came from Dalkeith to Glasgow to be minister of the most populous parish in Scotland—the Barony. Here he was inducted in July ; and next month he married Miss Ann Mackintosh, a daughter of William Mackintosh, Esq. of Geddes, and the sister of his friend John Mackintosh, " The Earnest Student." Their first house was in Woodlands Terrace, then considered the west end of the city. It stood high, and its upper windows commanded a wide prospect. In front lay the valley of the Clyde, and over the intervening roofs and chimneys his eyes used to rest with delight on the masts of the shipping in the river. Farther away, and beyond the smoke, were the Cathkin Hills, the Harlet Neb, and the Braes of Gleniffer ; whilst the back windows commanded a view of Campsie Fells. The glow of sunrise or of sunset on these hills was a great delight to Norman Macleod, and he often made his guests come upstairs to share in the pleasure.

The stir and bustle of Glasgow to him were thoroughly congenial. He loved the city, and was proud of the enterprise and generosity of its kindly citizens. The very noise of the busy streets was pleasant to his ears. He used to sit in his study in the quiet of the winter morning, and would be made aware that six o'clock had struck by hearing the thud of a great steam-hammer in the valley of Clyde, to which a thousand hammers ringing on a thousand anvils at once replied, telling that the city had awakened to another day of labour. It was his habit to rise very early, and after giving the first hour to devotion, he wrote or studied till breakfast time. Every Saturday he took the only walk of the week which had no object but enjoyment. He generally walked to J. M'Leod Campbell's house, which was two miles out of town, and the two cousins then walked out to the country. But in whatever direction he went, the day seldom ended without his visiting the Broomielaw, where he used to wander with delight among the ships and sailors, criticising hulls and rigging, and watching the discharging of foreign cargoes. Every Sunday he preached to crowds, that filled every seat and passage. His congregation always included a great many of the poor and working classes. In 1857 he began to hold Sabbath evening services for the very poor, none being admitted but those in their working clothes. The church was crammed at these services, and many hundreds were reclaimed.

In 1860 Dr Norman became editor of *Good Words*, and during the following ten years he contributed to it " The Old Lieutenant," " The Starling," &c. &c.

Norman Macleod said, " The Free Church claim to be the Church of the Covenanters ; they are welcome to consider themselves the church of the past ; it is enough for me that the Church of Scotland is the church for the people of to-day." No man had more influence than he in moulding and leading the Church, so as to rally the population of Scotland round it once again. There was a warmth and a manly robustness about Norman M'Leod that acted like a magnet. The Sabbath controversy raged in 1865, and his attitude on this question was made the excuse for starting the Barony Free Church. Dr Macleod was elected Moderator of the Church in 1869, after his return from India,—for it was his good fortune to visit many lands, Russia, America, India, and Palestine. At last he was taken to that country from which there is no return. He had removed his dwelling-place in 1859 to Adelaide Place, 204 Bath Street, and there he died on Sabbath, 16th June 1872, passing peacefully away. All the city made a great lamentation for him ; but his grave is out at Campsie, beside the grey hills he loved so well. Norman Macleod's death was the " scaling of the byke,"—the loss of the recognised centre for a large circle.

DAVID LIVINGSTONE.

DR LIVINGSTONE, on his father's side, had a Highland ancestry. " My great-grandfather," he says, " fell at the battle of Culloden, fighting for the old line of kings, and my grandfather was a small farmer in Ulva, where my father was born. Finding his farm insufficient to support his numerous family, my grandfather removed, in 1792, to Blantyre Works, a large cotton manufactory on the beautiful Clyde, above Glasgow ; and his sons, who had received the best education the Hebrides afforded, were gladly taken as clerks by the proprietors, Monteith & Co." They afterwards all enlisted or were impressed as soldiers or sailors, except Neil, Dr Livingstone's father, who became a tea dealer in Blantyre. There the doctor was born on 19th March 1813. When ten years of age he was sent to work for his daily bread in the cotton mills. Although his hours were from six in the morning till eight at night, he found means and ways of acquiring a good education. The famous religious awakening in the neighbourhood took place when he was sixteen, and Livingstone came under its influence. It was not until he was twenty, however, that he made up his mind to go to

China as a missionary.   Denominationally he was a Congre-
gationalist, his minister being the Rev. John Moir, of Hamilton, of whose church his father was a deacon.   With the
view to follow out his purpose, he commenced to study
Medicine and Greek at the Andersonian College, during the
winter of 1836 and 1837.   His father and he walked through
the snow from Blantyre, and engaged lodgings for him in
Rotten Row, at two shillings a week.   As his landlady
helped herself to his tea and sugar, he removed to other
quarters in the High Street, where he paid two shillings and
sixpence, and was well treated.   In April he returned to the
mill, but during the summer attended the divinity classes of
Dr Wardlaw, who trained students for the Independent
churches.   Livingstone had a great admiration for Wardlaw,
and accepted his theological views.   To attend his lectures
he walked every day a distance of nine miles to and from
his father's house.   At first he received no pecuniary help
from any one, nor did he expect any, but his brother assisted
him for the second session.   His most intimate friend at
this time was a young man called James Young, who was
then an assistant in the Andersonian College, and who, by his
chemical knowledge, made himself a name and a fortune by
the purification of petroleum, and the manufacture of paraffin
and paraffin oil.   When his studies were sufficiently advanced Livingstone offered himself to the London Missionary Society, and was accepted.   He went to Ongar, in
Surrey, for additional training.   He is described then as "a
pale, thin, modest, retiring young man, with a broad Scotch
accent ; if you broke through the crust of his natural reserve,
you found him open, frank, and most kind-hearted, ever
ready for any good and useful work, and very fond of long
walks."   He was at that time an ardent teetotaller, and held
even then very strong views on the slavery question.   The
key of his character was his indomitable resolution.   The
young missionary returned to the north, and passed at
Glasgow as a licentiate of the Faculty of Physicians and
Surgeons.

"On 17th November 1840," says his sister, "we got up
at five.   David read the 121st and the 135th Psalms, and
prayed.   My father and he walked to Glasgow to catch the
Liverpool steamer."   The old man walked back with a
lonely heart to Blantyre, while his son's face was set in

earnest towards Africa. That morning, at the Broomielaw, they parted for ever on earth. His father died in February 1856, when, as the traveller wrote, " I was, at the time, on my way below Zumbo, expecting no greater pleasure in this country than sitting by our cottage fire and telling him my travels." By that time (1856) David Livingstone's fame was widespread. He received the degree of LL.D. from Glasgow University, £2,000 was raised as a public testimonial, and the freedom of the city was presented to him. His second visit home was in 1864 and 1865. On 24th May of the latter year he was called from the south to Hamilton to see his dying mother. She passed away on the 19th of June ; and Livingstone had a double sorrow, for about this time he learned that his son Robert had lost his life in the American war. He was wounded when fighting for the cause of the North, and died in a Southron prison, aged nineteen. The date of Livingstone's own death was 1st May 1873. No better site could have been chosen for his statue than George Square, so near his old haunts,—the Andersonian College, where he studied, and Dr Wardlaw's church, now the N.B. Railway Station, being within a stonethrow.

JAMES LAMBERT.

" There are deeds which should not pass away,
And names that must not wither."—BYRON.

THE story of James Lambert, the heroic cotton spinner, who saved more than eighty persons from drowning in the Clyde, and who lost his eyesight through attempting another rescue, is one of touching interest, but to know its best points the story must be read as it has been written by Mr Charles Reade, the novelist. Through a paragraph in a Glasgow newspaper he first learned of James Lambert's existence. It told of a drowning accident in the Clyde, and of an old blind man, led by his grandchild, beseeching the bystanders to lead him to the river that he might try to save the unfortunate one ; and when nothing could be done, of the old man bursting into tears and reproaching the people for not attending to his wishes, telling them they might have guided him to the spot by their cries. A line was added giving the old man's name, and mentioning that he had saved many lives in bygone times. Years passed before Mr Reade was able to carry out his purpose, then formed, of finding out that blind man, and it was only by the aid of detectives that at last he discovered him, in a humble house in the Calton, reduced to poverty. Mr Reade's narrative goes on to tell of James Lambert's career from boyhood. His supreme purpose in life seems to have been to save persons from drowning, and many a tragic incident is recorded. It was on the 2d October 1856 that in one such attempt he sprang into the icy river when warm, and the result was an illness which cost him his eyesight.

Perhaps his crowning feat was when he saved a number of his own comrades of Somerville's Cotton Mill. The small ferry-boat, in which too many had crowded, was pushed off from the bank whilst some were anxious to get out, seeing it was overladen. In the confusion the boat capsized. James Lambert was one of the passengers, and his swimming prowess was known to all. Every eye turned to him, and every hand sought to grasp him. His life-saving genius was now seen at its best. He had no thought of abandoning the people. " In the water, them that hadna a haud o' me had a haud of them that had, and they carried me down like lead." He was clutched and pinned by four or five, and had the weight of other twelve people hanging on to them. " I just strauchtened myself oot like a corp, and let them tak' me down to the bottom o' the Clyde, and then I stood upright and waited. I was the only ane grunded ye'll obsairve ; I gied a violent push wi' my feet against the bottom, and wi' me choosing my time, up we a' came. My arms were grippet, but I could strike oot wi' my feet, and before we reached the surface I lashed oot for the quay. We made a yard or a yard and a half, when doon they carried me again like lead." Drowning persons rise once or twice. By choosing the time James, by another effort, made twelve strokes, and brought the company two yards nearer the shore. Another such effort, and some help reaches from the land, and one or two are saved. He drives a couple into shallow water with his feet. When he got into seven feet of water he acquired the mastery, and pulled one and shoved another till sixteen or seventeen were landed. Knowing there were more in the river he sprang out into the Clyde, and saved two lasses by their long hair,—then a lad and lass, whom he parted and took ashore one in each hand. Yet another was rescued, and then he returned again, and searched and searched for more. Three poor girls were drowned, though he was not aware of it. He fainted himself; and his life might have been sacrificed, had not an old man fished him out with a hook-staff and pulled him ashore, when he swooned right away.

The scene of this deed was at the part of the river where the Suspension Bridge was made. When it was opened every passenger had to pay a toll for crossing it except two, —the bailie who performed the opening ceremony, and James Lambert.

HENRY BELL.

HENRY BELL was born at Torphichen in Linlithgowshire, 7th April 1767. He was the son of a mechanic, and worked for a time as a stone-mason. After some experience of ship modelling at Bo'ness and under the famous Mr Rennie, he came to Glasgow about 1790, where he wrought for years as a house-carpenter. In 1808 he removed to Helensburgh. His wife kept the chief inn there, whilst he spent his time making many experiments in mechanical projects. At last he succeeded in adapting steam for the purposes of navigation. Henry Bell had seen the "Charlotte Dundas" at work on the Forth and Clyde Canal, and of course by this was greatly helped in completing his work. James Watt had steadily refused to undertake the task of applying his steam-engine to ships, saying some one else must work it out. In 1812 Bell's "Comet" commenced to ply on the Clyde; he made the engine himself. The vessel was forty feet in length, and the engine was three horse-power; the year after it was increased to six horse-power.

It is disappointing indeed to know that Bell did not gain any material advantages from his enterprise. In his old age he would have been destitute, had it not been for the generosity of the people of Glasgow and other places, who raised a testimonial for him. The trustees of the Clyde granted him an annuity of £100. He died at Helensburgh, 14th November 1830. (See also pp. 192, 201, 204.)

JOHN MAYNE.

JOHN MAYNE, the author of "The Siller Gun," "Logan Braes," &c., was a native of Dumfries, and a contemporary of Burns. Born in 1759, he became a printer, and published the "Siller Gun" at Dumfries in 1777. He removed to Glasgow, and worked for Andrew Foulis, the famous printer to the University, till 1789, when he joined the *Star*, an evening newspaper, in which many of his beautiful ballads appeared. Mr Mayne lived to a ripe old age (14th March 1836), and was a religious, warm-hearted, happy man, and a good poet. His verses on Glasgow were published first in the *Glasgow Magazine* in 1783. They well deserve a corner in "St Mungo's Bells."

> "HAIL, Glasgow! fam'd for ilka thing
> That heart can wish, or siller bring!
> May peace, wi' healing on her wing,
>   Aye nestle here,
> And plenty gar thy children sing
>   The lee-lang year?
>
> Within the tinkling o' thy bells,
> How mony a happy body dwells;
> Where they get bread they ken themsels;
>   But I'll declare
> They're aye bien like, and, what precels,
>   Hae fouth to spare!
>
> If ye've a knacky son or twa,
> To Glasgow College send them a';
> Wi' whilk for gospel, or for law,
>   Or classic lair,
> Ye'll find few places hereawa
>   That can compare!
>
> .   .   .   .
>
> In ilka house, frae man to boy,
> A' hands in Glasgow find employ;
> Ev'n little maids, wi' meikle joy,
>   Flower, lawn, and gauze;
> Or clip, wi' care, the silken soy
>   For ladies' braws.

. . . .
Look through the town, the houses here
Like noble palaces appear ;
A' things the face o' gladness wear—
          The markets' throng,
Bis'ness is brisk, and a' asteer
          The streets alang !

Clean keepit streets ! sae lang and braid,
The distant objects seem to fade !
And then, for shelter or for shade
          Frae sun or shower,
Piazzas lend their friendly aid,
          At ony hour !

. . . .
Wond'ring, we see new streets extending,
New squares wi' public buildings blending !
Brigs—stately brigs, in arches bending
          Across the Clyde ;
And turrets, kirks, and spires ascending
          In lofty pride !

High ower the lave, St Mungo rears
His sacred fane, the pride of years ;
And, stretching upwards to the spheres,
          His spire, afar,
To weary travellers appears
          A leading star.

. . . .
'Tween twa and three, wi' daily care,
The gentry to the Cross repair ;
The politician, wi' grave air
          Deliberating ;
Merchants and manufact'rers there
          Negotiating.

It's not by slothfu'ness and ease
That Glasgow's canty ingles bleeze ;
To gi'e her inland trade a heeze,
          As weel's her foreign,
She's joined the east and western seas
          Together, roaring !

Frae Forth, athort the land, to Clyde,
Her barks, a' winds and weathers, glide ;
And, on the bosom o' the tide,
          Wi' gentle motion,
Her vessels, like a forest, ride,
          And kiss auld Ocean !

. . . .

Hence, Commerce spreads her sails to a'
The Indies and America ;
Whatever makes ae penny twa,
 By wind or tide,
Is wafted to the Broomielaw
 On bonnie Clyde !

Yet should the best exertions fail,
And fickle fortune turn the scale—
.Should a' be lost in some hard gale,
 Or wrecked on shore—
The Merchants' House makes a' things hale
 As heretofore.

Wi' broken banes should Labour pine,
Or Indigence grow sick and dwine,
Th' Infirmary, wi' care divine,
 Unfolds its treasure,
And turns their wormwood cup to wine,
 Their pain to pleasure !

O ! blessings on them and their gear
Wha thus the poor man's friends appear,
While mony a waefu' heart they cheer,
 Revive and nourish—
Safe thro' life's quicksands may they steer !
 Like Glasgow, flourish !

Whae'er has dauner'd out at e'en,
And seen the sights that I ha'e seen,
For strappin' lasses, tight and clean—
 May proudly tell,
That, search the country, Glasgow Green
 Will bear the bell ! "

SIR ARCHIBALD ALISON.

SIR ARCHIBALD ALISON, the historian, was born on 29th
December 1792, at Kenley in Shropshire, where his father,
a Scotchman, was curate. His grandfather had been Lord
Provost of Edinburgh. His mother was Dorothea Gregory,
of the wonderful house of professors, doctors, and philo-
sophers, that sprang from the famous cattle-lifter, *Jan Dubh
Gearr*, one of whom invented Gregory's mixture. Archibald
studied at Edinburgh, and became an advocate. When
quite young he visited the Continent. One of his most in-

timate friends was Patrick Fraser Tytler, the future historian of Scotland, whose cousin he married in 1825. His history of the French Revolution was commenced in 1829. He received the appointment of Sheriff of Lanarkshire from Sir Robert Peel in 1834. This important post, with its six substitutes, became in its way a kind of rival to the Court of Session. Alison generally chose his colleagues from the lawyers of Glasgow. In 1854 he received a baronetcy from Lord Derby. He made his abode at Possil House, three miles from the city (now the scene of the Saracen iron industry). Here he spent thirty-three years, working hard during all his leisure hours at his great undertaking the "History of Europe," and other literary works. Occasionally Sir Archibald's Toryism brought him into unpopularity, but he won the respect and esteem of the most Radical of his townsmen by the manly way he faced personal danger during the time of the Chartist riots in the west. He died on the 2nd May 1867, and was buried in the Dean Cemetery, Edinburgh. Sir Archibald's two sons became soldiers, inheriting their learned father's quality of bravery. They obtained the notice of Sir Colin Campbell in the Crimea, and he got both of them placed on his staff for the campaign of the Indian Mutiny. At Lucknow, Archibald, the present baronet, lost his left arm, and Frederick was wounded. Sir Colin looked upon both brothers as if they were his own sons; when sick he attended them like a father. Once when Frederick was dangerously ill with smallpox, nothing could persuade Sir Colin to leave his bedside, where he sat endangering his own life, till the lad threatened to fling a boot at his head. When the veteran had been created Lord Clyde, and returned home to receive all the honours his townsmen could render him, he was the guest of the Sheriff at Possil House.

A famous satirist described the learned Sheriff as "Mr Wordy, who wrote the history of Europe in forty volumes, to prove that Providence was always on the side of the Tories." A more appreciative and competent reviewer writes of him and his work, "Sir Archibald was not a genius, but he possessed, in a high degree, the talents which his 'History of Europe since the French Revolution' and its continuation required. The work he mapped out for himself was gigantic. The talents it chiefly demanded were immense industry in reading up and sifting materials, with the power of luminous arrangement, and these Alison possessed, joined with a real enthusiasm for picturing drama- tically the great epoch he had selected.   Sir Archibald took the opposite side from the Whigs.   The Jeffrey set were wonderfully clever, but they were also wonderfully con- ceited.   They have not, among them all, left as much evidence, capable of resisting the consuming tooth of time for two or three generations, as Alison's ' History.'   We do not mean that the latter is, in its present form and proportions, an immortal work ; but we have no doubt it is the quarry from which future historians will take their materials."   Sir Archibald, the present holder of the title, was born at Edinburgh in January 1826.

HENRY GLASSFORD BELL. ·

THIS gifted poet was born in Glasgow on 5th November 1803, and was the eldest son of Mr James Bell, of the Scot- tish bar.   He was educated at the High School of Glasgow and at Edinburgh University, and commenced his literary career in 1829 as editor of the *Edinburgh Literary Journal*, which post he held till 1831.   In 1830 he published, in prose, in *Constable's Miscellany*, the " Life of Mary Stuart," in which he stoutly maintains the queen's cause.   Before this some of his poems had appeared, notably that on the beautiful unfortunate queen, which we suppose is his master- piece.   In 1831 Mr Bell married, and at the same time abandoned literature as a profession, taking to law instead. From 1832 to 1839 he practised at the bar, during which time he entered the Town Council of Edinburgh.   In 1839 he came to Glasgow as Sheriff-Substitute to Sir Archibald Alison, where he speedily won a reputation.   He is said to have been the best judge that ever sat in the Sheriff-Court of Glasgow, and as a mercantile lawyer he had no equal. At that time the work in Glasgow was far too severe upon the learned officials ; but although his labours were unceas- ing, and his strength overwrought, he took great interest in the public life of the western capital.   He was one of the founders of the Royal Scottish Academy ; and often appeared as a public lecturer, for he was a capital platform speaker. Upon Alison's death, in 1867, Mr Bell succeeded to the chief Sheriffship. When his health broke down at last, though he had done the work of three men during his time, the Sheriff received what was considered by the people of Glasgow very shabby treatment from the Liberal ministry of the day. He died on the 17th January 1874, and was buried in the nave of the Cathedral, the city according him a public funeral.

DAVID NAISMITH,

THE FOUNDER OF THE YOUNG MEN'S CHRISTIAN ASSOCIATION.

As another instance of the energy of Glasgow, the name of David Naismith deserves to be kept in mind. He it was who originated the Young Men's Christian Association in Glasgow, and set the institution at work in other cities all over the world. He also started the City Mission of London. The grandson of Mungo Naismith, the self-taught architect of St Andrew's Church, he was born in Glasgow on 21st March 1799, and was brought up to business. His church associations were with the Independents of Nile Street; but his life-work was noted for being instrumental in welding the various denominations together for useful purposes. In 1821 he became secretary of the "Religious Societies of Glasgow," at the "Institution Rooms," 59 Glassford Street. Naismith possessed a marvellous power of organisation and capacity for work. He was a true reformer, and thoroughly sincere in his endeavours to benefit his fellows. He founded Young Men's Christian Associations and City Missions in London, Dublin, and in many places in France, the United States, and Canada. He visited fifty-five cities in North America. He died on Christmas Day 1839, aged forty, and was buried in Bunhill Fields, London.

SHORT BIOGRAPHIES.

DR PETER LOWE, founder of the Faculty of Physicians and Surgeons of Glasgow, spent his life amid varied scenes. Born in Scotland about the middle of the sixteenth century,

H

he practised for twenty-two years in France and Flanders. For two years he was surgeon-major to the Spanish regiment at Paris, and afterwards for six years followed the fortunes in the field of his royal master, the most stirring king, Henry IV. of France, " King Henry of Navarre."

The date when he returned from the Continent and took up his residence in Glasgow is not known. In 1598, in consequence of ignorant persons intruding into the practice of surgery, James VI. granted Dr Lowe a privilege, under the privy seal, of examining all practitioners in surgery in the west of Scotland.

ROBERT BAILLIE, a learned Presbyterian minister, was born in Glasgow in 1599. Whilst minister of Kilwinning he opposed the attempt to introduce the Book of Common Prayer, and was present at Duns Law with the Covenanting blue-bonneted army, of whose proceedings he has left us an account. After the Restoration he was made Principal of Glasgow University (23rd January 1661). He was a staunch Presbyterian, and refused a bishopric. He died in 1662, aged sixty-three. He is the subject of Carlyle's sketch, " Baillie the Covenanter."

ROBERT and ANDREW FOULIS.—The brothers Robert and Andrew Foulis were famous printers and publishers in their day in Glasgow. Robert was born in 1707, and commenced life as a barber. In 1739 he began business as a bookseller, and soon after took his brother into partnership. They became printers to the University, and published many classical books. Robert established the first academy in Glasgow for the instruction of the young in sculpture and painting. This was the first school of fine arts in Great Britain. Andrew Foulis died in 1775, and Robert during the following year.

DOUGAL GRAHAM, a famous rhymester òf Glasgow, spent his earlier years " on the road " as a chapman. He witnessed some of the events in Prince Charlie's campaigns, which he recounted in verse. He became a printer in Glasgow, and ultimately bellman of the city. His chapbooks formed the chief stock-in-trade of the flying stationers for a long time after.

SIR THOMAS MUNRO, K.C.B., came of a good Glasgow race of merchants, and was born in the city in May 1761. The American Revolutionary War brought his father from affluence almost to ruin. Thomas spent two years at the University, and as a youth was an expert swimmer and athlete. He became a midshipman on the East India Company's ship " Walpole," but afterwards joined the army. In 1780 he served as ensign with the Madras Native Infantry, and took part in the Mysore War, and also fought against Tippo Saib in 1790. He was raised to a high official position in 1792, which his talents and valour had won for him. In 1799 he was made governor of Canara. He visited home in 1819, and was made a Commander of the Bath in November. He received a baronetcy five years later.

He died in 1827 as he was preparing to return home to Glasgow. An equestrian statue by Chantry was erected to his honour in Madras. He was known in the provinces he governed as " the father of the people." " The .population which he subdued by arms he managed with such address, equity, and wisdom that he established an empire over their hearts."

JAMES GRAHAM, author of "The Sabbath" and other poems, was the son of a writer in Glasgow, and was born there on 22nd April 1765. After spending his boyhood in St Mungo's city, he migrated to Edinburgh.

JAMES BEAUMONT NEILSON, the inventor of the hot-blast in its application to the smelting of iron, was born at Shettleston, near Glasgow, on 22nd June 1792. His father, Walter Neilson, was at that time an engine-wright or engineer, in the employment of Mr William Dixon, iron-master, at the Govanhill collieries. His two sons both rose to eminence. John, at the Oakbank Foundry, Glasgow, designed and made the first iron steamboat in 1825. He became an ironmaster, and lived to a good old age, his sons becoming extensive colliery proprietors in Lanarkshire. James B. Neilson, in 1817, became engineer, and after-wards manager, of the Glasgow Gas Works, which position he held until 1847. He introduced clay retorts instead of iron, and as early as 1826 he heated his retort-ovens entirely by the waste coal tar as liquid fuel; and used sulphate of iron solutions to remove the ammonia found so injurious to pipes and gas-fittings, &c. He invented the "swallow-tail" burner, which has since been used all over the world. None of these inventions he patented, but gave them to the Gas Company, which reaped substantial benefit. As a boy he had received a slight education, but in after-life he made up for this by diligence and perseverance. His patent for the hot-blast was taken out on 1st October 1828, but he suffered great persecution from the leading Scotch ironmasters, who united together and tried to break his rights. Their litigation only ended when the House of Lords decided in his favour. The total law expenses amounted to £40,000. Neilson made a moderate fortune out of his invention, and the country benefited by it to the extent of £1,200,000 per annum. Mr Neilson married an Ayrshire lady. He died at his country house on 18th January 1865. His son is Mr Walter Montgomery Neilson, locomotive engine maker and engineer, of Glasgow.

CHARLES MACINTOSH, F.R.S., was born at Glasgow, on 29th December 1766, and his name has become famous as the inventor of several chemical manufactures, and of waterproof cloth. He secured a contract with the Glasgow Gas Company to receive all the tar and other ammoniacal products of the distillation of coal in gas-making. After separating the ammonia, in converting the tar into pitch, the essential oil naphtha is produced, and it occurred to Mr Macintosh to turn this substance into account as a solvent of caoutchouc or india-rubber. He succeeded in producing a waterproof varnish, and established the manufacture of waterproof articles, first in Glasgow and afterwards in Manchester.

In 1828 Mr Macintosh joined his friend Mr J. B. Neilson as co-partner in working the hot-blast patent. He established the making of Prussian blue and prussiate of potash. He died on 25th July 1843, aged seventy-seven.

KIRKMAN FINLAY was one of the most enterprising manufacturers and merchants of Glasgow. He was born in the Gallowgait in 1772. As soon as the East India Company monopoly was broken up he entered that market. It was he who freighted the first Clyde ship for India. She was called "The Earl of Buckingham," 600 tons, and sailed for Bombay early in 1816. Next year he sent the "George Canning" to Calcutta; and in 1834 the first steamship, named after himself, also sailed to Calcutta, all laden with cottons. He was a prominent citizen and a keen volunteer, and died at Castle Toward in 1842.

ROBERT POLLOK, author of "The Course of Time," was

born in 1799 in the parish of Eaglesham, Renfrewshire, and was a student of Glasgow University, where he took his degree of M.A. He next attended the Divinity Hall of the United Secession Church in Glasgow under the Rev. Dr Dick. He died of consumption on 18th September 1827, and was buried at Millbrook, near Southampton. " His immortal poem is his monument."

DR JOHN LOVE, of Anderston (Clyde Street Chapel of Ease), was an eminent member of the Establishment in his day, and his name will long be remembered. He was one of the six men who, in an upper room in London, in 1795 founded the London Missionary Society. Lovedale, one of the principal stations of the society in South Africa, was called after him. Dr Love was a learned man and a deep theologian. Sheriff Barclay tells of an old woman who travelled far every Sabbath to hear him. Upon being asked, " But do you understand the Doctor?" her reply was, "Where is the man that understands Dr Love?"

Of DR JOHN MUIR, St James's Church, Great Hamilton Street, a very able man of bygone days, some good stories have been told. It was said that he used to mark his " heads" in shorthand on his finger nails, and that this led to the saying he has his sermon "on his finger-ends." During the ten years' conflict he was a non-intrusionist, and went to the very edge of coming out, but drew back at the last hour, joining the famous "forty thieves" led by Dr Leishman of Govan. Dr Muir was quite equal to the occasion, for on the Sabbath after the Disruption he preached from 2 Sam. xv. 11, " And with Absalom went two hundred men out of Jerusalem, that were called ; and they went in their simplicity, and they knew not any thing."

The REV. J. MORELL MACKENZIE came of a north country family, and was a young man of marked ability, and a bright genial disposition. He studied in Glasgow, and succeeded Greville Ewing as pastor of Nile Street Congregational Church. He also acted as colleague to Dr Wardlaw in the Theological Academy of the Independent Churches, and was the intimate companion of the late Dr Lindsay Alexander. His career was all too short. In the summer of 1843 he sailed in the steamer "Pegasus" from Leith for Hull to visit his friends. The unfortunate vessel struck on the Goldstone Rock, off the Farne Islands, on the night of the

20th July, when nearly all on board were drowned. Some. of the survivors told how they had seen Mr Mackenzie on the quarter-deck surrounded by the other passengers on their knees praying. He was quite cool and collected in the immediate prospect of death, and his voice rose calm and firm amid all the excitement of that trying moment. The distinguished physician of our day is the nephew and namesake of Morell Mackenzie, whose story awakened such interest at that time.

Dr WILLIAM ANDERSON was born in 1799 at Kilsyth, where his father was the Relief minister. Trained at Glasgow College, he entered upon his lifework as pastor of John Street Relief Church in March 1821, and from first to last kept up a good reputation for pulpit ability and uncommon common-sense. He always had the courage of his convictions, and used his MS. in the pulpit when it was considered almost a crime to read a sermon. Dr Anderson was a keen politician, and fought in the foremost rank for Catholic Emancipation, the Abolition of Slavery, and the Repeal of the Corn Laws. He espoused the side of the North during the American War. After having had a single-handed spell of thirty years, he received the help of a colleague. As a preacher the Doctor used to display great warmth, and has been known to cast aside not only his gown but his wig during the heat of his discourse. His humour was of a quiet but very effective kind. Upon one occasion a preacher of uncommon gush had appeared in the west, and created no small sensation in U.P. circles. Every one was loud in his praise. "What a grand head he's got," was the eulogistic remark of one elder. "Ay,—o' hair," the doctor quietly said. Dr Anderson died on 15th September 1872, aged seventy-four.

The REV. ALEXANDER M'LAREN, D.D., of Manchester, the prince of preachers as he has been called, was a Glasgow boy. His father, a merchant of the city, was pastor of the Scotch Baptist Church, which now worships in John Street, and was a man of marked ability. Young Maclaren was educated at the High School and College of Glasgow. Through the influence of the Rev. David Russell, of Eglinton Street Congregational Church, he was led to a decision whilst yet a youth. His family removed to London in 1841, where he studied for the Baptist Church. He was a dis-

tinguished student. His first charge was at Southampton.
From thence he came to Union Chapel, Manchester, in 1858.
His reputation as a preacher and teacher of the very first
rank is unchallenged.

WILLIAM BLACK, the novelist, was born in Glasgow in
1841. Educated at private schools, he intended to become
an artist, and studied for a short time in the Government
School of Art in the city, but eventually he took to jour-
nalism, joining the staff of the *Weekly Citizen* while yet in
his teens. In 1864 he went to London, and wrote for the
magazines. In 1865 he acted as special correspondent for
the *Morning Star* during the Franco-Austrian war. His
first novel, "Love or Marriage," appeared in 1867, and was
not a success. "In Silk Attire" followed in 1869; then
"Kilmeny," and the "Monarch of Mincing Lane;" but his
first real hit was in 1871 with "A Daughter of Heth."
"Strange Adventures" was published in 1872. Next year
the most popular of all appeared, "The Princess of Thule."
For four or five years Mr Black was assistant-editor of the
Daily News.

In one of Mr Black's latest and most enjoyable novels
"White Heather," the scene is changed from Sutherlandshire to St Mungo's city, and certain conditions of Glasgow
life are graphically delineated. The following verses are by
Ronald Strong, the love-stricken gamekeeper :—

"O Glasgow town, how little you know
  That Meenie has wandered in
  To the very heart of your darkened streets
  Through all the bustle and din.

A Sutherland blossom shining fair
  Amid all your dismal haze,
Forgetting the breath of the summer hills,
  And the blue of the northern days.

From Dixon's fire-wreaths to Rollox's stalk
  Blow, south wind, and clear the sky,
Till she think of Ben Clibrig's sunny slopes,
  Where the basking red-deer lie.

Blow, south wind, and show her a glimpse of blue
  Through the pall of dusky brown ;
And see that you guard her and tend her well,
  You, fortunate Glasgow town !"

WILLIAM BLACK.

A volume could be filled if we were to notice all the

eminent men of Glasgow. Time and space fail to tell of Thomas Graham, the Master of the Mint; of Bell, the traveller; of the brothers John and William Hunter, the anatomists; of all the eloquent divines by whose preaching of the Word, Glasgow has flourished; of Alexander Rodger, the Radical poet, and his "Whistle Binkie" brethren. The statesman and the preacher's voice is silent, however loud and sharp their notes sounded when rung out by the bells of their day, but the softer, lighter touch of the poet, although struck in a "minor" key, has left an echo that is distinctly heard down through all the years. William Miller, who was born in the Briggait and who never lost his Glasgow accent, stands unrivalled in his school, the "Laureate of the Nursery." No finer poem has been sung on any city than that by our own Alexander Smith on Glasgow. Robert Buchanan, who spent his childhood in our midst, and who was trained in the old College, has still his hand on the rope that rings St Mungo's Bells.

THE FIRST MECHANICS' INSTITUTE.

THE originator or pioneer of Mechanics' Institutes and Libraries was Dr George Birkbeck. Born at Settle, Yorkshire, in 1776, he received the chair of natural philosophy in the Andersonian University when only twenty-three years of age, and during his citizenship in Glasgow devoted much time and labour striving to help the working men and lads to habits of self-culture.

The honour of starting the first Mechanics' Institute has been claimed for London, but it belongs to Glasgow. This is placed beyond all doubt by the *Mechanics' Magazine* published in this city, where may be found a paper headed, "Constitution and Rules of the Glasgow Mechanics' Institution for the Promotion of Arts and Sciences," and from which it appears that it was opened on 5th November 1823, about four months before the London one. The rules were passed on 19th and 25th February 1824, and it was incorporated on the 22nd March of that year, Dr Birkbeck being appointed its honorary patron. In the *London Mechanics' Magazine* for 11th October 1823, the proposal to establish an institute in London was first submitted to the public.

Dr Birkbeck, who had betaken himself to London, advanced £3,700 for the erection of a lecture-room. He delivered the inaugural address in London on 24th February 1824. Other towns soon followed the good example; the parent institution at Glasgow continued to flourish, and to head the movement which it had originated; and in grateful remembrance of their former instructor they placed a portrait of Dr Birkbeck within the institution, where it may still be seen.

A collection of 2,000 volumes was soon got for the Mechanics' Library.

The present building in Bath Street is known as the College of Science and Arts, and contains a library of 8,000 volumes.

MILITARY ITEMS.

THE GLASGOW REGIMENT—VOLUNTEERS.

IN 1778, when the American War was threatening to destroy the trade of the city, Glasgow raised a regiment of soldiers to serve against the revolutionists; £5,000 was subscribed in a few days, and £10,000 in all was contributed by the citizens for the purpose. The regiment was embodied on Monday, 26th June, amid enthusiastic cheers, the chiming of the Tolbooth bells, &c. It became the 83rd regiment, and was sent to Minorca in April 1779; after some service it was disbanded in 1783.

In 1779 a company of fifty Highlanders, who had enlisted for the 42nd and 71st Highland regiments, were marched to Leith and ordered to embark as part of this 83rd Glasgow regiment. They refused and mutinied, objecting to wear the breeches, and the result was that much blood was shed. The mutineers were fired upon at Leith by the South Fencibles, and forty in all were killed or died of their wounds, whilst a captain and some of the Fencibles were killed besides.

The 71st has long been known as the Glasgow Regiment. Its official designation now is the Glasgow Highland Light Infantry. Since about 1881 its soldiers have worn the kilt. The following are the circumstances of its beginning :— Lord Macleod, son of the Earl of Cromarty, was out in the

rebellion with Prince Charles. A few days before Culloden
he led a party of Jacobites as far north as Thurso, but his
father and he were unluckily captured by a company of the
Sutherlandshire Militia at Golspie, as they were about to
embark for the Prince's headquarters. The Earls of Cromarty and Kilmarnock, with Lords Balmerino and Lovat,
were the chief prizes that fell into the hands of the Government for punishment, and of them all only Cromarty escaped
execution. The story of how his young wife interceded for
him is one of pathetic interest. His son, Lord Macleod,
was also pardoned. After spending many years abroad he
returned home at the outbreak of the Colonial War, and
raised a regiment of eleven hundred men, chiefly on his old
family estates in the north, of whom he became colonel. A
second battalion of this regiment was next raised in 1778,
and chiefly in Glasgow. It was numbered the 73rd, but
afterwards became the 71st, and it has ever since been connected with Glasgow. Its colonel chose a wife in one of
St Mungo's daughters, and the regiment was recruited from
and in many ways identified with the town.

At the battle of Fuento D'Honore in Spain the 71st bore
the brunt of the fight. When the contest seemed to be
going against the British, Colonel Cadogan waved his hat
and cried, " Now, my lads, charge them down the Gallowgait," the scene of the conflict resembling that old Glasgow
thoroughfare. The Glasgow fellows rallied with a cheer,
and, pressing on, soon drove the French out at the point of
the bayonet. A monument to the gallant colonel's memory
may be seen in the Cathedral.

There was a mutiny among the Breadalbane Fencibles in
Glasgow on the 1st December 1794. The disturbance was
owing to some of the regiment having been arrested. Their
comrades released them, and there was a good deal of in-
subordination, but the men soon came to their senses.
Three of them voluntarily came forward and surrendered
themselves to stand trial as atonement for the whole. Four
men were condemned, and were taken to Edinburgh, but
only one of them, Alexander Sutherland or Sandison, a
native of Caithness, was shot on Musselburgh Sands. He
met his fate with becoming penitence and fortitude.

It was on this occasion that an incident occurred characteristic of the relationship which existed between officers

and men in those days, and which shows the Highlander's high sense of honour. Whilst on the march to Edinburgh, one of the prisoners, named Macmartin, persuaded his officer to permit him to return to Glasgow to settle a matter of importance with a friend before his death, promising to overtake the party. The captain accepted his word of honour, but after lingering on the road as long as he dared, and the soldier not appearing as he had promised, at last the officer arrived at Edinburgh Castle minus one of his prisoners, when, just at the last moment, Macmartin rushed forward, pale and trembling lest his officer had incurred any ill consequences. Is it surprising that men of that kind of fibre proved unconquerable on every field of battle ?

During 1793 two battalions of infantry and one squadron of cavalry volunteers were raised in Glasgow. The first paid for their own clothing, and were five hundred strong ; they wore red coats. The second were clad in blue and scarlet, and numbered eight hundred. They were well drilled, and became thoroughly efficient ; the cavalry was also a serviceable body. These corps were all disbanded at the peace in 1802, but next year the war-cloud broke, and again Glasgow came to the front with over five thousand volunteers. The yeomanry are the representatives of the cavalry then embodied. There were eight battalions of infantry, including a fine band of seven hundred Highlanders in full Highland costume. The trades and the grocers each mustered six hundred men.

During the French War there was always a regiment in the Barracks in the Gallowgait, generally of English militia.

Recruits for the Highland regiments are got in great numbers in Glasgow and Edinburgh, but it is worth while noticing that a large proportion of recruits so procured are genuine Highlanders by birth or descent and name.

OLD GLASGOW.

HAVING given an account of historical events and incidents that have taken place within Glasgow, and noticed a few of the most eminent citizens, we will next glance at the older streets and buildings of the city, and will endeavour to tell

briefly all that is worth knowing about them or that is likely
to be of general interest.

There are not a few good people of Glasgow who can
devote days and weeks investigating Continental antiquities
and curiosities, whilst they remain all their lives in utter
ignorance of the few relics of antiquity that may still be
seen within sound of "St Mungo's Bells." No doubt the
squalor which possesses and haunts the regions of the past
in our city, is a drawback to a proper appreciation of them ;
but this reason does not deter the tourist of antiquarian
turn of mind from exploring the Cowgate and Canongate
closes of Edinburgh, and should not frighten the genuine
sons and daughters of St Mungo. Glasgow more than most
towns is a city of the present, and takes no time to look
behind. It has a past, however, and one of genuine interest
which is too much forgotten. Let our west-end young
ladies take a tour to the east some fine afternoon, and see
for themselves the grand old tower of the Merchants' House
in the Briggait, the Ship Bank at the corner of the Briggait
and the Saltmarket, St Andrew's Church and Square, the
Burnt Barns in Great Hamilton Street, the Saracen's Head
Inn in the Gallowgait. Let them penetrate some of the
Saltmarket closes and view the old-world architecture there;
and if something more than buildings should awaken their
interest, they will be none the worse of having their hearts
moved to do something for the miserable inhabitants of
their own city.

THE HIGH STREET.

FEW Scottish burghs have undergone more serious alterations
during recent years than Glasgow. The work of demolition
begun by the City Improvement Trust, necessary as it was
from a sanitary point of view, played sad havoc with that
central portion of the city around which many memories
lingered ; and the vast extension of railway operations in
the heart of the city threatens to complete the destruction of
most of the landmarks in its history. Old buildings have
been removed to give place to erections constructed more
in accordance with modern requirements, and the antique
portions of Glasgow are rapidly disappearing.

One of the last, and one that was sorely grudged, was the

old front of the College from the High Street. Its façade
was a good example of the Scottish Jacobean architecture of
the fifteenth century, and is believed to have been the work of·
Sir William Bruce. The old College was built later, chiefly
from 1632 to 1662. The front was three hundred and five
feet in length, and was surmounted by a steeple one hundred
and forty-eight feet high. The North British Railway having
acquired the ground, the College buildings gradually had to
give way to larger blocks. The old façade has been carefully preserved, and may be seen re-erected at the Hillhead
entrance to the University.

One of the "quaintest bits of Old Glasgow" yet
standing is to be seen in the close No. 101 High
Street. It is the only remaining relic in this locality of the
old timber-fronted houses, and cannot long survive. After
the terrible fire which broke out on 17th June 1652, and
which devastated many of the closes "baith bak and fore"
in the Saltmarket and Trongait, the Town Council forbade
the erection of any such timber-fronted houses in future, so
it is evident that this house was built before the·middle of
the seventeenth century.

The houses in 267 High Street are genuine relics of the
times of the Reformation. The decorated doorway and
the ample stair prove that they must have belonged to some
of the leading civic rulers, and there is little doubt from their
appearance that they were the town houses of some of the
powerful noblemen who governed Glasgow at that period
before the merchant class had risen to power. The High
Street used to be much steeper, but has been lowered; all
traces of the Bell o' the Brae—the site of the "Mercat
Cross" of Glasgow—have been destroyed. It stood at the
junction of the High Street with Rotten Row and the Drygait.

The "Mercat Cross" is spoken of as having a key. It
was probably a tower resembling the market cross lately
restored in the High Street of Edinburgh. The Cross is
said to have been changed to the Tolbooth corner. There
was a cross there in 1426, but the "Mercat Cross" was also
standing at the Bell o' the Brae in 1560.

The old house at the corner of Nicholas Street and High
Street with the crowstepped gable, is said to have been built
·as early as 1560.

Rotten Row was so called from having been the Routine

Rue or procession street. We think it would be an improvement if the old spelling were again adopted. In early times
all the houses in Rotten Row had gardens behind. Like
Castle Street it was occupied by the clergy. A port stood
at the east corner of Balmanno Street, beside which there
was the dwelling-house of the Dean of the Chapter, whose
glebe has preserved its name—Deanside—for six hundred
years. There are some very old houses in Rotten Row;
that at the west corner of Taylor Street is believed to date
from the middle of the seventeenth century. Antiquarians
have decided, from the style of architecture and masonry,
and the ample staircases of Union Court, Rotten Row
(leading to the High Street), that it dates from the pre-
Reformation period.

THE CATHEDRAL.*

A DESCRIPTION or history of the Cathedral is beyond the
limits of our space. The subject would require a volume,
and it has received the attention of competent writers. The
venerable pile is rich in historic memories. It was built long
ere Bannockburn was fought. Here has sounded the voice
of thanksgiving for that and other deliverances from the
English. Within its walls, after the National League and
Covenant had been signed, the Church of Scotland
assembled, and sounded their first clear note of resistance
to the pretensions of an infatuated king, and the strife was
fairly commenced that was to cost his family the kingdom.
Here sat Cromwell, with calm imperturbable countenance,
whilst old Zachary Boyd lectured and scolded him with a
courageous impertinence seldom wanting in a certain type
of the Scotch clergy.

The Cathedral externally is 329 feet in length, by 63 feet
in breadth, and the tower is 225 feet high. The nave
measures 155 feet by 60 feet, and is 90 feet in height. The
number of windows in the Cathedral is 159. The display
of stained glass is more abundant and brilliant than in any
other edifice in Great Britain. The number of columns is
147. The crypt is 125 feet in length.

---

* See " Bishop's Palace," page 22.

The Bell of the Cathedral was presented by a relation of John Knox. It was accidentally cracked in 1790, but was recast. It is twelve feet one inch in circumference, and rings the curfew every night at ten. In a book with such a title as ours, it is appropriate that the inscription on the Bell should be given in full.

"IN THE YEAR OF GRACE

1594

MARCUS KNOX,

A MERCHANT IN GLASGOW,

ZEALOUS FOR THE INTEREST OF THE REFORMED RELIGION,

CAUSED ME TO BE FABRICATED IN HOLLAND,

FOR THE USE OF HIS FELLOW-CITIZENS OF GLASGOW,

AND PLACED ME WITH SOLEMNITY

IN THE TOWER OF THEIR CATHEDRAL;

MY FUNCTION

WAS ANNOUNCED BY THE IMPRESS ON MY BOSOM,

*ME AUDITO VENIAS DOCTRINAM SANCTUM

UT DISCAS;

AND

I WAS TAUGHT TO PROCLAIM THE HOURS OF

UNHEEDED TIME.

195 YEARS HAD I SOUNDED THESE AWFUL WARNINGS,

WHEN I WAS BROKEN

BY THE HANDS OF INCONSIDERATE AND UNSKILFUL MEN.

IN THE YEAR 1790

I WAS CAST INTO THE FURNACE,

REFOUNDED AT LONDON,

AND RETURNED TO MY SACRED VOCATION.

READER,

THOU ALSO SHALT KNOW A RESURRECTION,

MAY IT BE UNTO ETERNAL LIFE.

THOMAS MEARS, FECIT, LONDON, 1790."

---

* "Come, that ye may learn holy doctrine."

THE NECROPOLIS.

THE Necropolis occupies a hill of trap rock two hundred and thirty feet above the Clyde. About half a century ago it was the Merchants' Park, or Fir Park.

John Knox's monument was erected before the place was made a cemetery. Of the scene at the Necropolis Alexander Smith says :—"The grand Cathedral, filled once with Popish shrines and rolling incense, on one side the ravine, and on the other John Knox on his pillar, impeaching it with outretched arm that clasps a Bible."

The name Necropolis is formed of two Greek words meaning "the city of the dead." The entrance is by the Bridge of Sighs, which crosses the Molendinar Burn,* now entirely covered over. At the gate may be observed two shields with the arms of Glasgow and of the Merchants' House.

Turning to the left we reach the Jews' burying-ground, an enclosed space. Under the capital of the column at the entrance is the inscription in Hebrew, "Who among the gods is like unto Jehovah?" and on the pedestal Byron's lines beginning, "O weep for them that wept by Babel's streams."

On the hill-top near John Knox's statue are monuments to James Ewing of Strathleven, Dr Dick, Dr Black, and J. H. Alexander of the old Theatre Royal. Further south is a monument to William M'Gavin, author of "The Protestant." There are also memorial-stones for Michael Scott, author of "Tom Cringle's Log," Motherwell the poet, Edward Irving, Dr Ralph Wardlaw, Dr Heugh, Charles Tennant of St Rollox, and others.

In Sighthill Cemetery, not far from the Necropolis, is a monument to Baird and Hardie, who were executed at Stirling in 1820 during the political troubles.

THE BARONY.

FOR more than two hundred years (from 1596 to 1801) the old Barony congregation worshipped in the Crypt of the Cathedral. No one can forget the scene in " Rob Roy,"

---

* Molendinar is said to mean the stream that turns the mill-stones. In 1750 the citizens living in the Briggait were wont to use its waters when brewing ale.

when Francis Osbaldistone receives the mysterious warning while among the worshippers. The Barony can boast of some eminent ministers, not the least of whom was Donald Cargill (see page 50). The last who preached in the Crypt was Dr John Burns, whose ministry was remarkably prolonged. At his death in 1839, Dr Burns had been seventy-two years minister of the Barony, his own age being ninety-six. He was ahead of Robert Raikes in starting Sunday schools, and he was at the front in every good work, taking a keen share in the anti-slavery movement, &c. On communion occasions he used to preach to overflow congregations in a large tent. Dr Burns was the father of the Messrs J. & G. Burns, the steamship owners, and the grandfather of Mr David M'Brayne.

The Barony parish is the most populous in Scotland. The old church, which has just given place to a modern building, was built in 1798, during the pastorate of Dr Burns. For some thirty years he had preached in the Crypt. The kirk of 1798 was a peculiar-looking structure. Never was a good word said in its favour until it was decided to demolish it, when some notes of admiration were sounded. It was the scene of Dr Norman Macleod's ministry.

Whilst we are in the vicinity the following true story is worth telling. The minister of a Free Church, situated not far from the Barony, was one day sent for to visit a sick man. Upon reaching the house, and before proceeding to administer the spiritual stimulus or comfort, he made some inquiries about the past life of the patient. "I suppose," said the clergyman, "your husband did not attend any means of grace, did he?" "Oh! ay, reg'lar; he went always to Dr Norman Macleod's at the Barony." "Then why did you send for me and not for Dr Macleod?" he asked in some surprise. "Weel, ye see, sir, it's a very bad and infectious complaint, and we didna like Dr Norman to run ony risk, so we called on you." The feelings of that F.C. divine may be left to the imagination without further note or comment.

    .   .   .   .

Love Loan used to be part of Dobbie's Loan. Christina Doby was the proprietrix of a house and garden on north side of the Drygait in 1507. In 1800 Dobbie's Loan was a beautiful green extending from the Barony Glebe to Port

I

Dundas. It is believed to mark the line of an old Roman road. A house in St James Road is a silent reminder of the time of the window tax—a living witness of those dark ages.

––––––––

THE TRONGAIT.*

GLASGOW CROSS—THE TOLBOOTH—ROB ROY—THE SHIP BANK
—CANDLERIGGS—KING STREET—STOCKWELL STREET.

THE name Trongait dates from about 1550. About sixty years before then James IV. granted to the Bishop of Glasgow and his successors the right of having a free tron or weighing machine in the city. The older name was St Thenaw's Gait. So it is designated in 1426. A chapel dedicated to St Thenaw, and St Thenaw's Well and Burn, were in or near St Enoch's Square. James III., in confirming an old grant of wax to the Cathedral, in 1426, directed that half a stone of it should be given for the light at the tomb of St Thenaw, "in the chapel where her bones lie," near the city of Glasgow.

In olden days the four streets—High Street, Saltmarket, Trongait, and Gallowgait—had on each side a row of piazzas of considerable length. There was a port at the west end of the Trongait, and another at the Gallowgait.

The old Cross of Glasgow stood at the centre formed by these four streets. The actual stone is said to have been buried in St Andrew Square, no doubt as a relic of Popery. The Cross or Tolbooth Steeple (built in 1625), however, still commemorates the spot, and with its noble crown forms a prominent landmark of Old Glasgow. The tower is all that remains of the Tolbooth, the adjoining building was erected about seventy-five years ago.

––

* We adopt the old and true spelling of such names as Drygait, Trongait, and Gallowgait. Dr A. H. Miller, in "Quaint Bits of Old Glasgow," says :—" In the Scottish vernacular the word *gait* means a road, whilst *yett* is a gate or doorway, but a very modern corruption has destroyed their significance. The Trongait is the street leading to the Tron, and has no reference to any doorway. The Gallowgate Port, if spelled in the modern way, is ridiculously tautological. No such confusion exists either in the Latin charters or the Council Records of Glasgow."

TRONGAIT, 1770.

What the Heart of Midlothian was to Edinburgh, this was to Glasgow. Round it a hundred proud memories cluster. Here, in the hour of their country's need, whole regiments have sprung into being. Here St Mungo's Bells have rung their song of victory amid the loud huzzas of the rejoicing townsfolk. Here many of the sturdiest champions of the Covenant were confined. Here the most bumptious of bailies have shown themselves off to the wonder and admiration of their compeers; and here too not a few of St Mungo's citizens have dangled gracefully at the end of a rope.

The Tolbooth was built in 1636, and was a high quaint house of five stories. The windows had strong iron stanchions. The ground floor was occupied by the town clerks. The Council chamber was on the flat immediately above. The entry having proved too small and narrow, the large

TOLBOOTH STEEPLE.

outside stair was made, upon which the magistrates were wont to stand and drink George III.'s health, tossing over their empty glasses to the crowd below.

In "Rob Roy," the old Tolbooth is the scene of the famous midnight interview when Bailie Nicol Jarvie is first introduced. We refrain from making any quotations from "Rob Roy." Every one of St Mungo's sons must be familiar with the story, and to all of them we would only

say, Read it once again and you will enjoy it more than ever.
No such picturesque account has been given of Old
Glasgow, and the Bailie is a characteristic specimen of the
Glasgow citizen to this day. Sir Walter's romance brings
up the old scenes and customs of 1715 with photographic
fidelity and vividness. The Bailie and Mattie still lend a
halo to the Saltmarket, where also flourished his father the
deacon, and one almost expects to find Rob Roy still lurking
behind some of the pillars in the crypt of the old Cathedral.

Next to the Tolbooth was the old Town Hall, and in
connection with it the Tontine, still to the fore, but reduced
into a drapery warehouse. It was built in 1782, by some
of the merchants of the city on the Tontine principle, and
formed a hotel, club, news-room, and exchange of Glasgow.
The covered pavement underneath was the favourite
parade ground of the great merchants of the town. Time
has wrought sad changes here, and even the "old Tontine
faces" * have been removed.

The Cross or Tolbooth Steeple is 120 feet in height.
The bells were set up in 1736 and 1739, and cost £611.
They were repaired in 1843. The chimes consisted of
twenty-eight bells, and they used to be played by hand every
afternoon, between two and three, in the following order :—
Sunday, "The Easter Hymn;" Monday, "Gilderoy;"
Tuesday, "Nancy's to the Greenwood gone;" Wednesday,
"Tweedside;" Thursday, "The Lass o' Patie's Mill;"
Friday, "The Last Time I came o'er the Muir;" Saturday,
"Roslin Castle." Recently an execrable set of bells has
been put up. The music they produce is of a very
indifferent character; they are not played by hand, but
by the turning of a crank. The large bell is of foreign
make, and is the oldest in Glasgow,—the oldest of "St
Mungo's Bells."

The equestrian statue of William III., the hero of Boyne
Water, was a gift from Mr James M'Rae, Governor of
Madras Presidency, and was erected in 1735.

The Tron Church was originally built in 1487; a burying-
ground surrounded it long ago. The quaint old tower,

---

* The "Tontine faces" may now be seen in a side court adjoining
Messrs Fraser & M'Laren's Warehouses, 10 Buchanan Street. They
were carved about 1732, by Mungo Naismith, the architect of St
Andrew's Church, then a foreman mason.

which stands out in the street, and is pierced and arched for the foot passage, dates from 1637. It is 126 feet high. The church used to be called the Laigh Kirk, the Cathedral being the High Kirk. It was rebuilt in 1794, and about 1815 was the scene of Dr Chalmers's services. Sir John Moore, the hero of Corunna, was born in Donald's Land, —now Nos. 60 to 90 Trongait,—opposite the Tron Steeple, but the old building has been removed. The oldest house standing in the Trongait is No. 133 ; it bears the date 1595.

THE SHIP BANK.—Of the many private banks that were carried on in Glasgow in the olden time, the first was commenced in January 1750, by five wealthy merchants, and opened in the Briggait. It was popularly known as the Ship Bank, as each of its bank notes bore a ship for the device. This flourishing institution was finally merged in the Union Bank. The original building is still standing at the south corner of the Saltmarket and Briggait. In 1776 the business was removed to the south-west corner of Glassford Street, to a building afterwards occupied by Mann, Simpson, & Byars, but then adjoining the Shawfield Mansion.

This bank used to be shut for an hour between one and two, to allow for dinner. The great man of the institution (says Sheriff Barclay), old Mr Robert Carrick, used to come from his house at Mount Vernon in state every day, and arrived at the back door of the Ship Bank at 9.30. His chariot was drawn by two plough horses, which were driven very slowly, and the old millionaire sat encompassed by baskets of vegetables, which had been grown in his garden, and which his man sold in the greenmarket in the Candleriggs.

King Street and Candleriggs were formed about 1724; the first was made through gardens, and the other through cornfields. A candle-work stood near the present St David's (Ramshorn) Church, hence the name Candleriggs was given. The Bazaar occupies the ground of the old Glasgow bowling-green. The City Hall is built above the Bazaar, on a series of pillars, and contains an immense organ.

King Street was opened in 1722-24, but the feus were slowly taken up. It was long known as the New Street. Some of its original buildings still show their weather-worn faces among their middle-aged neighbours. M'Nair's Land on the west side was built by Robert M'Nair, grocer and

fruit merchant in the Trongait.   He was born in 1703, and
carried on business in partnership with his frugal helpmate
under the title of "Robert M'Nair and Jean Holmes in
Co."   Their shop was brilliantly decorated with the view of
attracting country customers, and they advertised extensively the merits of their goods in the newspapers.   They
were the first of the "Polytechnic" and "Colosseum" school,
and became very wealthy.   Their house in King Street was
one of the finest in Glasgow of its time.   The keystones of
the arches were made with carved heads, in imitation of the

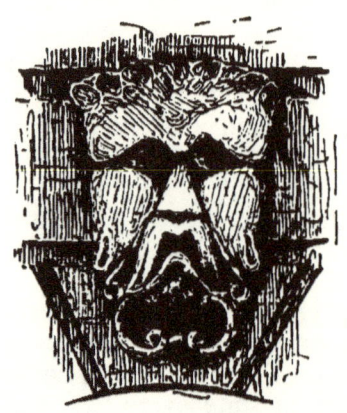

KEYSTONES IN M'NAIR'S LAND, KING STREET.

Tontine faces.   M'Nair next built a country house in
Camlachie, and named it Jeanfield after his thrifty wife.
Economical to the last, the worthy couple themselves acted
as architects of the building, and succeeded in planning a
very droll-looking edifice.   They omitted to arrange for
stairs inside the house.   M'Nair died in 1779.   Jeanfield
Cemetery occupies the site of the old dwelling-place, and
commemorates his saving Jean.

During the great flood in 1782, when the Clyde over-
flowed its banks, boats were seen sailing in King Street.

Stockwell Street is one of the ancient thoroughfares of the
town.   The Covenanters built a dyke at the river end as a
means of defence against Charles I., and made the Water
Port.   When Prince Charlie occupied the Shawfield Mansion,
which looked right down Stockwell Street, Lord George
Murray and many of the Jacobite officers found quarters in
Stockwell Street itself.

THE WYNDS.

IN this volume there is scant notice of the Free Church, chiefly because we have dealt with subjects that are of older date than the Disruption. In the following passage from "Work in the Wynds," published in 1865, we have an interesting account of work that forms an important phase of Glasgow life. It possesses not only historic information, but a fine picturesque effect. Should it for a moment be thought too serious for a book such as this, all we can say is that St Mungo's Bells have ever been identified with the preaching of the Word. The history of the Wynd Mission seems to send a gleam of hopeful sunshine into the foulest close in Glasgow. It shows that however degraded and miserable the denizens of these squalid quarters may be, the process of rescue and restoration is always going on. Strong arms and willing hands are ever stretched down to help those who have sunk so low, back into the way of well-doing once more.

"The Wynds of Glasgow are in the heart of the city; long, narrow, filthy, airless lanes, with every available inch of ground on each side occupied with buildings; many of them far gone, yet packed from cellar to garret with human life. Grouped near the Laigh or Low Kirk, otherwise called St Mary's, called also the Tron, because of the weights and measures tested there, the wynds were at first the streets, clean, though narrow, between the well-built mansions with their gardens and orchards that gave air and room for life. These wynds opened from the Trongait into the Briggait, and for many a day the good city clustered around. In the Briggait, close to the main bridge, were the mansions of lairds and merchants. Here stood the first Merchants' Hall, beside which rose, two hundred years ago, the noble spire that still looks down upon the Guildry Court, and which has seen the city, then of 8,000 inhabitants, spread almost out of sight with its present half a million. Among the churches early planted was the Wynd Kirk, a large and much frequented place of worship, where the judges on circuit went, and where the fashion and wealth of the city appeared.

"But gradually, as the city extended, the wynds fell into other hands. St Andrew's Square, to the east of the Salt-market, and Glassford, Virginia, and Miller Streets, received into larger mansions the richer men, and the orchards and green places in the wynds became built over to make the most of the ground. They thus became arteries to long winding veins or 'closes,' as they are fitly called, running up and down through the thick built spaces dense with flesh and blood; and only thereabout, when you carefully felt your way, could you make out any vital pulse at all. At length, some sixty or seventy years ago (the date was 1807), the Wynd Kirk was removed, and its site turned into the Kail or Green Market, and the present St George's was built in Buchanan Street; many of the people bewailing that it was removed so far into the country! But even then there were many respectable families living in the old roomy houses, with their dark wainscot and marble chimney pieces, families whose sons are now among the merchant princes. But these families also moved to other newer streets and squares, and the old houses became subdivided and sublet to humbler people; yet still in the memory of persons lately or now living, the voice of psalms and family worship, morning and evening, was heard from many a dwelling there. The Tron Church still remained a favourite place of worship. It was near the old Exchange and the Cross, and when Dr Chalmers preached his famous sermons there, on the Thursday afternoons, the church was crowded with the best of the city, breathless under his burning words. During his ministry the wynds could not be forgotten. Many a merchant and lawyer was induced to spend some hours in the week visiting the poor and teaching their children. Men like Daniel Stow, the founder of Normal Schools, who first reduced his theory to practice there, laboured for years, and not in vain; for after they had ceased through age and infirmities to devote their time and strength, their hearts would warm at the mention of the wynd or close where they had laboured; and they would delight to tell how, out of their thirty or forty Sabbath scholars, so many had become ministers, or doctors, or merchants, or in humbler places were married, and living godly lives at home and abroad.

"But still the wynds deteriorated. Many a large building, yielding a large rental, was left without repairs. From the influx of thousands of Roman Catholics from Ireland; from there being so many dark devious dens, to which the thief and the harlot, like beasts of prey, could retire, and from which, as night came down, they might creep out to seek their prey ; from the gradual exclusion to a large extent from the district of the sober, industrious, God-fearing native element ; from the multiplication of whisky-shops ; from the wild orgies of Saturday night, and the annual saturnalia of the Fair (rather the foul) holidays, with their shows and dancing-booths ; from the old churches gradually losing their hold of the district, by losing the members that lived in it and watched over it ; from all such reasons, the wynds became worse and worse every year. The Tron Parish Church before the Disruption, and the Tron Free Church after, under the pastorate of Dr Robert Buchanan, still held up the old flag, and continued to lead successive regiments—all volunteers as for a forlorn hope—to rescue even the few that might be saved. In addition to the parish school, relinquished with the parish church, Dr Buchanan, by the help of various friends, had purchased a candle manufactory in the Old Wynd at a cost of £1,100, and had turned it into a school. Another was opened in a hayloft in the Briggait. Sabbath schools were organised for children and adults ; an unusually able missionary, James Hogg, full of sympathy and graphic power of speech, was appointed; and finally, through the Free Church Building Society, a new Wynd Church was projected, and was opened in 1854, on part of the old historic site. The foundation stone was laid by Mr William Campbell of Tulliechewan, a man who spent half his income for years before his death in good and noble work, and who helped to build this synagogue."

The story of the wynds is a chronicle of religious revival work, of which at that time the Free Church seemed to have the monopoly. It is a fashion to sneer at everything like excitement in religion. We leave the facts to speak for themselves. " By their fruits ye shall know them."

The Free Wynd Church was opened in 1854, for the Rev. D. M'Coll, on part of the site of the Old Wynd Kirk, near King Street. It was overfilled, and a new and larger place was built,—the Briggait Free Church,—whither the congregation repaired in 1858. Mr Howie got the Wynd place of worship, and it was soon again overcrowded. Pastor and flock moved to Trinity Church, and the Wynd was again deserted, but Mr Wells next, by the same evangelistic effort, gathered a congregation in the old building. They went to the Free Barony. A fourth gathering was brought in and worshipped in the ' Wynd,' under Mr Riddell's care. They in time migrated to Augustine.

Each of the new churches—the Briggait, Trinity, Barony, and Augustine—was seated for eleven hundred, and all were well filled. These facts of gospel success stand alone in the history of the modern Church ; but the same kind of redemptive work is going on to this day in Glasgow, and is being crowned with success no less encouraging.

VIRGINIA STREET.

MILLER STREET—COCHRANE STREET—INGRAM STREET.

VIRGINIA STREET was the first of the new streets, and was opened in 1753, soon after the removal of the West Port, by Provost Andrew Buchanan of Drumpellier, and his son George, who built the Virginia Mansion at the head of the street. Both belonged to the aristocratic class—the Virginian tobacco merchants of scarlet cloak and cocked hat notoriety. Andrew was in office in 1745, when Prince Charlie's army came to the city. On the Jacobites demanding from him a list of the names of those who had subscribed money against their cause, he refused, saying he himself had subscribed double as much as any, and that he was ready to die for his loyalty. The Virginia Mansion was a grand house. It had extensive grounds, and an uninterrupted view all round, the Candleriggs alone obstructing the prospect in one direction. The Union Bank now occupies its stance. George Buchanan died in 1769.

The first house actually built in Virginia Street was the Thistle Bank. The City of Glasgow Bank afterwards occupied its site. Next was built a dwelling-house which is still to the fore as the Old Apothecaries' Hall. After this the Virginia Mansion itself was erected, at the top of the street; and soon after, in 1760, Mr Alexander Spiers's house was built beside it at the north end.

Alexander Spiers was married to George Buchanan's sister, and he afterwards bought the Virginia Mansion itself from Buchanan's son.   Mr Spiers was one of the famous four young men who made Glasgow.

No. 21 Glassford Street, through to Virginia Street, was being finished as the head-office of the City of Glasgow Bank when the bank failed.   It is now the drapery warehouse of Mann, Byars, & Co.

DOORWAY OF HOUSE IN MILLER STREET.

MILLER STREET.

MILLER STREET commenced life in 1762, as a most aristocratic west-ender.   It was called after its owner, John Miller of Westerton, a rich brewer, and contained a number of fine town mansions, two of which (Nos. 42 and 78) survive to this day. Mr Miller's own house was at the south-east corner. On its site the Western Bank was built. It was started in 1832, and the present building was erected in 1840. The bank succumbed in November 1857.

Mr Walter Stirling, the founder of the Stirling Library, lived in Miller Street. He was a merchant in the Trongait, and bought a house in Miller Street on 4th August 1779. He died in 1791, aged sixty-eight, bequeathing his house and library to the city. The present library was built on the site of his house.

COCHRANE STREET.

COCHRANE STREET was made in 1787, and commemorates the high-spirited provost who recovered the money from Parliament for what the city had been compelled to pay to Prince Charlie. He was three times provost, and married a daughter of Provost Peter Murdoch. Provost Cochrane died in 1777. His monument in the nave of the Cathedral bears a Latin inscription, the conclusion of which has been translated :—" Eloquent and erudite was he among friends and at the convivial board; even when aged he was pleasant and merry."

INGRAM STREET.

IN 1711 INGRAM STREET was a country road between hedges, and was known for a long time after as the Back Cow Loan. It got its present name from Mr Andrew Ingram, who was provost in 1762 and 1763. At first the only building was a large inkle manufactory. The warehouse of Messrs J. & W. Campbell was built upon its site. The elevations of this building were drawn by Mr Billing, the author of " Baronial and Ecclesiastical Antiquities of Scotland." The style is a mixture of Elizabethan and Scottish Baronial. The first premises of the firm were at No. 5 Saltmarket. The old Highland Kirk used to stand in the Back Cow Loan, on the site now occupied by the British Linen Company's Bank. Ingram Street contains many important buildings. The Union Bank, with its enormous granite pillars and colossal figures, is the most imposing. The old Athenæum is opposite. Hutcheson's Hospital and the Ramshorn Kirk possess historic interest. The Bishop's lands of Ramnishorne are mentioned as far back as 1241.

HUTCHESON'S HOSPITAL.

THE original Hutcheson's Hospital was erected in 1641, on the north side of the Trongait, at the foot of Hutcheson Street, and was taken down when that street was made. The present building dates from 1805, was designed by David Hamilton, and cost £5,200 sterling, and the site £1,450.

Its position in Ingram Street, looking down Hutcheson Street, and its tall spire, give it an imposing appearance. The façade is ornamented with statues of the founders, George and Thomas Hutcheson, which, with the tablet, clock, and bell, were brought from the old hospital.

The story of Hutcheson's Hospital and its founders is a striking illustration of the truth and philosophy of the parable of the mustard seed. The institution in its wealth and influence has enormously out-grown the wildest dreams of the founders, but it remains and will always remain a monument to their kind hearts and shrewd foresight. No good deed ever loses its reward. Not many are so conspicuously crowned with success as the gift of the Hutchesons. The good that men do lives after them, and we sometimes think that the results that follow a noble purpose or deed make their blessing felt long before they come to the light, and act with reflex force upon the doer. The sower as it were anticipates the harvest, and is blest by it before ever the green blade has sprung up. At all events the brothers George and Thomas Hutcheson served their day and generation well, maintaining a blameless reputation. Born fully three hundred years ago, they were yet in their teens when the crowns of England and Scotland were set on one man's head, and he a Scot. The long weary warfare between north and south was at last at an end, but during the latter years of their lives Scotland was all up in arms again, this time to resist the meddling tyranny of her own king, Charles I.

The father of the founders of the hospital was John Hutcheson, an old rentaller under the Bishop of Glasgow. George, the elder of the brothers, who seems to have made the money, was a public notary and writer in Glasgow. Two things were said of him by his townfolks. He was scrupulously honest, and he was moderate in his charges.

He seems to have never married, and died in 1640. Besides what he bequeathed to the hospital, he left considerable estate, which his brother Thomas inherited. Portions were also left to three nephews, the sons of his sister, but the heirs of two of these men became poor men, and died inmates of the hospital. Thomas Hutcheson was also a writer. He was keeper and clerk to the Register of Sasines of Glasgow. His wife was Marion Stewart, but there is no mention of any children. Thomas is always designated " Master," and " of Lambhill." He is supposed to have been a graduate of Glasgow University.

George's mortification is declared to be for aged decrepit men, above fifty years old, of honest life, and who are known to be destitute, being merchants, craftsmen, or of any trade, without distinction. The annual rent of the principal sum was to be spent in building and decorating the hospital. When this had been done, he expected that the funds would maintain eleven old men. George Hutcheson died fifteen days after making his will, and it had not been witnessed, but his brother got the deed ratified, and added to the amount.

On 9th March 1641, Thomas made a further gift of 20,000 merks to educate and bring up twelve orphan boys, sons of burgesses of Glasgow. Altogether the amount left for these two purposes by the brothers reached the sum of 70,000 merks. Thomas also bequeathed 2,000 merks to the University of Glasgow for a "Bibliothecary," and £1,000 Scots to restore the south quarter of the buildings, which were ruinous.

He died on 1st September 1641, aged fifty-two, and by his own directions, was buried beside his brother, on the south side of the Cathedral, where his tomb may be seen. His wife was also buried there.

Thomas Hutcheson had authorised the provost and other patrons to lay out the sums, mortified by his brother and himself, upon lands in the neighbourhood of Glasgow. They commenced forthwith to purchase,—near the College in 1642; and in 1650 from Sir Robert Douglas of Blackerston they bought one-half of Gorbals and Brigend for £40,666. 13s. 4d. Scots, the Town and Trades' House having acquired the other half between them. At first the investment seemed to have been unfortunate and unprofitable; the crops were trodden down and destroyed during the wars of Charles II. and Cromwell, and the patrons were nearly obliged to send their old men away for want of funds, but the city authorities came to their assistance, and matters soon improved. For a time the trust did no more than maintain the twelve men and twelve boys, but gradually its wealth increased as feus were taken up. In 1659, after the Gorbals lands had been paid, the net revenue of the hospital was £160 sterling; in 1700 it had increased to £300; in 1750 to £390. Land had been bought in other parts of the city which turned out equally well. The ground near Hutcheson Street, Meadowflats, where is now West George Street, Garngad Hill, &c., became the property of the trust.

Over a century and a half ago old women were admitted to a share in the benefits of the institution. Recently there were eight hundred names on the pension roll, and in the school in Crown Street two hundred boys were receiving a sound and liberal education. Steps have since then been taken still further to extend the usefulness of the trust. One of the largest undertakings of the managers was the building of Hutchesontown Bridge, at the foot of the Saltmarket (foundation stone laid 18th August 1829). Its place was taken by the Albert Bridge, founded in 1870.

Old Hutcheson's Hospital was a quaint two-story building, with a frontage of seventy feet to the Trongait. Its upper windows, seven in number, were gabled; there was a stately chief entrance door, and a steeple of the Flemish order rose from the roof to the height of one hundred feet. The foundation stone was laid by Thomas Hutcheson himself, on 19th March 1641, and the cost of the hospital was £26,000 Scots. In 1795 the old hospital had fallen into decay, and it was resolved to open up Hutcheson Street, and to erect a new building at the top. No pensioners have ever lived inside the present hospital. It was used as a school for a time, and here the business of the trust is transacted. The hall is now occupied as a clearing-house by the banks of the city.

Lambhill, the seat of the Hutchesons, was near Possilpark. Next to Hutcheson's Hospital, in John Street, is the handsome, though somewhat peculiar-looking U.P. church. It has an Ionic colonnade, and was built on the site of the older church which was so long the scene of the labours of the famous Dr William Anderson.

GLASSFORD STREET.

THE TRADES' HOUSE—THE MERCHANTS' HALL.

GLASSFORD STREET was opened in 1796. The garden of the Shawfield Mansion used to extend to Ingram Street—the Back Cow Loan.

Next to the Savings Bank is the Trades' Hall, which belongs to the incorporated trades of the city,—the hammermen, cordiners, weavers, &c. The design was by Mr Adam. The dome and somewhat ponderous architecture have a good effect.

The Trades' House is composed of the deacon, convener, and collector, with deputies from each of the fourteen incorporated trades, as follows :—Hammermen, 6 ; Tailors, 6 ; Cordiners, 6 ; Maltmen, 6 ; Weavers, 4 ; Bakers, 3 ; Skinners, 3 ; Wrights, 3 ; Coopers, 3 ; Masons, 3 ; Butchers, 3 ; Gardeners, 3 ; Barbers, 3 ; Bonnetmakers and Dyers, 2.

The oldest records now belonging to the Trades' House bear the date of 1605, but it was in existence as a corporation before that time. The House has met in Glassford Street for nearly a hundred years. The purchase of the lands on the south side of Glasgow, known as Tradeston, was a fortunate investment. The most noteworthy incident in the history of the Trades is the stand they made against the destruction of the Cathedral (see page 28). The Trades' House and the Merchants' House were to some extent rival institutions.

Facing the other side of the Trades' Hall, in Hutcheson Street, is the Merchants' Hall, a splendid Grecian building, with six lofty Ionic columns. It has been appropriated for the Sheriff Small Debt Court and other offices, and forms now only a part of the range of buildings known as the County Buildings, whose true front is to Wilson Street. These County Buildings occupy all the space between Wilson Street on the south, Ingram Street on the north, Hutcheson Street on the west, and Brunswick Street on the east. This Merchants' Hall in Hutcheson Street was the successor of the old building in the Briggait, of which only the steeple remains. The Merchants' Hall of to-day is on the northwest side of George Square, and forms one of the most prominent and palatial buildings of the city.

THE SALTMARKET.

THIS famous street was known as the Waulkergait or Fuller-gait, until about the middle of the sixteenth century. Here there used to be a colony of Fullers or Waulkers, for whose washing-tubs the green banks of the Molendinar and Clyde proved convenient. The industry of waulking or fulling was connected with the purifying and dying of wool and the making of cloth, and originated the surnames Walker, Fuller, Fullerton, and Fulton. Walkinshaws is probably taken from Waulkin-fields.

The more recent name of the street would be adopted through the custom of exposing all produce for sale in the open street at the Market Cross. Dealers in certain commodities gradually gathered together in particular places near the Cross, to save time and facilitate business. In 1686 the Town Council decreed, "For the better keeping of the calsay red (clean) about the Cross, ordaines the piges to stand behind the kreilis, hard by the kock stoole (the original of the pillory), and the salt boynes to stand about Dowhill's yett and downwards, and the fruit standis rownd about the Gairdhouse."

The title-deeds of property on the east side of the Salt-market, written two hundred years ago, declare that the owners shall have the privilege of fishing in the Molendinar Burn.

On the east side of the Saltmarket are the model tenements of workmen's dwelling-houses erected by the City Improvement Trust in 1887. The area which they occupy is the site of Silvercraigs Land, the house where Oliver Cromwell took up his abode in 1650. The extent of the new block; including the playground, is sixteen hundred square yards. There are twelve houses of one room, thirty-one of two rooms, five of three rooms, and eight single and four double shops. The designs were by Mr Carrick and Mr M'Donald. There is a resident caretaker, who takes the oversight of the sanitary affairs of the tenements. The former dwellings were cleared out and razed by the Improvement Trust about 1875. The large room where Cromwell had held his levees had degenerated into an auction hall, and the land had become a hotbed of vice and disease through overcrowding.

On Thursday, 17th June 1652, a fire broke out in the

K

city, and both sides of the Saltmarket were totally consumed.   After the fire, when the street was rebuilt, the
houses on both sides
were made with piaz-
zas under them, the
outer line of the
buildings resting upon
pillars, thus forming
an arcade.

On 3rd November
1677, fire again de-
vastated the town.
This time it broke
out at the head of the
Saltmarket, through
the malicious act of
a smith's apprentice
boy.

The grandest of all
the dwelling-places of
the Saltmarket was
Provost Gibson's
house, with its eighteen
stately pillars (see pp.
45 and 192). It stood
at the north-east cor-
ner of Princes Street,
then called Gibson's
Wynd. Two disasters
befell it.   It had been
sublet and subdivided
till it belonged to
fifteen proprietors.
They made so many
alterations and im-
provements, that half
of the building sud-
denly came down, on
3rd March 1814. Of
the nine families who

OLD STAIR, 28 SALTMARKET.

inhabited it only one person lost his life.   On 16th February
1823, owing to the southern portion of the tenement having

received similar treatment, it fell with a great crash. The inhabitants had been warned out two days before, but again one life was lost.

No street has known greater vicissitudes than the Saltmarket of Glasgow. The genius of Sir Walter Scott has thrown around it a quaint charm, which no amount of social decadence can possibly efface. "The comforts of the Saltmarket" are famous all over Christendom. In olden times it was the residence of the great and wealthy. In "Quaint Bits of Old Glasgow," attention has been directed, not before time, to a number of old houses in the Saltmarket, which well deserve more than a passing glance.

In close No. 28 Saltmarket a timber-fronted house is still standing. It must have been built before 1650, for all such wooden erections were forbidden in that year on account of the recent fire. The staircase is very curious.

In Robb's Close, 122 Saltmarket, is another of these old timber-fronted lands. The house at the head of the close is supposed to have been the town dwelling-place of the Andersons of Dowhill.* From 1655 to 1658 John Anderson of Dowhill was provost of Glasgow, and his burgh house was "near the middle of the Saltmarket." His son and namesake took a prominent part in the affairs of the city, and stoutly resisted the tyranny of Charles II.'s government. In 1676 certain ardent Presbyterians brought across six thousand stand of arms from Holland in a ship belonging to him, and concealed them in Glasgow, but the plot proved abortive. In 1688 he was one of those sent to offer the crown of the United Kingdom to William and Mary, and he represented Glasgow in the Convention of the Estates from 1689 to 1702. He was provost of the city from 1689 to 1704. Sir John Moore was one of his descendants.

In the first court east of the Saltmarket in Greendyke Street is a peculiar old staircase, which is quite unique in Scotland. It has a semi-octagonal tower, entirely covered with blue slates. From the style of structure it is supposed to date from the beginning of the eighteenth century.

---

* According to M'Ure, John Andersons, elder and younger of Dowhill, with James Peadie, John Luke, Ninian Anderson, and Captain John Anderson, owners of the ship "Providence," were the first to import "cherry sacke" to Glasgow, and this was before Walter Gibson had commenced his foreign trade.

The rickety wooden house at the corner of Saltmarket and Greendyke Street, at the Green, is the original Mumford's Theatre, a favourite place of entertainment thirty years ago.

MUSICIANS OF MUMFORD'S THEATRE.

THE BRIGGAIT.

ABOUT the beginning of last century the Briggait was the most important street in Glasgow. Here not only stood the Merchants' House, or Hospital, but the premises of most of the leading business firms.

There is no more picturesque object in the city than the tower and spire of the old Merchants' House, which still remains in this sadly altered locality. In its palmy days the building comprised a fine hall known as the Guild Hall. The Guild Book of 1659 contains the resolution of a meeting of the merchants that a new house and steeple be erected. The same authority says it was nearly eight years in building. The designer, Sir William Bruce, afterwards was architect to Charles II., and was the most eminent of his day. The tower has three turrets, and with the spire is two hundred feet in height.

According to the Council Records, the Dean of Guild and Dean Convener were recommended in 1663 to "provyd for ane knock and ane paill of belles to be put in the steeple now in building in the Briggait," and at the same time it was ordered that "the tounes armes be fixeit on the belles." It is recorded in 1736 that "Robert Fulton, Coppersmith, be paid 232 pounds Scots for making a new jack pinnet (pennon) and new ensign, raising the foremast and mainmast, making a new rudder, and other reparations on the ship on the Briggait steeple."

The Merchants' Hall used to be the scene of many a merry dance. Thither in sedan chairs our grandmothers were wont to be carried, looking as young and fresh as any of their happiest descendants now. The merchants removed to Hutcheson Street, and sold the hall in the Briggait in 1817 for £7,500. It was taken down during the following year. The tower now belongs to the Corporation of Glasgow. It is needless to say that the large flower garden which surrounded the hall has long since vanished. The Merchants' House in George Square is the descendant, we suppose, in the third generation of this Briggait house; both still exhibit the ship very conspicuously.

Besides the venerable tower, the chief object of interest here is the original office of the Ship Bank, which was established by five wealthy merchants in 1750, and which still stands at the south corner of the Saltmarket and Briggait. It was the first bank in Glasgow (see page 133), and its notes, with the well-known device of the ship, were held in great esteem, especially by the West Highlanders, who preferred them to all others.

ARMS OF THE SHIP BANK.

The town house of the Campbells of Blythswood stood on the south side of Briggait; its gardens extended to the river, but both have entirely disappeared.

Goosedubs is a modern name. It used to be called Aird's Wynd, after Provost Aird who held office during the troubles of 1715 and 1725—the Jacobite Rebellion and the Shawfield Riots.

The Stone Pulpit outside Briggait Free Church is a kind of war veteran that has stood the battle and the breeze. Here there used to be frequent riotings. The Irish Roman Catholics objected to be preached at, from it, in this their own particular preserve of the city, for the Briggait was the stronghold of the Irish until recently, when the railway crossed it so often that its denizens had to follow the example of the old dons, and betake themselves to other regions.

The fishmarket lends importance, if not enchantment, to this old commercial thoroughfare.

THE OLD BRIDGE.

STOCKWELL Bridge took the place of the Old Bridge of Glasgow, which for centuries was the only approach to Glasgow from the south. The ancient structure was a very high steep bridge, and was built by Bishop Rae, assisted by the pious Lady Lochaw, who defrayed the cost of the third arch from the north side. There were eight arches, and the bridge was twelve feet wide. Bishop Rae was raised to the see in 1335, and died in 1368. The bridge was very badly built, and showed a great ignorance of architectural science on the part of the builders, yet it stood till July 1671, when part of it came down. In 1776 it was improved, and made ten feet wider. In 1821 Telford had it in hand, and strengthened it. In 1850 it was demolished.

In " Glasgow Past and Present," Mr John Carrick says : —" For four hundred years it formed the only channel of communication between the north and south banks of the Clyde at Glasgow. The Regent Murray, with his infantry and a strong auxiliary force of Glasgow burghers, crossed it to shatter the last hopes of Queen Mary at Langside. Cromwell and his troopers,* if they did not use it, must have admired it, for stone bridges were at a premium in those days. The luckless James VII., when Duke of York,

---

* As Cromwell approached Glasgow by way of Hamilton upon the occasion of his second visit, it is more than likely that he did cross the bridge.

was lodged and feted sumptuously by Provost Bell within a stone-throw of it; and it was of no small service to his descendant, Charles Edward, and his foraging parties, during the ten days he recruited in Glasgow, previous to the fatal field of Culloden. How many tales could it tell of the dignity of the princely churchmen of Glasgow in days ere Archbishop Beaton fled with the relics and the records and the golden candlesticks; and how eloquent could it be on the thousands upon thousands sterling which have been received in doles and mites by the generations of beggars who thirled themselves on its pathway, with their blindness and age, and deformities and loathsome sores, and troops of orphan children lent out at so much a day ! ”

Glasgow Fair used to be held at the north end of the bridge until about seventy years ago.

At the corner of Stockwell Street and Great Clyde Street stood an old-fashioned Flemish-built house, whose gable fronted the river. Here the burgh's dues, or the “ common good of the city,” were collected. It was situated close to the West Port, and was convenient for receiving “ an egg out of every bushel of eggs, and a bawbee for every barrel of sour milk that crossed the bridge.”

GORBALS.

THIS ancient name is evidently of Celtic origin, and is pro- bably derived from some of the following roots :—*Gar*, rough ; *garvt*, enclosure, field ; *bal*, a village ; *bal*, wide, level. A leper hospital was founded by Lady Marjory Stewart of Lochow, granddaughter of Robert II., on St Ninian's Croft, Gorbals, in 1350, during the reign of David I.* The hospital was a thatched building. Long ago leprosy was a prevalent disease, and was supposed to have been ' brought by crusaders from the Holy Land. Even Robert the Bruce had fallen a victim to it. In 1584 the number of lepers in Lochow was six. It seems that the lepers were allowed to enter the city :—“ October 1610, It is ordainit that the lipper of the hospital sall gang only on

* Hospital Street and St Ninian Street, near the Clyde, commemorate the benefaction.

the calsie syde near the gutter, and sall haif (have) clapperis
on his feet and ane claith upon their mouth and faces, and
sall stand afar off quhill they resaif almous."

It was Lady Marjory who gave these lands the name of
St Ninian's Croft. They became the property of Hutcheson's Hospital in 1790, and were feued out by the directors
of that institution and called Hutchesonston. The village
was begun in 1794, and a bridge over the Clyde from the
Saltmarket was built about the same time.

The tradition long lingered of the Regent Murray's
troopers, after the battle of Langside, riding through the
Gorbals on their way back to Glasgow, and of them wiping
their bloody swords on the manes of their horses as they
approached the city.

The greater portion of the south side was sold by Sir
Robert Douglas (in 1650) to the magistrates for behoof of
the Corporation, Hutcheson's Hospital, and the Trades'
House, hence the names Hutchesonston and Tradeston of
these divisions.* The hospital had a right to half the barony,
for which they paid £3,388. The Corporation acquired the
westmost portion, extending from West Street to Kinning
House Burn, and including an irregular bit between Pollokshaws Road and Eglinton Street, which now forms Gushet-
faulds C.R. Station. Hutcheson's Hospital got the portion
of Gorbals between Eglinton Street and the Blind Burn. At
first the investment led them into trouble, for during the
disturbances of the civil wars of Charles II. and Cromwell's
time, their cornfields were trodden down and their harvests
lost, and no revenue was forthcoming. Coalfields were
worked in Gorbals as early as 1655. About 1775 the Gorbal authorities used to banish delinquents to Glasgow. In
1786 William Menzies opened in Gorbals the first licensed
distillery in Glasgow; there were only three before it in Scotland, Burns's " Dear Kilbagie," and two others. Muirhead
Street, Gorbals, near the Clyde, was named after Bailie
Robert Muirhead in 1798. The first mill was here, and
sent a stream of hot water into the Clyde, in consequence of which the street was called Warm Water Street.

---

* The value of the Trades' proportion of the Gorbals Lands, which
cost originally £1,726, was estimated in 1884 at £124,000.—*Notes to
" Glasgow Past and Present."*

Norfolk Street was formerly known as Rutherglen Loan. Wide, open, modern streets have taken the place of the twisted old Main Street of Gorbals, with its many thatched houses. The high land on the west known as The Ark, and on the east the baronial tower of the Elphinstones, are no longer to the fore. The latter was a fine old building, with stone oriel windows and ·outside oaken staircases. It was the home of a good friend of St Mungo's city (see page 35), but in the latter days fell into the occupancy of foreigners from the Emerald Isle, and was condemned in 1849.

There used to be an island in the Clyde which was claimed by the Gorbal boys. Here pitched battles were of frequent occurrence between them and invaders from Glasgow, when fists and stones and sticks were freely used. If the Gorbal youths were hard pressed, they used to send for the Gorbal weaver lads, who, at once leaving their looms, rushed to their help, and generally turned the battle against the enemy. Extraordinary to relate, owing to an earthquake in 1754, this scene of tumult and strife sank under the waters of the Clyde.

Dean Ramsay tells the following :—"An old shoemaker in Glasgow was sitting by the bedside of his wife, who was dying. She took him by the hand, ' Weel, John, we're gawin to part. I hae been a gude wife to you, John.' ' Oh, just middling, just middling, Jenny,' said John, not disposed to commit himself. ' John,' says she, ' ye maun promise to bury me in the auld kirkyard at Stra'von, beside my mither. I couldna rest in peace among unco folk in the dirt and smoke o' Glasgow.' ' Weel, weel, Jenny, my woman,' said John soothingly, ' we'll just pit ye in the Gorbals first, and gin ye dinna lie quiet, we'll try you syne in Stra'von.' "

LAURIESTON.—In 1802 Mr Laurie, a timber merchant, and famous land and building speculator, feued from the hospital trustees the Kirkcroft, where he soon laid out and built that part of the city which bears his name. He had a weakness for grand sounding names,—Portland, Cavendish, Bedford, Salisbury, Warwick, and Cumberland Streets were all of his christening. Bridge Street he called Bloomsbury; and Eglinton Street, Marlboro,—but these afterwards were changed.

Bridge Street Caledonian Railway Station was made at

first from the Methodist chapel of the Rev. Valentine Ward. It still fronts the east.

TRADESTON.—The Trades' House of Glasgow are superiors of this part of the town, hence the name. They draw an immense revenue from it. The site was commenced to be feued upon in 1790, when it appeared as a village among green fields. Mavisbank, Greenbank, Plantation, Haughhead, and Cessnockbank were all nice villa residences fronting the Clyde, with green fields behind. No other houses were nearer than the quiet village of Govan, with its one street of thatched cottages and a cross street to the ferry, its denizens finding recreation for their hours of rest in watching the salmon fishers drawing the salmon from the Clyde.

Little Govan, a village of handloom weavers, once occupied the stance of Dixon's Ironworks. The trade deserted them, and after ineffectual attempts were made to revive their special industry, the community was broken up and scattered, and their houses pulled down to make way for a private estate, which in turn gave place to Dixon's Ironworks. This great enterprise was begun by an Englishman, Mr William Dixon, a native of Newcastle-on-Tyne. He came to Glasgow to be manager of a colliery about 1780. It was said he bought the ironworks for an old song not very long after. In 1837 the "bleezes" were in full blast.

POLLOKSHAWS.—"Shaws" is an old word, meaning woods, and the proverb about "the queer folk in the shaws," which the inhabitants of Pollokshaws resent so much, is believed to have originated in the ancient notion that there were fairies in the woods.

GOVAN.

THERE was a settlement of Culdees at Govan in very ancient times. Afterwards, in 1147, a monastery is referred to as existing at that date. After the Reformation the old church of Govan was the scene of the ministry of Andrew Melville. Till 1820, an open tract of one and a half miles separated Glasgow from Govan. As late as 1832 it was customary for Glasgow people to go to Govan for salmon suppers on Sunday (see "Barclay's Poems," 1832). It is "pleasantly situated

GLASGOW FROM THE GREEN, 1795.

on the south side of the Clyde." Govan lives chiefly by shipbuilding, but has numerous public works, including two silk mills, the oldest of which, near the river, belongs to Messrs Morris, Pollock, & Son, and was the first in which silks were spun in Scotland. Govan grew so fast as to be-come the eighth burgh (royal, parliamentary, or otherwise) in Scotland. The population in 1871 was 19,899, and in 1881, was 51,783. The former parish church had a spire which was an exact copy of that at Stratford-on-Avon, but a newer building has taken its place. Dr J. M'Leod is the incumbent of the parish, which is one of the richest in Scot-land. The Elder Park, presented by Mrs Elder, and opened in August 1885 by Lord Rosebery, is a valuable acquisition to the industrial community of Govan.

TITWOOD used to be spelt Tiltwood, and was probably in ancient times the scene of lance and helmet smashing.

GLASGOW GREEN.

" I've wandered mony a nicht in June,
    Alang the banks o' Clyde ;
Beneath a bright and bonnie moon,
    Wi' Mary by my side."

THE town used to possess three public greens. There was the Merchants' Park, which is now the Necropolis; our present Green, formerly known as the New Green; and most important of all, and the most fashionable resort of our great-grandmothers and their sweethearts, was the Old Green. It occupied the space between Jamaica Street and the old Stockwell Bridge. In 1720 there were one hundred and fifty large trees shading its walks, whilst the Clyde flowed clear and bright beside it. No wonder that it was a favourite promenade.

The present Green once formed part of the Bishop's forest. It now covers an area of one hundred and eight acres. The King's Park has been long the scene of military manœuvres.

M'Ure, writing in 1736, says, " The second park is that which is commonly called the New Green, adorned with pleasant galleries of elm trees, and situated upon the south-east corner of the city, and is enclosed with a stately stone

wall two thousand five hundred ells in length, and fenced
on the south with the river of Clyde ; it hath all the summer
time betwixt two and three hundred women bleaching of
linen cloths, and washing linen cloths of all sorts in the
river Clyde, and in the midst of this enclosure there is a
useful well for cleaning the cloths after they are washed in
the river; likewise·there is a lodge built of free-stone in the
midst of it, for a shelter to the herd who waits upon the
horses and cows that are grazed therein."

In 1754 there was a subsidence of about ten feet of part
of the High Green, and an island in the river where bleaching used to be done disappeared at the same time. The
cause is supposed to have been an earthquake, and as they
were prevalent at that period there seems little reason to
doubt the theory. The most of the Green, and a good part
of the city besides, is now undermined by collieries. It is
said that no excavation had taken place on the part which
subsided.

Nelson's Monument, an obelisk one hundred and forty-
four feet high, was erected in 1806. Near the monument
formerly stood the herd's house. A hundred and twenty
cows used to be pastured on the Green. The Camlachie
Burn and the classic Molendinar unite their waters near the
English church. An avenue of trees was taken off in 1819
to form Great Hamilton Street and Monteith Row. An interesting fact about the Arns Well, in the Green, is that it was
when at this spot during one of his usual walks that James
Watt first conceived the idea of the double condenser of the
steam-engine. The Flesher's Haugh, an angle at the south-
east corner, that is washed on three sides by the Clyde, was
the scene of Prince Charlie's review, after the retreat from
Derby (see p. 65). In 1804 a big elm tree was flourishing
on the Low Green. Under it, half a century earlier, a
bright group of ladies stood and witnessed Prince Charlie
reviewing his troops. The Prince's army was about equal
in numbers to that of the Regent Murray in 1568. In 1814
Lord Moira reviewed double the number, for 7,000 were
present at that time under arms on the Green. These
numbers look small now-a-days.

In 1750 a military execution took place on the Green.
John M'Leod, a Highland soldier, was shot for having
deserted to the Jacobites in 1745. The severity was the

cause of great resentment, and considerable ill-feeling was shown to the officers and regiment by the people of Glasgow.

In 1776 the early Baptists used to immerse their converts in the Clyde, at the west end of the Flesher's Haugh, where there was a sloping sandy shore.

The Gymnasium was the gift of a native of Glasgow, residing in Manchester.

ST ANDREW'S EPISCOPAL CHURCH.

OPPOSITE the west end of the Green is St Andrew's Episcopal Church, the oldest of that denomination in Scotland, and built about 1756. It is a neat square edifice, a wall and railing surrounding its few gravestones. The vulgar of a past generation nicknamed it "The Whistling

ST ANDREW'S EPISCOPAL CHURCH.

Kirk," on account of the organ. For a long time St Andrew's was a very fashionable place of worship. All the west - country aristocracy had sittings in it, and rows of carriages were to be seen in attendance. From its records it appears that 100,000 baptisms, and as many marriages, have taken place within its walls.

The Shuttle Street Secession congregation excommunicated Andrew Hunter, mason, for his great sin in building
the Episcopal meeting-house (26th April 1756). This was
the first Secession church in Glasgow. They removed to
North Albion Street, and several of the largest United Presbyterian congregations in the city are directly descended
from them.

ST ANDREW'S CHURCH.

ST ANDREW SQUARE—CHARLOTTE STREET.

A LONG time was spent in building St Andrew's Church.
It was commenced in 1739, and only finished in 1756.
The architect was a self-taught mason, Mungo Naismyth,
grandfather of the founder of the Young Men's Christian
Association. The portico was the first flat arch in the city,
and the masons who were engaged in the work had such
grave doubts of its stability that they would not remove its
supports. A company of labourers, well primed with John
Barleycorn, were bold enough to take the risk. The
square was not built till thirty years after, but a green
surrounded the church, the grass grown on which used to
be sold by the magistrates. When the square was finished,
about 1787, it became the residence of the wealthiest men
of the city, Virginia Street being a sort of rival in select-
ness. The Old Cross of Glasgow is said to have been
buried in the square or kirkgreen.

Vincent Lunardi made a balloon ascent from St Andrew
Square in November 1785, descending near Hawick, a
distance of seventy miles, two hours after. The balloon
was afterwards exhibited suspended in the nave of the
Cathedral.

On the north side of St Andrew Square is Mr Quarrier's
Orphan Home.

Dr Craig was first minister of St Andrew's Church; Dr
William Lockhart the second; and Dr Ritchie, the third, was
appointed in 1802. He it was who introduced an organ,
which occasioned considerable disturbance in the city in
1807, and the innovation led to the Doctor's removal to
Edinburgh. It is said that the first instrument he brought
into the church was the famous little organ which had been

made by James Watt, who had worshipped in St Andrew's in earlier days. Dr Candlish was at one time assistant minister of St Andrew's.

Charlotte Street was made on a market-garden, the rent of which had been three hundred and sixty-five merks Scots annually, and the street was long known as Merk Daily Street.

Charlotte Street was opened by Mr Archibald Paterson, who was Mr David Dale's partner,* and was called after George III.'s Queen. It still preserves its genteel appearance, and many of the old houses are in use as family dwellings. Mr Dale's house was at the south-west corner, nearest the Green. Mr Paterson's was next door. When Greendyke Street was widened, a slice was taken off David Dale's old garden. Mr Paterson was a modest unassuming man, and built the first Independent Church in Glasgow, at his own cost. It was in Grayfriars Wynd, and was nicknamed the Candle Kirk, because Mr Paterson was a candlemaker. He occasionally preached, but Mr Dale was the pastor of the congregation. Dale Street and Paterson Street on the south side were called after them. These streets were near a second church that was built, and are a little way west from and parallel with Eglinton Street. The old Scots Independents, whose church is in Oswald Street, are the descendants of Mr Dale's flock. James Watt was often to be seen sauntering through Charlotte Street on his way to and from the Green.

THE GALLOWGAIT.

THE GALLOWGAIT—LITTLE SANCT MUNGO—THE SARACEN'S HEAD—THE GALLOWMUIR—THE WITCH LOAN.

THE Gallowgait was so called from its being the road to the muir, east of the city, where stood the gallows. It bore the same ominous designation as early as the days of Wallace, and is mentioned in an old document written in 1327. The street now extends for two miles to Camlachie; but, as a built street, it formerly only reached to the East Port (Dove-hill Lane); beyond, it was known as Camlachie Loan.

* See page 83, "David Dale."

In 1736 most of the houses in the Gallowgait were of two stories, and the majority were thatched. A good many of them still remain. Regarding Spoutmouth Loan, off the Gallowgait, it was recorded long ago, before Loch Katrine was pressed into the service of the city:—"The Spout Wynd has four cisterns of very fine sweet water," and this explains the name.

LITTLE SANCT MUNGO.

The East Port stood a few yards west from Dovehill Lane. On the left-hand side, just outside the port (on north side of Gallowgait, past Dovehill Street), there is an interesting spot. Here long ago stood "Little Sanct Mungo," an old Popish chapel, surrounded by a burying-ground. It was built during the reign of James IV. This chapel, after having become superannuated, was converted into an hospital or residence for lepers, "without the gaits of the city" (see Gorbals, page 151), for which special purpose it had been bought (1593) by the magistrates. It was also used during the visitation of the terrible plague. In later times the ancient eerie kirkyard was believed to be haunted; an honest penny was made out of it all the same, however, by letting it for grazing purposes. It was surrounded by trees.

After the East Port had been taken away (about 1749), there being a want for a good large hotel in Glasgow, the magistrates interested themselves to provide one, and the site they fixed upon as the most desirable was the deserted kirkyard of Little Sanct Mungo. They advertised the spot, and it fell into the hands of Robert Tennent, who undertook to erect an inn according to the ideas of the magistrates. In order to encourage him he was permitted to use the Archbishop's Castle as a quarry; and here, above the old graves, was built in 1755 the far-famed Saracen's Head, which is still to the fore. It contained thirty-six fine rooms and a dancing-hall, and was for many a year the chief hotel in Glasgow.

THE SARACEN'S HEAD.

The Saracen's Head was long the chief rendezvous of all distinguished strangers, and the place selected for balls, county meetings, public dinners, &c. &c. The sporting Duke of Hamilton regularly put up there, and many of the

Scotch nobility danced in the spacious ball-room, at county and other balls. Dr Samuel Johnson, on his return from his tour in the Hebrides with Boswell in 1773, lived in the inn.

It has been described as a handsome three-story building, and there was an enormous signboard, with a most ferocious-looking Saracen, to attract the passing stranger. So remorseless and hard-hearted are cities in their onward march. Could savages be more callous in their behaviour, than these townsmen dancing on the very graves of their ancestors! Amidst all their feasting and frivolity, had they no fear of wakening those who were lying so quiet below? The wine brought up from the cellars that so closely neighboured the tombs, must have had a queer flavour, it might certainly possess "body"!

The Saracen's Head is a solid substantial-looking house yet, though its glories have long since passed away. It deserves notice as being altogether a sort of resurrection building, having been founded on dead men's bones, and composed of stones that once formed part of the old episcopal palace that stood near the Cathedral, as we have already stated. The ball-room became a candlework. A carriage entry to it is now the lane called Great Dovehill; whilst the entrance to the stables was by a private lane skirting the east side of the hotel, and is now called Saracen Lane.

The famous Saracen Foundry began life in this lane, which business Mr Walter Macfarlane started in 1851. The Saracen Works at Possil Park now cover from eleven to twelve acres of ground, all under roofing, and employ from 600 to 1000 men.

Robert Tennent who built the Saracen's Head was the brother of Hugh Tennent, the ancestor of the Tennents of Wellpark Brewery.

CAMPBELL STREET.—The ground near was purchased from Sir John Moore's father, Dr John Moore, who is immortalised in Moore Street, off Gallowgait. He opened Campbell Street in 1784. Churches had been expressly forbidden to be built in some of the adjacent streets by their charters, so three were erected in Campbell Street,—the Burgher, the Anti-burgher, and the Relief. It is still a stronghold of the U.P.'s. Graem Street (also off Gallow-

L

gait) was made and named after Mr Graham, a writer, about the same time.

Dovehill was probably so named after the wild doves, whose nests were in the woods there. A monkish tradition said it got the name to commemorate a visit of St Columba, —the dove.

MacFarlane's Observatory was erected by the University in 1757, near where is now MacFarlane Street, off the Gallowgait, but at that time this ground was within the College gardens. Astronomical instruments had been presented by Alexander MacFarlane, Esq., of Jamaica. The first open-air amusements in Glasgow took place in the College gardens during the summer of 1850, — various athletic games, bands of music, balloon ascents, and fireworks. The morality and propriety of such relaxations were discussed to a great extent in pulpits and newspapers. The scheme did not succeed.

St John's Parish Church, a massive Gothic building, stands on rising ground at the head of MacFarlane Street, at the east side of the Gallowgait, and not far from the Barracks. It was built for Dr Chalmers, and the district was the scene of his labours and of Edward Irving's (see page 94).

The old Gallowmuir is now occupied by the Cattle Market, and is traversed or built over by some seventeen streets. One of the lines of crossing used to be called the Witch Loan and is a very ancient thoroughfare. It was the track made across the muir by the workmen who were building the Cathedral and who lodged in Rutherglen, Glasgow being unable to provide accommodation for so many strangers. They crossed the Clyde by a ford. Many generations after, some mysterious malady having attacked the cattle of the townsfolk they were supposed to be bewitched. A running stream and change of air and pasturage were prescribed, and this proved an effectual cure. They were daily driven to the Clyde and the path taken by the sick and convalescent cows was the old masons' road, which was called in consequence the " Witch Loan." Abercrombie Street, Young Street, and Belgrove Street are the aristocratic daughters of the old Witch; the first of these was named after Sir Ralph.

The Barracks were built in 1795, at a cost of £15,000, and

could accommodate one thousand men. The first occupants were the Argyleshire Fencibles. Many a gallant regiment went right from the Gallowgait Barracks to the continental battlefields, and many returned with thinned ranks, always receiving a warm welcome in Glasgow. The 71st Light Infantry was raised in the town, and was designated the Glasgow Regiment. They wore tartan trews and smart Scotch bonnets, and were commanded by Colonel Cadogan, who with his black horse was long spoken about by the past generation. Many of the Glasgow lads fell with him at Vittoria. A tablet in the nave of the Cathedral records his name and bravery.

THE BUTTS.—The Easter Common was a large open waste which stretched east and north from the old College. Weaponschaws used to be held at one place, which was called in consequence the Butts. By an Act of the Scots Parliament of 1425 every man between sixteen and sixty had to attend the weaponschaws. In 1578 the fines levied upon the burghers who did not attend the practisings were devoted to causewaying the town. In 1543, during the childhood of Queen Mary, the battle of the Butts was fought (see page 20), when the Earl of Lennox and the citizens of Glasgow were defeated, and the city given up to pillage.

The Butts extended to Ladywell Street. Until 1765 the place of execution was there, but at that date it was changed to Howgatehead, near the Monkland Canal basin. The Easter Common was sold or feued by the Corporation.

CALTON.

CALTON—THE BURNT BARNS—BRIDGETON.

CALTON at the beginning of last century was known as Black Fauld,—which meant the fold for black cattle. The district lies immediately south of the Gallowgait. In later times nearly all the inhabitants were weavers, who lived in two-roomed houses, one room containing the loom. During the strike and riot of the weavers, 3rd September 1787, three men were killed and several wounded.

The chief points of interest in Calton are the Burnt Barns and Balaam's Pass. Tradition says the former were barns

that were burnt at the time of Wallace's victory at the Bell o'
the Brae. Balaam's Pass is the popular and mysterious name
for the passage between London Street and Great Hamilton
Street.   The Burnt Barns Inn was situated so as to inter-
cept the wayfarer on his road to and from Rutherglen and
the south.   It was established as an inn in 1679, but has
undergone alterations.   St Andrew's Lane, Balaam's Pass,
and Great Hamilton Street, mark the line of an ancient road
from Saltmarket to Rutherglen.   Great Hamilton Street and
Canning Street form the leading thoroughfare of Calton. At
Barrowfield Toll a quick turn to the right conducts us to
Main Street, Bridgeton.

It is supposed that the name of Tureen Street, in Calton,
has been corrupted from Touraine; one of the first feuars was
a Frenchman named Bagniolle.

Very long ago—in 1226—Shettleston is referred to in
a document, and is spelt Schedenston.

It was the third John Walkinshaw of Camlachie who projected the village of Bridgeton.   It dates from 1777, when
the bridge to Rutherglen was made, and it used to be occupied by a community of weavers.   The bridge joins the
famous lands of Barrowfield and Shawfield.   It has five
steep arches, and is said to resemble the Auld Brig of
Glasgow.   Dalmarnock Bridge is about as crooked-backed,
but it is not so aged. It is a wooden structure.

In 1783 David Dale and George Macintosh founded
Barrowfield, the first Turkey-red work in Great Britain.

MOUNT VERNON, three miles east of Glasgow Cross, was
named by Andrew Buchanan, the founder of Virginia
Street, after a great tobacco plantation in Virginia, from
whence he imported tobacco.   It was the plantation of the
brother of George Washington.   The House of Mount
Vernon, in Virginia, was long the residence of the President,
and is still standing.

CAMLACHIE.

THE WALKINSHAWS — EARLY COAL-MINING — SLAVERY IN
GLASGOW—PRINCE CHARLIE AND A CAMLACHIE BEAUTY
—GENERAL WOLFE.

To the many Camlachie and its associations savour of
nothing but vulgarity.   Let us inquire into the past history

of the place and see what can be done to make it interesting. The name is Celtic, and is supposed to mean the muddy bend of the burn. Camlachie Brig appears in a document of 1590, and Camlachie itself is mentioned as far back as the time of William Wallace. It is that part of the city between the Gallowgait and Parkhead, and was situated on the old highway of traffic to Edinburgh and the east.

The soil was of a good arable nature, but much of the early importance of Camlachie and that district was owing to the collieries, which were opened there very long ago. The oldest coalmasters in the West of Scotland were the Grays of Dalmarnock, one of whom, John Gray, laird of Carntyne, a zealous Covenanter, opened up coalfields about 1630; he died in 1687. His intimate friend and neighbour was John Walkinshaw, a Glasgow merchant and the first laird of Western Camlachie. He left £100 to the poor of the Merchants' House of Glasgow.

His son and namesake was a magistrate of Glasgow, and one of the merchants who fitted out the "Lion" privateer to cruise against the Dutch. It was probably he who married the daughter of "Bailey the Covenanter." He died in 1689. Both he and his father were wealthy. These Walkinshaws of Camlachie belonged originally to a Renfrewshire family, and had risen to distinction in Glasgow (see page 220).

The third John Walkinshaw was singularly unlucky. In 1705 he bought a great part of the lands called Easter Common, east of the city, and including the Golf Hill, and laid out the village of Barrowfield,* which in later years, after the bridge to Rutherglen had been built in 1775, was called Bridgeton. Mr Walkinshaw lost a fortune in unremunerative coalmining, and in other matters was equally unsuccessful. Like all his family he was a keen Jacobite, and married a lady of the same political principles. She was a sister of Sir Hugh Paterson of Bannockburn, who was married to the Earl of Mar's sister. Mrs Walkinshaw was popularly known as Lady Barrowfield. She brought her husband a handsome fortune, and in course of time ten daughters but no son.

At the 1715 rebellion Mr Walkinshaw and Sir Hugh

---

* The Regent Murray's army in 1568 was encamped on the Barrow or Burgh Field.

came out with the Earl of Mar and fought at Sheriffmuir, where Walkinshaw was taken prisoner. His wife found access to his prison in Stirling Castle, and by exchanging clothes with her husband and remaining in his stead he effected his escape. She was thirty-two years of age at this time, having been born in 1683.

Walkinshaw's estates and possessions were forfeited ; but two years afterwards he was pardoned, and returned to Cam-lachie. Evil fortune still clung to his pecuniary affairs, the coal mines never paid, and he had to part with the most of his land and collieries.

It was in 1720 that he built the famous Camlachie House, which is still standing (see page 169). It was surrounded by twelve acres of ground. Ten years after-wards, March 1730, he had to sell "the coall craigs and coall seems, with the whole coall heughers, winnace men, and other servants whatever, belonging to the said coal works . . . water pumps, roup bucketts, and generallie the whole other materialle belonging to the said coal works."

In an old coal tack, of about the same date, relating to the Camlachie or Barrowfield collieries belonging to John Walkinshaw, "the tenant has power to keep the said coal hewers, winnace men, and other servants att their work or business, and to apprehend and incarcerate such of them as shall flye, run away, or refuse to come back when desired."

At that time coal was sold in Glasgow at one shilling a cart of ten cwt., so, in spite of the bondage of the miners, colliery proprietors did not make much money at the busi-ness.

John Walkinshaw's widow lived to be ninety-seven (1780), and was generally called Lady Barrowfield. Her later years were spent in Carrubber's Close, Edinburgh. One of her ten daughters attained notoriety in connection with Prince Charles. Miss Clementina Walkinshaw was one of the Jacobite young ladies who waited upon him at the Shawfield Mansion in December 1745. (One writer mentions her uncle's house at Bannockburn as the first place of meeting.) She was a mere girl then, but after the Prince had been in France for a short time, he induced her to follow him. The attachment was unfortunate. Although one of the most beautiful women of her day, her comparatively humble rank stood in the way of marriage with the Prince. She obtained great ascendancy over him, which caused the estrangement of his friends. They were afraid that she might betray them, because her sister was a housekeeper at Leicester House, but she had entered that service before the rising of 1745.

Dr King, in his "Anecdotes of his Own Times," says :— "In the year 1745, when Charles Edward was in Scotland, he had a mistress whose name was Walkinshaw, and whose sister was at that time, and is still, housekeeper at Leicester House, at the Dowager Princess of Wales' (George II.'s). Some years after Prince Charles was relieved from his French prison and conducted out of France, he sent for this girl, who soon acquired such a dominion over him that she was acquainted with all his schemes, and trusted with his most secret correspondence. As soon as this was known in England, all those persons of distinction who were attached to him were greatly alarmed ; they imagined that this wench had been placed in his family by the English ministers; and considering her sister's situation, they seemed to have some ground for their suspicion ; wherefore, they despatched a gentleman to Paris, where the Prince then was, who had instructions to insist that Mrs Walkinshaw should be removed to a convent for a certain time. But her gallant absolutely refused to comply with this demand ; and although M'Namara, the gentleman who was sent to him, urged the most cogent reasons and used all the arts of persuasion, to induce him to part with her, and even proceeded to assure him, according to his instructions, that an immediate interruption of all correspondence with his most powerful friends in England, and in short, that the ruin of his interest, which was now daily increasing, would be the infallible consequence of his refusal; yet he continued inflexible. M'Namara stayed in Paris some days, endeavouring to reason the Prince into a better temper, but finding him obstinately persevere in his first answer, he took his leave with concern and indignation, saying, as he passed out, 'What has your family done, sir, thus to draw down the vengeance of Heaven on every branch of it through so many ages?' In all the conferences with M'Namara, the Prince declared that it was not a violent passion, or indeed any particular regard, which attached him to Mrs Walkinshaw, and that he could see her removed from him without any concern ; but he would not receive directions, in respect to his private conduct, from any man alive.

"The result was that his friends resolved no longer to endanger their lives in his cause."

The singular devotion of the "powerful English Jacobites," and their anxiety to rise in arms on his behalf years after the opportunity had gone by, affords a characteristic contrast to the conduct of his northern friends. We cannot help doubting every point of the story. We question the genuineness of the English devotion ; we do not believe in the perfidy of Clementina ; nor, lastly, in the sincerity of the Prince's protestations of his indifference to her.

We are prepared to stand up for the honesty of the Glasgow girl, the traditions of whose country and family were all true to the core in that undertaking.

The Duchess of Albany was the Prince's daughter by Miss Walkinshaw. She was an accomplished and amiable lady. Charles long refused to legitimise her, but she was supported by her uncle, the Cardinal York, who gave her six thousand crowns per annum.

In September 1787 a deed was recorded in the parliament of Paris, whereby Charles at last removed the stigma from his daughter's name, creating her Duchess of Albany, and constituting her his sole heir. She died in 1789, in consequence of a fall from a horse, being then about forty years of age, and left £20,000.

Camlachie House, built in 1720 by John Walkinshaw, is still to the fore, and used to be surrounded by a garden. It became the property of Mr William Orr, who bought the mines, &c., of the Walkinshaws; and in 1749 and 1750 was the residence of General Wolfe, the hero of Quebec. After the battle of Culloden in 1746, he had taken his share in some hot work on the Continent, and had seen the Duke of Cumberland out-generalled and thrashed by the French.

Now, in 1749, he was in command of the regiment which occupied Glasgow. There were no barracks then, but the soldiers were quartered on the inhabitants. Colonel Wolfe became the occupant of Camlachie House, having been received by Mr William Orr of Barrowfield. Whilst in Glasgow the young officer engaged a teacher to come from Glasgow to assist him in studying Latin and Greek. He was a frequent guest at Mr Orr's fine house of Barrowfield, and enjoyed the hospitality of the leading inhabitants. He wrote some rather severe remarks upon the mercenary spirit of the Glasgow young ladies.

Camlachie House is a two-story building. It stands a little way east of the corner of East Nelson Street, and has

CAMLACHIE HOUSE (GENERAL WOLFE'S RESIDENCE).

degenerated into a whisky tavern. It contained six good fire rooms, besides kitchen, garrets, &c. Built by John Walkinshaw in 1720, ten years before he died, his wife and daughter lived in it until 1734. Clementina's childhood's days at least were spent here, though she went to France for her education.

RUTHERGLEN.

In these days of rampant Radicalism, and the universal belief in the *Vox populi vox Dei* theory, it is almost dangerous to refer to the ancient but far decayed burgh of Rutherglen; but here it remains, within two miles of Glasgow Cross, a permanent warning of certain dangers of democracy. As far back as the reign of David I., when Glasgow was yet a mere village governed by its bishop, Rutherglen was a royal burgh, with its provost and bailies. Both towns had a fair start, in shipping and trade, and for a time the older one seemed to lead; but alas, how soon it fell behind in the race. The chief reason seems to have been, that whilst Glasgow was being ruled by men of energy and character, who knew what was for the good of the community, the Radical burgh, with its popular elections and other privileges, gave itself up to local squabbling and bickering. This appears several times in the records of the rival towns. In Glasgow, a close burgh, the magistrates elected themselves,—the merchant interest was supreme. They carried Clyde navigation bills through Parliament, and were ever alive to the development of the city. It was the mercantile genius—the mercantile instinct—that at first made Glasgow. In later days the mechanical ascendancy of our shipbuilders and engineers have more than maintained the supremacy of the Clyde.

During Queen Mary's reign the townsmen of Glasgow, Renfrew, and Dumbarton made an agreement to work on the Clyde for six weeks at a time to remove the ford at Dumbuck, and make other improvements. These burghs had no greater interest in clearing away the obstacles than Rutherglen had, but she seems to have stood aloof with folded hands, and allowed her sisters to do the work. In 1755, when the magistrates of Glasgow consulted Smeaton about the deepening of the river, Rutherglen again stood back. Before the Clyde Navigation Acts were passed (1750), and before the Broomielaw Bridge was built (1768), there were frequently more vessels to be seen at the quay at Rutherglen than at Glasgow. They were frequently to be seen sailing up under the arches of the Old Bridge to Rutherglen until the latter year.

Rutherglen possesses not a little historical interest. It is very often mentioned in Scottish story. Its strong castle was often brought into prominence during the wars. Alexander Smith speaks of "The long straggling burgh of Rutherglen, with the church tower which saw the bargain struck with Menteith for the betrayal of Wallace." A small quaint steeple it is, compared with the new lofty tower of the Town House.

THE COVENANTERS AT RUTHERGLEN.

IT is the 29th May 1679, and the anniversary of the Restoration. A bonfire has been kindled in the chief street of the old burgh of Rutherglen in honour of the event, when a company of stern-visaged horsemen ride in from the country and interrupt the proceedings. The leaders of the party are Hackston, Burleigh, and Hamilton, and their following has been gathered from among the "chased or tossed" men from the surrounding uplands. Claverhouse's dragoons are in Glasgow,* but the movements of the Covenanters give no evidence of fear or haste. They tramp out the bonfire, and, after singing and prayer, make a public protest against the proceedings of the Government, which they affix to the Cross, committing to the flames all the Acts of the Scottish Parliament that have been passed in favour of Prelacy. These openly declared rebels are immediately joined by many of the peasantry. Marching to the southwest, they take up their position on Loudon Hill. Thither in hot haste goes Claverhouse, with one hundred and fifty of his rough troopers. The Covenanters move down to a boggy piece of ground, about a mile from the hill, where the battle of Drumclog is fought (Sunday, 1st June 1678). The Scots Greys, for this was the regiment's first engagement, and their unmerciful chief, are met hand to hand by men of as stern a mould. Not only is the position of the peasant infantry impregnable, but the charge of the mounted Covenanters shatters the ranks of the dragoons, thirty of whom are killed, and the rest are chased from the field in discomfiture and confusion. The soldiers received but scanty sympathy from the burghers of Glasgow upon their arrival there. Next day the insurgents were repulsed in their attack upon Glasgow ; but Claverhouse deemed it expedient to leave immediately after.

Rutherglen Bridge connects the famous lands of Barrowfield, or Burghfield, and Shawfield. The weavers of Rutherglen used to be mighty anglers at Dalmarnock ford.

---

* Wilson in his "Impartial Account," 1750, says, "June 1st, Claverhouse came with a troop of dragoons from the new garrison in Glasgow ;" but by the biography of Claverhouse (in "English Worthies") it appears that the leader himself was in Falkirk on 29th May, as a letter of his was written on that day at Falkirk. Some of his dragoons, however, witnessed from a safe distance the doings of the Covenanters at Rutherglen.

ARGYLE STREET.

THE BLACK BULL INN—DUNLOP STREET.

THIS, the main street of the city, runs from east to west almost parallel with the Clyde for about a mile, and in continuation of the Trongait. The only fatal mistake yet made by the city was in allowing the Caledonian Railway to cross Argyle Street. They have disfigured one of the finest streets in the kingdom. In olden days it was called the Westergait, and was quite open, with a few small thatched houses here and there. St Enoch's Croft extended to Jamaica Street, and the Lang Croft from Candleriggs to Queen Street. These were used as gardens or cornfields. M'Ure, who wrote in 1737, says :—" The city is surrounded with cornfields, kitchen and flower gardens, and beautiful orchyards, abounding with fruits of all sorts; which by reason of the open and large streets send forth a pleasant and odoriferous smell."

The two oldest houses lately standing in Argyle Street were the Buck's Head Inn, at the corner of Dunlop Street, which was built as a mansion for Provost Dunlop in 1750, and further east the old dwelling-place of Provost Murdoch, built during the same year. They were both merchants and bankers in the Briggait, and both attained the provostship. The Buck's Head has been cut and carved beyond all recognition now, but the other house still preserves its main features, and may be at once recognised by the ornamental urns on the top.

The West Port was removed in 1751. Before then Argyle Street was a country road leading to the mills at Partick and to Dumbarton. Most of the thatched cottages on either side were occupied by small brewers or maltmen. They made a sort of home-brewed ale, and used to deliver it to the townsfolk each day. Before the reign of tea and coffee commenced, this ale was the orthodox breakfast beverage of all classes. The west half of Argyle Street continued to be called Anderston Walk till far into the present century, and was an open roadway. Anderston was a separate village, and early in the century a carrier used to travel every day between it and Glasgow. Maxwell Street was made in 1771, by John Maxwell, writer, and Stephen

Maxwell, coppersmith, and named after them. St Enoch's Kirk was built in 1780. St Enoch Square used to be a square of private houses, with a rail-enclosed garden. The present St Enoch's Church was built in 1827, from designs by David Hamilton. The spire of the old church was preserved. St Enoch Railway Station and Hotel occupies the whole of the east side of St Enoch Square, and is one of the finest buildings of the kind in the kingdom. It was finished at a cost of over £500,000, in 1880. It is lighted by the electric light. The glass roof of the station is five hundred and thirty feet long, two hundred and five feet wide, and eighty-five feet high. St Enoch Burn, which crosses Argyle Street between Buchanan Street and Union Street, was the old Royalty boundary until 1846. The space between Argyle Street and the Broomielaw, as far west as M'Alpine Street, was previously within the Royalty. The then West End, viz., Blythswood Hill, was outside of the boundary.

THE BLACK BULL INN.

THE West Port stood a little way west of Glassford Street. A cattle market used to be held just outside the gate, and there formerly stood on the site of the second tenement west from Stockwell Street, on the south side of Argyle Street, a quaint old hostelry, with thatched roof and antiquated gables. It bore the sign of the Black Bull Inn.

About 1750 it was thought necessary to provide additional hotel accommodation. The Saracen's Head Inn was erected at the East Port in the Gallowgait in 1755, and in 1758 the Highland Society built the new Black Bull Inn, on the north side of Argyle Street, at the south-east corner of Virginia Street, on ground which had been part of the garden of the Shawfield mansion.

The new Black Bull had a somewhat singular beginning. At the request of a few Highland gentlemen, George White-field preached a sermon on behalf of poor Highlanders (June 1757). It was in the High Churchyard, and he begged so lustily from the immense audience that the biggest collection ever made in Scotland was taken. The Glasgow Highland Society had been formed before 1727. Chiefly with this money they bought land west of the West Port, on which they built the Black Bull Inn, and this formed the chief source of their income afterwards. Many

a young Highlander has been clothed and educated off the
profits of the establishment.

The first landlord, James Graham, was the proprietor of
the old Black Bull Inn, on the other side of the street, and
he transferred the name.   The new inn comprised twenty-
three bedrooms, six parlours, one large hall thirty-seven feet
square, a kitchen, six cellars underground, a dwelling-house
consisting of a back-room and shop both underground,
stables for thirty-eight horses, hay and corn lofts, coach-
house, byre, &c.   It survived the Saracen's Head, which fell
from its high estate in 1791.   From 1758 till 1825 the
rental had been increased to twelve times its original figure,
and it continued to be a hotel until 1849, although the
lower portion had been made into shops.   In 1849 the
Black Bull became the drapery warehouse of Mann, Simpson, & Byars, and the same firm, under the name of Mann,
Byars, & Co., still occupy the premises.

DUNLOP STREET was laid out about 1750 by Colin Dunlop,
Esq. of Carmyle, provost, banker, and merchant, who died
in 1777.   His old mansion is still standing; and as the
oldest house in Argyle Street, is worthy of more than a
passing glance.   No difficulty will be experienced in identify-
ing the building.   Its triangular entablature and large ornamental urns at once catch the eye.   Next house but one,
and at the corner of Dunlop Street, was the famous Buck's
Head Inn.   It was built at the same time as Mr Dunlop's
by Provost George Murdoch, but has undergone repeated
transformations.   It succeeded the Saracen Inn as the chief
hotel of the city.   Now it seems to have been altered beyond recognition.   How these proud old city magnates
would open their eyes could they revisit Argyle Street, and
see to what base uses their grand mansions have been put,
and how much they have been eclipsed by modern neighbours !   It was Provost Murdoch who laid the foundation
stone of Jamaica Bridge on 29th September 1768.   The
first feuar of Dunlop Street was Dr Moore, the author of
"Zelucca," and father of Sir John Moore.   His former
house was at Donald's Land, No. 88, on north side of Trongait, where Sir John was born.   Desiring a more fashionable
residence, he built one on west side of Dunlop Street, No.
22, and here Sir John spent his boyhood.

JAMAICA STREET.

JAMAICA STREET AND BRIDGE—THE OLD GREEN — THE
BOTTLE WORKS—OSWALD STREET—JAMES WATT STREET
—ANDERSTON, &c.

JAMAICA STREET was not finished till 1772 ; the builder
was a mason, John Adam, of Adam's Court. The river end
of the street was shut up by a building which crossed it, till
in 1768 the first Broomielaw Bridge was built. After Jamaica
Street was made, Union Street continued to be occupied
with gardens.

Long ago the ground beside the river between Jamaica
Street and Stockwell Bridge was innocent of stone and lime.
It was the public green of the town (see page 155).
M'Ure, in 1736, says :— " The old green is only fenced
round with palisadoes, and no stone wall, but that loss is
made up by one hundred and fifty growing trees round the
green, pretty large. Within this green is the Ropework,
which keeps constantly twenty men at work, and the proprietors thereof can furnish as good tarr'd cable ropes, and
white ropes untarr'd, as any in Britain. On the west end of
this green is the Glasswork." Brown's " History of Glasgow "
says :—" Bottlemaking was carried on for many years on a
stance a little way east of Jamaica Bridge, where a few workmen at a three-pot furnace were able to supply all the demand,
and filled up three months of the year working for bottlemakers
in Edinburgh. The annual suspension of the fires gave rise
to the popular notion that it was necessary to stop lest
salamanders would breed." The situation of the bottlework
was about Howard and Dixon Streets. It was a great nui-
sance, and sent up huge volumes of smoke. Its cone, one
hundred feet in height, is a prominent object in old pictures
of Glasgow. The Custom-house was built on part of its site.
Before the days of the bottlework, a wood extended along
the river side.

The Royal Circus, or Riding School, was on the west side
of Jamaica Street. It became the tabernacle of the Rev.
Greville Ewing. His congregation removed to Nile Street,
afterwards to Waterloo Street, and now worships in Hillhead. The Jamaica Street Bridge was built (1834) of stones
from the quarry at Queen Street Railway Station. It cost
from £30,000 to £40,000. The architect was T. Telford.

Oswald Street was named after the father of James Oswald, M.P., who bought the land on speculation. The Custom-house is built on the western boundary. He gave Howard Street its name in honour of the great philanthropist. Fox Street was called after that famous statesman. The Oswalds of Glasgow were eminent merchants. The family was derived from or connected with the town of Thurso. In 1745 R. and A. Oswald were strong Jacobites. They and some others negotiated successfully with Prince Charlie, whilst on his southward march, and prevented his coming to Glasgow, as is shown by the records of the Town Council thanking them for their service. Richard Oswald rose to distinction. He became a merchant in London, and acted as one of the plenipotentiaries from the Court of Great Britain at the settlement of 1783. He was a friend of Benjamin Franklin.

JAMES WATT STREET.—Denholm, writing in 1798, says: —"James Watt Street was formerly called the Delpht-house Lane, as the Delpht-house, or Pottery, stood there; but its designation was changed to commemorate the great inventor, as he had once obtained a small room in the pottery that he might prosecute his studies outside of the burgh."

Brown Street, Carrick Street, and M'Alpine Street, mark the site of the old bleaching fields of Brown, Carrick, & Co., and are named after the three partners in this firm, which was the leading one in Glasgow. Their warehouse was in Bell Street. Mr Carrick was the famous manager of the Ship Bank.

Washington Street was named by the lady owner of the land thereabouts, early in the century. She was a Foxite-Radical, and given to literary pursuits; and, in choosing the name, wished to show her admiration of the great President.

The three contiguous streets, Campbell Street, Mains Street, and Douglas Street, are all connected with the Blythswood family. Colin Campbell, who was provost in 1661, was married to Mary, daughter of John Douglas of Mains. Their grandson eventually succeeded to the Blythswood estate.

ANDERSTON was laid off and named after Provost John Anderson of Dowhill and the Gallowgait, on part of his lands of Stobcross, in 1725. He was the grandfather of Sir John Moore's mother (see page 87). There was a little colony of forty Frenchwomen brought to Anderston in 1768 to begin the spinning of fine yarn. The village was erected into a burgh of barony in 1824.

Finnieston was named after the Rev. John Finnie, who had been tutor to the Orrs of Barrowfield. The village was laid out in 1768 by Matthew Orr, who died in 1786. Five years later, the unlucky coal mines of Camlachie proved the ruin of the Orrs.

THE CAMPBELLS OF BLYTHSWOOD.

THE Campbells of Blythswood are descended from one of the oldest mercantile houses in Glasgow. They were traders in Queen Mary's days, when there were only 4,500 inhabitants in the city, and grew with its progress. In the house of one of them, Robert Campbell of Elie and Silvercraigs, Oliver Cromwell took up his quarters in the Saltmarket in 1650. The estate of Blythswood formed part of the Gorbals land, and was bought in 1661 by Provost Colin Campbell from the creditors of Sir George Elphinstone, whose old castle used to form such a picturesque mark in Main Street, Gorbals. The "Blythswood annexation lands," north-west of the city, were acquired for a very small price in 1670 by the same provost. During the time of Major Archibald Campbell, M.P., feuing was commenced on these valuable acres. This gentleman had succeeded his brother, Colonel John Campbell, who was killed in 1794 at Martinico, but was a prisoner in Toulon when the news reached him of his having succeeded to the large entailed estates. The father of these brothers had died in 1775, insolvent and involved in debt. Archibald got legal power to sell the Briggait mansion and other parts of the estate. He it was who bought the lands north-west of the city, which have since become so valuable,* and upon which so much of the new town has been built. Where now are so many handsome streets were wont to be fields and orchards ; the neighbourhood of Glasgow long ago was famous for fruit.

---

* Dugald Bannatyne, William Jack, and Dr Cleland opened Bath Street in 1800. The Blythswood rent roll was then £223 per annum ; in 1837, when Cleland wrote, the feus amounted to £12,500, with seventy-five acres still to feu. The feus were one shilling and sixpence per yard.

M

PARTICK.

THE REGENT'S MILL—CLAYSLAP MILLS.

THE bishops of Glasgow had a residence at Partick, or
Perthec, as it was then called, before 1277. It is believed
to have stood on the bank overlooking the junction of the
Kelvin and Clyde. The archbishop used to live here before
the Reformation.

Captain Thomas Crawford of Jordanhill built an arch of
the bridge of Partick over the Kelvin, where his name and
arms are still to be seen. He was provost of Glasgow, 1578-
1603, having been nominated by the Regent, the Earl of
Lennox. It was during his term of office that the Cathedral
was endangered.

The Regent's Mill, on the east bank of the Kelvin, adjoining the Old Dumbarton Road, stands on historic ground.
It is built on the site of the ancient wheat mill which was
gifted to the Incorporation of Bakers by the Regent Murray,
after the battle of Langside in 1568, in recognition of the
satisfactory manner in which the bakers of Glasgow had
supplied his troops with bread. The mill and lands remained in possession of the incorporation for three hundred
and nineteen years, and proved a valuable possession. The
present building is at least the third that has occupied the
site. Before the battle of Langside the name was the Archbishop's Mill, but it was then changed to the Bunhouse. A
new building was erected in 1828, but it was burned down
in February 1885. The new mills belong to Ex-Provost
Ure. Both Mr Ure's forefathers and Mrs Ure's have been
connected with the Incorporation of Bakers for seven generations. The name of the new Regent's Mill will serve to
hand down the story.

In addition to the Partick mills, the bakers also possessed
the adjoining mills at Clayslap, on the Kelvin. The Clayslap Mill was bought by the Incorporation of Bakers about
1771. It was formerly a snuff-mill. Above the entrance is
a shield with the arms of Glasgow and the date 1654.

.   .   .   .

The operations in connection with the laying out of the
Victoria Park, Whiteinch, have led to the discovery of a
good many tree fossils of considerable size embedded in

freestone. They are believed to be specimens of the family *Lycopodii*, herbaceous trees of gigantic growth, nourished under atmospheric and climatic conditions which no longer exist on the earth's surface.

. . . . . .

Dwellers in some of the grandest streets in the west end may be a little scandalised to learn that much of their quarter has been undermined by collieries. Concerning an old pit are a couple of curious stories. About the locality of Woodside there was a wood, and in the wood some old disused pits. Into one of them a certain Lieutenant Spearing unfortunately fell. His experience was extraordinary. He lived at the bottom, fifty feet down, without food for seven days, until some friends, who were searching in the wood for his body, heard his cries and rescued him. This was in 1769. In 1773 no fence had been made, and a washer-woman next, who was gathering brambles and hazel nuts in the wood, fell into the same pit. She reached the bottom unhurt, and fortunately had with her a supply of bannocks. Three days passed, and she heard the Sabbath bells ringing in the city ; but no one heard her cries until a labourer happened to pass that way. He not only delivered her, but soon after they were united in the bonds of wedlock.

. . . . . .

ST ROLLOX.—The Chapel of St Roche was founded in 1508 by Thomas Mureheid, canon of Glasgow, and stood alone on a moor, where is now St Rollox, the latter name being a corruption of St Roche.

St Rollox Chemical Works (Messrs Tennant, Knox, & Co.), for making sulphuric acid, chloride of lime, soda, soap, &c., are the largest of the kind in the world, and employ twelve hundred hands. The chimney, built in 1843, cost £12,000, and is 455 feet high. Townsend's is still higher.

"In Possil Moss," says Rennie in his "Essay on Peat Moss," "a leathern bag containing about two hundred silver coins of Rome was found." The Moss is supposed to have been formed since the time of the Romans. Possil is spelt Possele in 1241, and is then mentioned as belonging to the Bishop of Glasgow. The estate of Possil Park was the home of Sir Archibald Alison, the historian. It is still the scene of heavy productions.

QUEEN STREET.

QUEEN STREET used to be the Cow Loan by which the townsfolk's cattle were wont to march to the common pasturage of Cowcaddens. It was by it and St Enoch's Gait that Oliver Cromwell entered Glasgow in 1650; and Prince Charlie and his army followed by the same route in 1745. The street was widened and causewayed in 1766, and named Queen Street in honour of the then young grandmother of Queen Victoria.

Long ago, where the Exchange is now built, there used to stand a thatched farm-house, with a big midden on either side. George Square was then a stagnant lake, where many a cat was drowned.

The Royal Exchange was built in 1829. It cost £60,000, and is one of the finest buildings in Glasgow,—Corinthian pillars and a beautiful lantern tower being the distinguishing features. The architect was David Hamilton. The Royal Exchange originated about 1770, through a coffee-room being opened where a few merchants might meet and see the newspapers. The accommodation not being sufficient, they clubbed together on the Tontine principle and built the Tontine Hotel in the Trongait, which was the chief rendezvous of the merchants of the city till 1829, when the present Royal Exchange was erected. The Exchange occupies the site of the mansion built by Mr William Cunningham of Lainshaws, one of the famous four Virginian merchants of last century. It was completed in 1780, and was a splendid house. It 1819 it was remodelled, and converted into the office of the Royal Bank. Ten years later the property changed hands, and the Exchange was built round it, the old house being that part of the Exchange immediately within the portico. The Royal Bank built premises in the square close behind.

In front of the Royal Exchange is the splendid equestrian statue of the Duke of Wellington by Baron Marochetti. The man and horse are of bronze, and the attitude is life-like and spirited. On the four sides of the pedestal are relief groups of " Assaye " and " Waterloo," " The young soldier leaving the plough," and " The return from the war." The statue cost £10,000.

The North British Railway Station occupies the site of an

old quarry, whence building stone was got for a considerable part of the city. Its frontage to George Street includes the chapel of the Rev. Dr Wardlaw, where he preached until his death.

GEORGE SQUARE.

GEORGE SQUARE was commenced in 1786. It was long a railed-in enclosure, from which the public were religiously kept out, till the Corporation, in trying to arrange with the proprietors of the neighbourhood for the purchase of the square so that the town's people might have access to it, discovered to their astonishment that it belonged to the town.

The good folks of Glasgow, as they often inform the stranger, keep all their stock of monuments in one place. This arrangement saves tourists the bother of looking about the city for statues, as the favoured spot—George Square—happens to be near one of the chief railway stations. The first statue was that to Sir John Moore, erected in 1819 by public subscription. The monument to Sir Walter Scott dates from 1837; the column, which is eighty feet high, is by David Rhind, and the statue by Ritchie, both of Edinburgh. The equestrian statues to the Queen and Prince Consort are by Baron Marochetti. The other statues are Sir Robert Peel, by Mossman; James Watt, by Chantrey; Thomas Graham, late Master of the Mint, and James Oswald, M.P., both by Brodie, of Edinburgh. Near the middle of the Square stands Robert Burns, raised by one shilling subscriptions, and the work of Ewing, of Glasgow. It was unveiled on 25th January 1877, by Lord Houghton. The bronze statues of two soldiers occupy the front of the Square, looking southwards. They are the work of two great sculptors. Sir John Moore is by Flaxman, and Lord Clyde by Foley. Both generals were natives of Glasgow. Another no less gallant hero, David Livingstone, is commemorated in bronze at the west side of the Square, and no more telling statue could be desired to show the manner of man he was,—the attitude unassuming and unaggressive, both the face and figure conveying the idea of decision and indomitable courage, whilst the face exhibits the manliness of the soldier and the tenderness of the philanthropist. No more appropriate place could have been chosen for a statue of the great missionary (see page 103).

George Square is surrounded by some noble buildings, of which the new Municipal Palace is the grandest. It has reduced Sir Walter's height considerably, and for a Scottish edifice it seems to display an extraordinary crop of "twelve apostles" and other images. The west side of the square is occupied by the Merchants' House, with the old ship still crowning its vane in memory of the "sea adventurers" of two centuries ago (see page 148), and the Bank of Scotland, with the colossal Atlas of Mossman. Whilst the Post Office and a drapery warehouse form the southern line, some white-washed veterans still hold their own on the north, in defiance of modern ideas.

THE MUNICIPAL BUILDINGS.

IT was not till the year of grace 1625 that St Mungo attained such dignity and dimensions as to require a public building in which to transact the business of the city. Just at that time, however, ships of thirty or forty tons burden were actually beginning to come as far as the Broomielaw, and it burst upon the Council that Glasgow was becoming a centre of some importance. And so, in 1625, the building which is still represented by the Cross Steeple was erected by the Hon. James Inglis, then Lord Provost of the city. That was an auspicious day in the town's history. It is true that the council-chamber, court-house, prison, and other public departments, were comprised within the walls of the building at the Cross, but the city fathers were not so ambitious then as they are now, and they were content to know that the erection of the municipal buildings marked a stage in the city's progress and development. For well-nigh two centuries the structure performed its functions, although long before that time it was felt that ampler accommodation was needed. It was not, however, till the Hon. James Black assumed the chair of office as Lord Provost that the final step was taken, and the black dingy building constructed at the west end of Glasgow Green, in that part now known as Jail Square. In 1842 removal again became necessary, and the Corporation migrated to the south side of Ingram Street. Thirty years later, in 1872, the building was greatly enlarged. It extended down Hutcheson and Brunswick Streets.

Quite ten years ago it began to be felt that the public business of the city was unnecessarily cramped and confined, and it was felt also that for the credit of the city a more commodious and convenient structure was a thing to be desired. For a year the matter was only talked about, till 1876 when Lord Provost Bain formally tabled a motion on the subject, but six years elapsed before it was given practical effect to.

The chosen design was that of Mr William Young, of London, and it is the product of his genius which is shown in George Square to-day. When the fact transpired that the successful competitor happened to be a native of Glasgow, the townsfolk were delighted. It was originally intended that the cost of the buildings should not exceed £150,000—this of course exclusive of site,—but it was felt that this sum would not pay for a structure which would be a credit to the city. Wiser counsels prevailed, and Mr Young designed a building to be erected at a cost of a round quarter of a million. The foundation stone was laid on Saturday the 6th of October 1883, with Masonic honours. A general holiday was observed in the town, the sun shone out brightly on the event, and probably such pomp and pageantry were never seen in the city before. It was calculated that quite 200,000 witnessed the ceremony at some part of its stages. On George Square alone, a huge platform was erected covering the entire area of the new building, on which ten or twelve thousand people found places. Lord Provost Ure laid the stone in its place, and when the sun went down and the darkness crept in, a blaze of illuminations, from one end of the city to the other, proclaimed the close of an event of the first importance in the history of Glasgow.

The building represents a free but dignified style of the period of the Italian Renaissance. It is surmounted by several towers, the climax being reached in a magnificent tower which frowns down on the grand entrance. There are four fronts, each surpassing the others in magnificence. The chief entrance faces George Square. Entering by it we find the great hall, with beautiful marble pillars, and huge sculptured figures. Ample accommodation will be found in the

new buildings for all the public departments which carry on
the business of the Corporation, while the Town Council
will be given greatly increased facilities in the way of com-
mittee-rooms and other useful and necessary apartments of
a semi-private nature. The buildings are practically fire-
proof; not a scrap of wood has been used, the floors are
composed of concrete and iron. As to the cost, it is almost
as uncertain as the date of the completion of the structure.
£250,000 was the sum originally fixed; but whatever their
cost, and whenever the date of their completion, everybody
will have reason to be proud of the new buildings. It is not
meet that Glasgow should lag behind other great industrial
centres in the kingdom in the matter of a fit and suitable
place wherein to transact its own business. It is our boast
that Glasgow is the second city in the Empire; the new
municipal buildings will help us to maintain that proud
reputation.

THE ANDERSONIAN COLLEGE AND ITS
FOUNDER.

THIS important educational institution was founded in
1795 by Dr John Anderson, Professor of Natural Philosophy
in Glasgow University. Unpretending in architectural style,
the plain building in East George Street is very commodious,
and it is equipped with a large and efficient professorial
staff, whose lessons in Science, Literature, and Medicine are
less costly than the instruction to be obtained at Gilmorehill. Every branch of university education is taught except
theology. In Music it has a very high standing, having an
endowed chair and a professor. Its Museum contains a
very interesting and valuable collection, and is open daily
from 11 to 3. Here may be seen the identical Newcome
model engine which Dr Anderson gave to James Watt to repair, and which was the cause of his applying himself to the
experiments which resulted in the discovery of the power of
steam. Newcome's model was in no sense a steam-engine,
but was worked by atmospheric pressure.

No fewer than 1,700 students attend the various classes,
and among those who have been numbered in their ranks
appears the name of David Livingstone. Dr Anderson was

forty-one years Professor of Natural Philosophy in the University. For many years he gave lectures to mechanics in the forenoon, and in other respects the Doctor was far in advance of his time, for by his will he enjoined that the ladies of Glasgow especially were to be admitted to his University, and thereby to be made "the most accomplished ladies in Europe." Dr Anderson's favourite studies were in gunnery and electricity, and he was prepared to give Prince Charlie the benefit of his knowledge in 1746, for he was among the garrison at Stirling Castle, and anxious to defend it against the rebels. His theories not being encouraged by the British Government, he visited France in company with the famous sea-rover Paul Jones, and exhibited his discoveries before military men there.

DUKE STREET prison occupies the site of a building belonging to the Duke of Montrose, which was known as the Duke's Lodgings. Its position is described as on the south side of the Drygait. It was a conglomeration of bits dating from ante-Reformation times, and was still unfinished in 1729. In the early part of the seventeenth century it belonged to the Stuarts of Minto,* several of whom from an early period were provosts of Glasgow.

The property came into the possession of the Montrose family near the close of the seventeenth century, and the buildings were altered and added to during the next fifty years. They were finally condemned, and demolished about 1850 or 1851. The Lodgings commanded a splendid view. Duke Street and Montrose Street probably derive their names from this source, although it has been said that the former was named after H.R.H. Frederick, Duke of York, second son of George II.

Duke Street was formed in 1794, and cut through Ladywell Street, Drygait, and the Buchts.

In 1850 Duke Street east of the Cattle Market was a country road, with several old-fashioned partly decayed mansions on its borders. The site of the present Dennistoun consists of the mansions and grounds of Golf Hill, Dunchattan, and Whitehill. The Dennistouns were proprietors of Golf Hill.

* The first Provost of Glasgow was John Stuart of Minto, 1454. His son or namesake fell at Flodden in 1513.

Ladywell Street derived its name from the Lady Well. Its old thatched buildings are almost the last of their kind in the city, and were doubtless in existence long before 1794,

THE LADY WELL.

when Duke Street was opened. The Lady Well is supposed
to have been sunk for the use of the common people.
There were priests' wells in the vicinity, which the laity were
not permitted to use. M'Ure refers to sixteen public wells
in existence in Glasgow in 1726. Owing to its proximity to
the Necropolis the authorities shut up the Lady Well as a
fountain. It had been used up to 1820. The inscription
it now bears is

THE LADY WELL.
Restored 1836 — Rebuilt 1874
by the
MERCHANTS' HOUSE OF GLASGOW.

ALEXANDRA PARK.

Alexandra Park contains about seventy-four acres, and
commands a view of Ben Lomond.

At a debate in the Glasgow Town Council some years
ago with regard to the laying out of the Alexandra Park, one
of the councillors proposed that a pair of swans should be
secured for the ornamental pond. This proposal was opposed
by another councillor, who suggested, as more suitable, that
a gondola should be placed upon the water. A third councillor, under the impression that gondolas were some rare
members of the feathered race, objected to gondolas being
placed upon the pond ; and being asked his reasons for
doing so, he innocently replied :—" Weel, ye see, if ye pit
gondolas upon the water they micht breed and hae young
anes, and lead the council thereby into expense; an' I'm for
economy on a' questions o' public expenditure."

BUCHANAN STREET.

ST GEORGE'S CHURCH—UNION STREET—SAUCHIEHALL STREET—BATH STREET.

BUCHANAN STREET, the premier street of the city, is comparatively modern, being only about one hundred years old
It was projected and named after Andrew Buchanan, one
of the old tobacco lords. It was opened in 1780, and was
a quiet west-end residential street, with retired houses like
those in Miller Street, and grass growing over half its
breadth. No shops were allowed. It was quite in the out-

skirts of the city, and at first went no further than the entrance to the Exchange, the farm of Meadowflats forming its boundary on the north. Families who lived in it used to give the farmer a small sum for permitting their boys to cross the Meadowflats, as a short cut to the Grammar School in George Street. St Vincent Street and West George Street were not made for many a day after. Gordon Street was called after a merchant of that name, whose paternal property was there. It was opened in 1802, twenty-two years after Buchanan Street. There were gentlemen alive in 1855 who had shot hares and partridges upon the ground now occupied by it.

ST GEORGE'S CHURCH originated two hundred years ago as the Wynd Kirk. It was built in 1687, during the time of the toleration of James VII., when Episcopacy was still dominant, by some sturdy Presbyterians who insisted on their right to worship in their own way. In 1764 a new building was erected, but it continued to be known as the Wynd Kirk until 1807, when it was transferred to Buchanan Street, and became St George's Church. The foundation stone was laid with much ceremony. There was a procession of all the dignitaries of the city, escorted by the 71st or Glasgow Regiment. Some of the church folks objected to the new site because it was too far west of their habitations. When it was built St Enoch's Burn ran gently behind. For fifty years Dr Porteous was the minister. He died soon after the new church was finished. The bell of St George's bears the inscription :—

" I to the church the people call,
And to the grave I summon all."

UNION STREET.—It is surely unnecessary to point out, or attempt to commend, the magnificent architecture designed by Mr Alexander Thomson—the renowned Greek Thomson. The splendid range of warehouses in Union Street at once arrest the stranger's attention. Their most striking feature is the line of short graceful columns supporting the massive entablature. Another of his choicest designs may be seen on the north side of Sauchiehall Street; and the St Vincent Street U.P. Church, with its enormous tower, are striking specimens of Mr Thomson's handicraft.

The building in Union Street now occupied by the *North British Mail* offices was for many years the church of the Unitarians, who now meet in St Vincent Street. The congregation originally worshipped in the Trades' Hall, where their minister, the Rev. James Totness, some seventy years ago, came into some prominence through his controversy on Socinianism with Dr Wardlaw. Mr Mitchell, of the Mitchell Library, belonged to this denomination.

RENFIELD STREET, one of the chief thoroughfares of the city, probably derived its name from Renfield, the country house of J. Campbell, Esq., on the Clyde west of Renfrew, and opposite Yoker, or Yocker as it used to be spelled.

SAUCHIEHALL STREET.

THIS fashionable promenade derives its name from the white willow or sauch trees which used to abound in the locality. Up till 1800 it was often a quagmire with nothing to be seen but its stunted willows and mud. It was known as the Common Loan. Gillespie's Ponds, near the west end, about India Street, formed the chief skating place for the townsfolk. The name was Sauchiehaugh, but in an ill-advised hour it was changed to Sauchiehall Street. Shield-haugh was altered at the same time to Shieldhall. Still, partly disguised though it be, how much better is such a distinctive Scotch name than the commonplaces New City Road, Great Western Road, &c.

Cambridge Street was formerly called Magazine Street, because of the arms and powder magazine being there.

BATH STREET.—Long before Loch Katrine was dreamt of for a water supply for the city a scarcity arose, the old wells were insufficient, and great inconvenience was felt, when William Harley, a manufacturer, sank wells in his property in Willowbank Street, on Sauchiehall Road, and sent carts round the town selling water to the inhabitants. He was a practical kind of man, and not only supplied bread and milk in the same way, but began public baths in the locality, which was called in consequence Bath Street.

The *Scotsman's Library*, 1825, says :—" Willow Bank is famous for its great milk establishment. A large portion of the population of Glasgow receive supplies from it. There are 180 cows, which are kept in two covered areas, in rows fronting each other. A steam-engine of four horse-power is used for churning the surplus milk, chopping hay and thrashing oats. At Willow Bank are also some fine hot, cold, and shower baths, which are much used by the inhabitants of Glasgow. Prices of bathing vary from 1s. to 3s.

THE PARKS.

For her population, Glasgow is not nearly so well provided with parks as many other large cities.

The Queen's Park, on the south side, contains about eighty acres, and cost the city £100,000. The grounds were laid out by Sir Joseph Paxton, the famous Scotch gardener, who planned the Crystal Palace. The name commemorates Queen Mary. The battle of Langside (see page 26) was fought on the ground immediately adjoining the southern border of the park.

Kelvingrove Park, or the West End Park, forms a portion of the old estates of Woodside and Kelvingrove, and was well wooded before it became the property of the city. The old white house now used as a museum was Kelvingrove House. (See also pages 155 and 187.)

CATHKIN BRAES.

Through the munificent generosity of a true son of St Mungo—Mr James Dick—the city has recently come into enjoyment of what will no doubt form a " joy for ever," the far-famed Cathkin Braes. Six hundred feet above the sea-level, they command a splendid view of the valley of the Clyde, the whole range of the Campsie Fells and Kilpatrick Hills, with the background of Ben Lomond and the alpine ranges of Argyleshire. The Braes are four miles distant from the Cross, but that is not a disadvantage. The locality was highly esteemed in the days before the railway train and excursion steamers afforded facilities for travel to more distant but not more enjoyable scenes. The Braes are well known to our older citizens. On the long summer evenings, and on holidays, which came seldom round in those days, they were the favourite resort of both old and young. The ground is diversified by stretches of woodland and natural terraces of traprock covered with rich turf. One condition of the gift was that the property must be left in its natural state, and certainly nothing could be finer than the soft sylvan beauty of the Braes,—their natural covering of bracken, yellow broom, and grass will be infinitely preferred to the greatest triumph of the landscape gardener's art. The historical associations are of a most interesting nature. On 4th April 1820 an army of Radicals gathered here to sally down on the devoted

The father of the foreign commerce of Glásgow was Provost Walter Gibson (1687–88). He converted the little
jetty at the Broomielaw into a harbour, and was the first to
import iron to the Clyde. His chief exports were herring
and other fish, and he brought home from the Continent
salt and brandy. He was a leading merchant of the city all
his life, and a somewhat ardent Episcopalian (see page 45).
His house, with its eighteen stately pillars, which stood in
the Saltmarket, was designed by Sir William Bruce, the
architect of Holyrood. It became the property of Mr
Francis Orr, and had two disastrous falls, which were caused
more by the spirit of modern improvement than by the
frailties of old age.

During Provost Gibson's time in 1688, the harbour formed
at the Broomielaw cost £1,666. 13s. 4d. Twenty-six years
before, the magistrates had bought thirteen acres of ground,
on which they planned and built Port-Glasgow. They there
made a harbour, and the first graving dock in Scotland,
—showing not a little faith and foresight.

In 1763 James Watt retired to a single room near the
Broomielaw (now James Watt Street), where, with one assistant, he grappled with the problem of the steam-engine.
Forty-nine years later, Henry Bell, of Helensburgh, launched
his little "Comet" on the Clyde, the pioneer of our steam
navigation. She sailed regularly from the Broomielaw,
commencing one summer day in 1812. The first steamboat
which ran upon Scottish waters was the "Charlotte Dundas"
(so named in honour of the sister of Lord Dundas, one of
the leading proprietors of the Forth and Clyde Canal), built
and engined by William Symington, a mining engineer, and
a native of Leadhills, Lanarkshire. Symington obtained his
first patent in 1785, and a second one in 1801. It was in
the latter year that the "Charlotte Dundas" ran, for in 1803
another boat was built and engined by Symington, also
named the "Charlotte Dundas." Thirty years since it was
stated in the *Glasgow Herald*:—"The machinery of the
'Charlotte Dundas' was so complete, that it is the opinion
of eminent engineers that the first practical steamboat (the
'Charlotte Dundas') was as perfect in principle and prac-
ticability as many of the steamboats now in use; and the
boat in question was the identical steamer which Robert
Fulton and Henry Bell minutely inspected and took sketches

of the machinery, whilst the vessel was steaming on the Forth and Clyde Canal in 1802,—a circumstance which enabled Fulton shortly afterwards to introduce steam navigation into America, and Bell to carry the invention to the Clyde." Fulton began to ply on the Hudson on 17th August 1807, and the "Comet" on the Clyde in 1812.

In "One Hundred Glasgow Men" it has been well said :— "Many cities claimed to have been the birthplace of Homer, and many waters claim to have been the birthplace of the steamer. But this at least is clear, the Clyde, if not the first in the race, soon took the lead, and by steady running it heads them all yet. The earliest steamers had not ventured beyond the loch, the canal, or the river. It was Clyde paddles that first lashed the salt water. The 'Comet' boldly put out to sea, and made various trips to the Highlands, to England, and to Ireland. She commenced to ply regularly to Fort-William on September 2, 1812. Early in 1814 the 'Elizabeth,' built by Wood of Port-Glasgow, steamed up the Mersey. In November 1814 the 'Marjory,' built by Denny of Dumbarton, began to ply between London and Margate. She steamed round Land's End, scaring the Cockney watermen when she appeared. The 'Argyle,' built by Martin of Port-Glasgow, followed her. The 'Rob Roy,' of 1818, was the first real sea-going steamer in the world. She was ninety tons, and thirty horse-power, built by William Denny of Dumbarton, and engined by David Napier. She first ran to Belfast, but was found too small, and then became the pioneer of the Dover and Calais passage. The French Government bought her, and changed her name to the 'Henri Quatre.'"

The early fame of the west ·of Scotland as the cradle of steam navigation, is largely owing to David Elder, a native of Kinross-shire. He may be regarded as the father of marine engineering upon the Clyde, and in his line was second to none. He died in January 1866, aged eighty-two. His son, John Elder, was also as eminent. Born in Glasgow on 8th March 1824, he soon made his mark in his profession. Associated like his father with the Napiers, he assisted him in drawing and constructing the Cunard steamers. In 1852 he joined the already famous firm of Randolph, Elder, & Co. In 1858 it became John Elder. During Mr Elder's connection with it, the firm constructed one

N

hundred and ten sets of steam engines, and built most of the vessels also. He resuscitated, improved, and brought into successful use James Watt's old idea of steam jacketing; and he it was who brought compound engines into use, effecting an enormous saving of coal. Mr Elder's early death in 1869, whilst in the flower of manhood, was a calamity to Glasgow. He was one of the handsomest as well as·one of the ablest of St Mungo's sons, and his goodness of heart and practical philanthropy endeared him to all his workpeople and townsfolk.

An interesting chapter might be written about the beginning of the great Clyde shipping concerns. A few words must suffice:—Messrs G. & J. Burns were the sons of the Rev. Dr Burns of the Barony Church (see page 128). They were engaged in the Irish trade, and originally ran twelve smacks across the Channel. David Hutchison was their head clerk or manager at that time. Their first steam vessel, the "Glasgow," dates from 13th March 1829. The Cunard Company was originated by the Burns' and Mr Samuel Cunard, a gentleman of Nova Scotia. He was without experience of shipping, but had influence to secure the Government contracts for conveying the mails to America, and got the Burns' to undertake the enterprise. The renowned company was formed in Glasgow, and the "Britannia," sailed on 4th July 1840, was their first steamer to cross the Atlantic. From that day to this (January 1888) the Cunard Company have never lost a passenger's life. With its origin and headquarters in Glasgow, first and last the Cunard Company have owned 78 and the Burns' 107 steamers, of a gross value of over £10,000,000 sterling. Every one of them has been built and engined on the Clyde. The Burns', as G. & J. Burns, continued to develop the Irish trade. Their lieutenant of the old smack days, David Hutchison, went into the West Highlands, where he is well represented by David M'Brayne, the nephew of the Burns'.

The founder of the Allan fleet was Mr Alexander Allan, a ship-carpenter of Saltcoats. He became captain and part owner of the brig "Jean," named after his wife, and was engaged during the Peninsular War in carrying cattle and other supplies to the troops. The "Jean" was the pioneer of the line. Captain Allan next sailed to Canada, and with his five sons developed a great carrying trade between

Montreal and the old country. In 1854 they launched their first steamer " The Canadian," and the same year Mr Allan died.

_____

THE CLYDE.

THE story is told of a Yankee, who, sailing up the Clyde with a Glasgow skipper, was expressing his contempt for our classic stream in very free terms. " Waal, now, you call this a river; I reckon it's only a sewer. If you could see our American rivers, you would never talk of this at all," &c. &c. The Scot replied, " Oh, ye needna' brag, you're indebted to Providence for your big rivers ; we made this ane oorsels."

The familiar saying that the Clyde made Glasgow, is doubtless true to a certain extent; but the skipper's statement that Glasgow made the Clyde, is quite as near the mark. The great energy of the citizens has gradually converted a shallow island-dotted stream into a shipping highway, and steep broom-clad banks into successions of quays. Says the *Bailie* :—" Among all the changes that have taken place in Glasgow during the last hundred years, the change that has passed over the Clyde and its banks is undoubtedly the most noteworthy. Once upon a time, travellers declared Glasgow to be one of the prettiest little cities in the country, and much of its beauty was due to the pleasant rural features of the scenery by the river side. The water—sparkling and limpid—ran wimpling to the sea between waving cornfields and knowes of yellow broom. In cosy sheltered corners, snug country houses studded its margin, and here and there old-fashioned hostelries offered rest and refreshment to the wearied wayfarer. The sleepy-eyed cattle cooled themselves in the shallows, and were startled from their drowsy contentment only when some restless silvery salmon splashed and leaped in the deeper pools. How we have changed all that ! The union with England that opened to us the trade of the world has taken the sweet country beauty from the Clyde. The river now rolls along dark and foul, its waters churned into perpetual agitation by countless steam vessels. The broom has given place to stone quays and grimy storehouses. Where the salmon sported, 'richly freighted argosies' now float, of a size that

never entered into the wildest imaginings of our early douce
Virginia traders.   The busiest energies of life are at work,
where formerly ' Flora and the country green ' held undisputed possession, and Scottish Izaak Waltons lounged the
lazy hours away.   We cannot regret the change, ugly as it
may seem in fastidious æsthetic eyes.   It has brought employment, and therefore happiness, to millions; it is the
result and the evidence of the ingenuity, the perseverance,
and the patience of our countrymen. ˙ A shallow uncertain
stream has been turned by steady labour and clear-sighted
enterprise into a great channel of commerce, that carries
to thousands of homes the blessings of daily bread, and
helps to keep the whole world from rusting in ignoble lotos-
eating."

About 1800 the Clyde below Jamaica Bridge was quite
narrow.   From the south side, near the bridge, a beautiful
green promontory reached half-way across the river.   Men
were often to be seen on the Broomielaw quays angling with
rod and line ; a long summer day would pass without a
single sail appearing to disturb their sport.

Formerly there were five islands or inches on the Clyde
between Govan and Renfrew (Blair's map of 1654)—Water
Inch, Whyt Inch, Buck Inch (or Packman's Isle), King's
Inch, and Sand Inch.   None of these survive.   The Clyde
Trust has been the death of them.

About 1830, John Galt, author of "Annals of the Parish,"
entertained a project for making Glasgow a sea-port, by
deepening the Clyde, and erecting a dam, with a lock at
Bowling Bay.   This, which was a favourite crotchet of his,
he said was the legacy he left to Glasgow, in gratitude for
the many good offices done to him by the inhabitants of
the city.

The people of Govan thought the Clyde Trust, in appro-
priating the river banks, had in that respect done them no
service, and consider that out of the enormous amount
received by the Trust a portion should be set aside to provide a park for Govan by way of a recompense.

The making of the Clyde, its harbours, and its docks, is
a work of which Glasgow has reason to be proud, for it
stands pre-eminent among· municipal enterprises and engineering achievements.   Fresh demands for extension
have arisen time after time, and each generation has had

the public spirit to extend the work of its predecessors. Since 1868 the "Nevada," the "Oregon," the "Austral," the "Alaska," the "Umbria," and the "Etruria," have been built and engined within sight of the harbour; and the "Servia," the "Aurania," and the "America" opposite the mouth of the Cart; whilst the "City of Rome," the largest mercantile steamer afloat (March 1888), has been brought up the river, been "canted" in the Queen's Dock, and been accommodated in our No. 1 Graving Dock,— no graving dock in Liverpool having at that particular state of the tide depth enough on its sill to take it in.

The men who have made the Clyde have known what they were about. They have not hazarded the public money, but, looking shrewdly ahead, have simply watched for the demand, and provided for it. As the shipping and the trade of the city have increased, the accommodation has been extended for their comfort and encouragement. Enormous as the expenditure has been, it has been good sound business from beginning to end. The Trust revenue, which was £3,319 in 1800, has grown about a hundredfold, being now some £300,000 a year, and still growing. As to what further extension of our harbour and docks may be required in course of time, it would be idle to speculate. When they come, the requirements will be met. That has been the case hitherto; and we do not doubt that the Glasgow of the future will be worthy of its past.

The *Scotsman* says of the river:—"It is quite true the Clyde somehow is not associated with the beautiful in nature, as the Tweed or the Dee is linked. When we think of it, we connect it with Glasgow, and see it running foul and turgid between quay walls and amid smoky surroundings at the Broomielaw Bridge. But every one who has fished the Clyde, or sketched on its banks, or even been whisked along its side by the train as it toils up the ascent from Carstairs to Beattock, knows that, while yet within sight of its parent hills, there is not a sweeter stream in Scotland. Its waters are limpid and bright; its flow serene and peaceful, as if the stillness and solitude of its birthplace had indelibly impressed itself upon it. It gets more talkative at Lanark, as it rushes down to the low country in a series of famous falls; and if its waters now begin to get drumly, its course has a certain picturesqueness even to the outskirts

of Glasgow. In its passage through the great city it is
terribly soiled, but it purges itself again in its noble estuary.
There we have beauty all around, and the eye is never satis-
fied with seeing, under their ever-shifting atmospheric effects,
the dark lochs and Highland hills, picturesque islands,
prettily wooded shores, and glorious sunsets of the estuary
of the Clyde."

FIRST IMPRESSIONS OF THE CLYDE.

By John Burroughs.

" Those who, after ten days of sorrowing and fasting in
the desert of the ocean, have sailed up the Firth of Clyde,
and thence up the Clyde to Glasgow, on the morning of a
perfect mid-May-day, the sky all sunshine, the earth all
verdure, know what this experience is ; and only those can
know it. It takes a good many foul days in Scotland to
breed one fair one; but when the fair day does come, it is
worth the price paid for it. The soul and sentiment of all
fair weather is in it ; it is the flowering of the meteorological
influences, the rose on this thorn of rain and mist. These
fair days, I was told, may be quite confidently looked for
in May; we were so fortunate as to experience a series of
them, and the day we entered port was such a one as you
would select from a hundred.

" The traveller is in a mood to be pleased after clearing
the Atlantic gulf ; the eye in its exuberance is full of caresses
and flattery, and the deck of a steamer is a rare vantage-
ground on any occasion of sight-seeing ; it affords just the
isolation and elevation needed. Yet fully discounting these
favourable conditions, the fact remains that Scotch sunshine is
bewitching, and that the scenery of the Clyde is unequalled
by any other approach to Europe. It is Europe, abridged and
assorted, and passed before you in the space of a few hours;
the highlands, and lochs, and castle-crowned crags on the
one hand, and the lowlands, with their parks and farms,
their manor halls and matchless verdure, on the other.
The eye is conservative, and loves a look of permanence
and order, of peace and contentment ; and these Scotch
shores, with their stone houses, compact masonry, clean
fields, grazing herds, ivied walls, massive foliage, perfect

roads, verdant mountains, &c., fill all the conditions. We passed an hour in front of Greenock, and then on the crest of the tide, make our way slowly upward. The landscape closes around us. We can almost hear the cattle ripping off the lush grass in the fields. One feels as if he could eat grass himself. It is a pastoral paradise. We can see the daisies and buttercups, and from above a meadow on the right a part of the song of a skylark reaches my ear. Indeed not a little of the charm and novelty of this part of the voyage was the impression it made as of going afield in an ocean steamer. We had suddenly passed from a wilderness of waters into a verdurous, sunlit landscape, where scarcely any water was visible. The Clyde soon after you leave Greenock becomes little more than a large deep canal, enclosed between meadow banks, and from the deck of the great steamer only the most charming rural sights and sounds greet you.

" You are at sea amid verdant parks, and fields of clover and grain. You behold farm occupations,—sowing, planting, ploughing,—as from the middle of the Atlantic. Playful heifers and skipping lambs take the place of the leaping dolphins and the basking sword-fish. The ship steers her way amid turnip-fields and broad acres of newly planted potatoes. You are not surprised that she needs piloting. A little tug, with a rope at her bow, pulls her first this way and then that, while one at her stern nudges her right flank and then her left. Presently we come to the shipbuilding yards of the Clyde, where rural pastoral scenes are strangely mingled with those of quite another sort. ' First a cow, and then an iron ship,' as one of the voyagers observed. Here a pasture, or a meadow, or a field of wheat or oats, and close beside it, without an inch of waste or neutral ground between, rise the skeletons of innumerable ships, like a forest of slender growths of iron, with the workmen hammering amid it, like so many noisy woodpeckers. It is doubtful if such a scene can be witnessed anywhere else in the world,—an enormous mechanical, commercial, and architectural interest, alternating with the quiet and simplicity of inland farms and home occupations. You could leap from the deck of a half-finished ocean steamer into a field of waving wheat or Winchester beans. The vast ship-yards appear to be set down here upon the banks of the

Clyde without any interference with the natural surroundings of the place.

"Of the factories and foundries that put this iron in shape
you get no hint; here the ships rise as if they sprouted from
the soil, without waste or litter, but with an incessant din.
They stand as thickly as a row of cattle in stanchions,
almost touching each other, and in all stages of development.   Now and then a stall will be vacant, the ship having
just been launched; and others will be standing with flags
flying and timbers greased or soaped, ready to take the
water at the word. . . . The vessels are launched diagonally
up or down stream, on account of the narrowness of the
channel.   But to see such a brood of ships, the largest in
the world, hatched upon the banks of such a placid little
river, amid such quiet country scenes, is a novel experience.
But this is Britain; a little island, with little lakes, little
rivers, quiet bosky fields, but mighty interests and powers
that reach round the world."

THE ANCIENT CANOES.

THE first canoe was found twenty-five feet below the surface
when the foundations of St Enoch's Church were being made
in 1780.   It contained a stone hatchet.   A second was discovered in the following year at the Cross, when excavating
the foundations of the Tontine.   In 1824 a third canoe was
found in Stockwell Street, and another in the Drygait.
While cutting a sewer in London Street a fifth was found.
It contained marine shells.   During extensive operations at
the widening of the Clyde, within the period embraced by the
years 1846 and 1854, no fewer than twelve canoes were discovered.   They were about nineteen feet down, and at
least a hundred feet from the edge of the river, and all lay
upon sand. · They were oak trees.

Ruder specimens · of vessels than these of our forefathers
it would be hard to imagine.*   A fallen tree, with a hollow
burnt out, the bow with no attempt at cut, and the stern
fitted with a sliding board.   Some of the canoes had
evidently been propelled with paddles; but others had been

---

* One is in Stirling's Library.

rowed with oars, for besides rough row-locks, there are ledges at the sides which had once supported seats, and on the bottom are cross-boards for giving the oarsmen a purchase with their feet. They are placed at such distances from one another as to show that the old boatmen were tall of stature. In every boat there is a big round hole plugged by a wooden pin. These holes, it is thought, were for filling the boats and hiding them under water.

· In one case a real cork was found, which has been a cause of wonderment, for there is no cork-growing country nearer than Spain. Only one of the boats was not a "dugout," but built with keel and ribs.

When these canoes were afloat, Gilmore Hill, Garnet Hill, and Garngad Hill would be islets in the ancient shallow sea which filled the whole valley from Cathkin and Gleniffer Braes to Campsie Hills. At a later period, the high steep streets of North Frederick Street, John Street, Montrose Street, Portland Street, and Balmano Street, that rise so abruptly off George and Duke Streets, formerly formed the banks of the estuary, whilst Argyle Street and George Square were still under water.

THOMAS CARLYLE.

THE INVENTOR OF THE STEAMBOAT—CARLYLE'S VISITS TO GLASGOW.

DURING their companionship at Kirkcaldy, Edward Irving and Carlyle made many walking excursions. Of one in 1817 the following reminiscences are especially interesting :—

"At Greenock," says Carlyle, "I first saw steamers on the water; queer little dumpy things, with a red sail to each, and legible name, 'Defiance' and such like, bobbing about there, and making continual passages as their business. . . . Not till two years later (1819, if I mistake not) did Forth see a steamer. Forth's first was far bigger than the Greenock ones, and called itself 'The Tug,' being intended for towing ships in those narrow waters, as I have often seen it doing. It still had no rival or conqueror, till (in 1825) Leith, spurred on by one Bain, a kind of scientific half-pay master R.N., got up a large finely appointed steamer, or pair of steamers, for London; which, so successful were they, all ports then set to imitating. London alone still held back for a good few years. London was notably shy of the steamship, great as are its doings now in that line. An old friend of mine, the late Mr Strachey, has told me that in his school days he at one time —early in the nineties, I should guess, say 1793—used to see, in crossing Westminster Bridge, a little model steam-ship paddling to and fro between him and Blackfriars Bridge, with steam funnel, paddle wheels, and the other outfit, exhibiting and recommending itself to London and whatever scientific or other spirit of marine adventure London might have. London entirely dead to the pheno-menon, which had to duck under and dive across the Atlantic before London saw it again, when a new generation had risen. The real inventor of steamships, I have learned credibly elsewhere, the maker and proprietor of that fruitless model on the Thames, was Mr Miller, laird of Dalswinton in Dumfriesshire (Poet Burns's landlord), who spent his life and his estate in that adventure, and is not now to be heard of in those parts; having had to sell Dalswinton and die quasi-bankrupt (and I should think, broken-hearted), after that completing of his painful invention, and finding London and mankind dead to it. Miller's assistant and workhand for many years was John Bell, a joiner in the neighbouring village of Thornhill. Miller being ruined, Bell was out of work and connection, emigrated to New York, and there speaking much of his old master, and glorious unheeded invention well known to Bell in all its outlines or details, at length found one Fulton to listen to him; and by ' Fulton & Bell,' about 1809, an actual packet-steamer was got launched, and lucratively plying on the Hudson River, became the miracle of Yankeeland, and gradually of all lands. These, I believe, are essentially the facts. Old Robert M'Queen of Thornhill, Strachey of the India House, and many other bits of good testimony and indication, once far apart, curiously coalescing and corresponding for me. And as possibly enough the story is not now known in whole to anybody but myself, it may go in here as a digression,—*àpropos* of those brisk Greenock steamers which I first saw and still so vividly remember; little ' Defiance,'

&c., saucily bounding about with their red sails in the sun, on this my tour with Irving."

"At Glasgow, I remember our glad embarkation towards Paisley by canal track-boat ; visit preappointed for us by Irving in a good old lady's house, whose son was Irving's boarder ; the dusty, sunny Glasgow evening ; and my friend's joy to see Brown and me."

"Irving in truth was the natural king among us, and his qualities of captaincy were indisputable. Brown, he, and I went by the Falls of Clyde. I do not recollect the rest of our route, except that at New Lanark, a green silent valley, with cotton works turned by Clyde waters. We called to see Robert Owen, the then incipient arch-gomeril 'model school,' and thought it (and him, whom, after all, we did not see, and knew only by his pamphlets and it) a thing of wind."

After Irving's settlement in Glasgow, Carlyle spent some days with him at 34 Kent Street in the spring of 1820, and noted, according to his habit, the outward signs of men and things. He saw the Glasgow merchants in the Tontine ; he observed them, fine, clean, opulent, with their shining bald crowns and serene white heads, sauntering about or reading their newspapers. He criticised the dresses of the young ladies, for whom he had always an eye. He saw and heard . Chalmers. "Never preacher went so into one's heart." But the chief interest in that Glasgow visit lies less in itself than in what followed it,—a conversation between these two young, then unknown men, strolling alone together over a Scotch moor. Carlyle also spent Christmas of the same year in Glasgow. He says :—"I will remember the first visit and pieces of the other, each of them a real holiday to me. By steamer to Bo'ness, and then by canal. Skipper of canal boat and two Glasgow scamps of the period, these are figures of the first voyage ; very vivid then, the rest utterly out. I think I always went by Bo'ness, and steam *so far*, coach the remainder of the road in all subsequent journeys. Irving lived in Kent Street, eastern end of Glasgow, ground floor, tolerably spacious room. I think he sometimes gave me up his bedroom, and went out himself to some friend's house."

THE INVENTION OF THE STEAMBOAT.*

IF the steamboat was not born on the Clyde, the man who invented it was. Patrick Miller first saw the light in St Mungo's city in 1731. His father belonged to Kirkcud-brightshire, and the son was a man of great natural ability. In his youth as a sailor he visited many parts of the globe, but he became a banker in Edinburgh, where he realised a fortune. He bought the estate of Dalswinton in Dumfries-shire, and built a fine house, but his retirement was spent in scientific pursuits. He made various useful inventions. Whilst engaged in making a paddle-boat he was assisted by James Taylor, a native of Leadhills, who is said to have suggested steam instead of manual labour for turning the paddle-wheels. Taylor was the tutor of Mr Miller's sons. He introduced him to William Symington, a mining engineer, then at Edinburgh, but a Leadhills man too, whom Miller employed to make up and fit to the paddle-wheel boat a new kind of engine Symington had just constructed and patented. On 14th October 1788 the first trial was made on the loch of Dalswinton. She ran five miles an hour, and was considered a success. The persons on board were Patrick Miller, William Symington, Sir William Monteith, Robert Burns (then a tenant of Miller), William Taylor, and Alexander Naismyth, the artist. Lord Henry Brougham, then a youth, stood on the lakeside and watched the experiment. In 1789 a larger vessel was fitted up at Carron foundry, under Taylor's supervision. She made two trials on the Forth and Clyde Canal. Patrick Miller had borne all the expenses. Want of funds prevented further effort.

In 1801 Symington, who had commenced business in Fal-kirk, fitted up another steamboat, the "Charlotte Dundas," which was inspected on the same day by Robert Fulton, from the United States, and Henry Bell, of Glasgow. (Henry Bell and John Bell may have been relatives.) Fulton launched his steamer on the Hudson in 1807, and Henry Bell started the "Comet" on the Clyde in 1812.

THE TWO "COMETS."

The first steamboat started by Henry Bell, in the summer of 1812, was called the "Comet," and plied between the

---

* See also pages 107, 192, 201, and 204.

Broomielaw and Greenock ; she was twenty-five tons register, and her engine was only four horse-power. On 2nd
September of the same year she commenced to run to Fort-
William, and continued on that route till 1820, when she
was wrecked. "On Friday afternoon at half-past four," says
a newspaper of December 19, 1820, "while passing through
Dorishmore, at the point of Craignish Rock, the 'Comet'
was struck with a strong gust of wind, which laid her on her
beam ends ; and in two minutes, owing to the great current
of tide and high seas and wind, was laid broadside on the
rocks. Every exertion was made for the landing of passengers and men, which was safely accomplished. On
Saturday morning she was a complete wreck."

The *Glasgow Courier* of July 14, 1821, gives the following information :—"New 'Comet' steamboat plying between
Fort-William and Glasgow.—On the wreck of the old 'Comet'
steamboat last winter, the majority of the proprietors, aided
by other gentlemen, in order to keep open a communication
found to be of such great public utility, commenced on a
more extensive and improved scale to erect a new boat. She
completed her first voyage from Glasgow to Fort-William
last Friday, in the short space of twenty-six hours, after
calling at the interjacent places at which the old boat used
to call. The proprietors have spared neither pains nor
expense in making the boat elegant, commodious, and substantial, and they are happy at being in a condition to assure
the public that their exertions have been rewarded with
complete success. The material and machinery of the boat
are of first-rate quality, and the workmanship in the different
departments is completed in the most masterly style. The
engines and boilers are, in particular, most excellent. She
has a great number of beds, with a variety of comfortable
bedding. She is commanded by a master of respectability
and much experience in her route of sailing (Captain Robert
Bain), and who has given the utmost satisfaction to the
public as commander of the old 'Comet,'" &c. &c.

By this time steam navigation had firmly established itself.
There were 150 steam vessels in Britain, representing a
tonnage of 16,000 tons, 5,000 horse-power, and costing half
a million. In 1821, "seventeen steam-packets sail from the
Mersey, twenty-nine from the Clyde, twenty from the
Thames, ten from the Forth, fifteen from the Tyne, four

cross the Irish Sea from Holyhead to Dublin, two between
Milford and Waterford, two between Bristol and Bath, four
from Belfast, four upon the Tay, ten upon different canals,
and, lastly, one plies upon Loch Ness, commanded by Mr
Henry Bell himself, who has been driven from station to
station, and seems doomed here to end his days in earning a
scanty and precarious subsistence."

The second "Comet" was fated to come to a disastrous
end. She was run down while on the voyage from Fort-
William by the "Air" steamboat off Gourock, on Friday
night, 21st October 1825, when some sixty-five persons
were drowned. The "Comet" carried no light. Captain
M'Innes was in charge, and the crew and stewards numbered
twelve. The disaster took place at two o'clock in the
morning, and of those on board only thirteen were saved.
The unfortunate vessel was twenty-eight tons burden, fourteen horse-power, and drew five feet of water. She had to
be a small narrow boat in order to get through the Crinan
Canal. "Peter Sutherland, the carpenter of the 'Comet,'
stated that M'Bride, the pilot, on approaching Kempach
Point, expressed a wish that a light should be exhibited in
the lanthorn, but he was told that there was no light to
spare till such time as they should arrive at Greenock, as
there was a scarcity of candles on board." New rules and
regulations in regard to lights, &c., came immediately after
into force.

INKLE-MAKING AND WEAVING.

THE POWER-LOOM.

INKLE-MAKING is said to have been introduced into this
country by Protestant refugees from Holland in the sixteenth
century. Inkles were linen tapes used for garters, apron
strings, &c. The inkle loom was a Dutch invention, the
secret of which they jealously guarded. But in 1732 Alexander Harvey, of Glasgow, at the risk of his life, managed to
bring over from Haarlem two of the Dutch looms and a
Dutchman to work them, and soon inkle-making became a
considerable industry in Glasgow.

Our city took an early place in the invention and improvement of the power-loom. The Rev. E. Cartwright, of Holland House, Kent, was the first to patent a loom for weaving

otherwise than by hand. Being in Matlock in 1784, he heard some Manchester men discussing the possibility of such a thing, and being of a mechanical turn he brought out a power-loom, which he patented in 1785, and again in 1787. It was a modification of the existing inkle or tape loom, which had made its way into England. In its turn the Cartwright loom found its way to the north. It was a rude machine, and had not been taken up by the trade, but some specimens of it had been set up at the hulks to be worked by the convicts. There in 1793 James Louis Robertson, of Dunblane, saw it at work, and brought two specimens of it back with him to Glasgow. These he set up in a cellar in Argyle Street, supplying the motive power by an unhappy Newfoundland dog working in a revolving cage.

The first two looms for weaving calico cloth by steam or water power were invented and brought into practical use by Andrew Kinloch, in 1793, in a court off the Gallowgait. He was assisted by an old clockmaker, and the money was furnished by four members of the Chamber of Commerce. Other forty looms were ordered to be made, and were subsequently wrought by water-power at Milton, near Bowling, till 1813. The bulk of them were transferred to the Abbey Close at Paisley, where they ended their days. But two were preserved at Milton as relics, and one of them was to have gone to the Exhibition of 1851, when unluckily the two were destroyed by a fire at Milton in 1850. In 1801 two of these Milton looms had become the patterns for a two-hundred loom weaving factory, set up at the 'Shaws by John Monteith, son of James Monteith, of Anderston, who in 1780 had set up the first web of pure cotton ever woven in Scotland. In 1804, again, two of the 'Shaws looms were taken as patterns by Archibald Buchanan, of Catrine, who so much improved them that he may be called the inventor of the power-loom of trade. From this beginning power-loom weaving spread rapidly here. Indeed at one time Scotland had a hold on the whole cotton trade that we can hardly now-a-days realise ; it seemed as if the trade was to have its headquarters north and not south of the Border. Scotland got the start, and Lanarkshire long had many more power-looms than Lancashire (which as late as 1817 had only 2,000 of them). Scotland has gradually increased her number, and in December 1885 she had 29,689 ;—but

England had jumped up to 528,765. In the spinning branch our glory has still more emphatically departed. Arkwright did his best to give this branch a set our way. He came down here in 1783 specially to push Scotch spinning, and he gave David Dale his personal help in choosing his site and laying out his famous works at New Lanark. It was not mere hope of gain that had brought Arkwright here. The English spinners had disputed his patents, and they had taunted him with his old trade of a barber. The injury and the insult had rankled ; and, when he returned home from David Dale, he told his English friends that he had put a razor into a Scotsman's hands who would shave the lot of them. It seemed as if it was to be so. Between Arkwright and Dale, New Lanark grew to be the first spinning mill of its day ; it became the pattern for others ; and as early as 1787 there were nineteen cotton spinning-mills in Scotland. Ichabod ! Ichabod ! In the last returns of the factory inspectors all Scotland has but 636,894 spindles against England's 40,000,000.

Some of J. Louis Robertson's looms were actually at work in the east end as late as 1835. In 1842 old Kinloch visited Glasgow, when he was entertained to supper in Marshall's restaurant, and presented with a purse and sixty sovereigns by the power-loom factory managers, tenters, and dressers, in consideration that he was the man who had perfected the loom, which now gives employment to hundreds of thousands in many parts of the world. Andrew Kinloch was born at Port-Glasgow in 1760.

The cotton industry gives employment to about thirty-four thousand persons in Glasgow. Two of the biggest factories are those of Messrs Galbraith at Oakbank and St Rollox. Silk, rope, flax, and jute factories employ over two thousand hands.

FLAKEFIELD.

Two young men named Wilson came to Glasgow about the end of the seventeenth century and commenced business. Both seem to have come from the same part of the country, and to have engaged in the same class of trade ; and their identity of name having led to many mistakes, one of them, in order to be distinguished from his rival, changed his altogether, adopting that of Flakefield, after Flakefield in East Kilbride, where his boyhood had been spent. This became his family patronymic.

A son of his learned the weaving trade, but enlisted about 1670 in the Cameronians, and was afterwards drafted into the Scottish Guards. During his fighting days on the Continent, he happened to procure a blue and white handkerchief that had been woven in Germany, and at the time the thought struck Flakefield that if it was his good fortune ever to return to Glasgow, he would try to make a cloth like it. He preserved a bit carefully. When discharged in 1700 he had not forgot his idea. He commenced operations; a few spindles of yarn fit for his purpose was all he could collect, the white was ill-bleached and the blue very dark, but they were the best Glasgow could turn out at that time. The first web was twenty-four handkerchiefs. The merchants were pleased with the stripes, and with the soft and delicate texture of the cloth, which was thin-set in comparison with Hollands and other cloth of the kind. A demand sprung up in town and country, and soon many looms were employed in the special manufacture. Glasgow became famous for this branch of the linen trade, and not long after Paisley, always "quick in the uptak," joined in. Unfortunately, as is the case so often with originators, Flakefield himself had been too poor a man, and did not reap any material advantage. When old he was appointed town-drummer in respect to his long service and good conduct in the army, and that position he occupied until his death.

OUR FIRST POLICEMEN.

BEFORE the Police Bill of 1800, the guardians of the city were the burgesses or freemen craftsmen. The magistrates of Glasgow, after many attempts from 1778 onwards, succeeded in 1800 in carrying a Police Bill, and ever since we have had police rates to pay. The account of the first police force in "Glasgow Past and Present," by Dr John Aitken, is a spicy reminiscence:—"We had sixty-eight watchmen, and nine day officers, and our impression was that this force was so large and overwhelming, that it would

drive iniquity out of the city as by a hurricane. On this
first night greatcoats and 'staves were served out to each
watchman. . . . Each man's number was painted on the
back of his greatcoat, between the shoulders, in white
coloured letters, about six inches long and of a pro-
portionate breadth. A lantern and two candles were also
served out to each man,—the one lighted, and the other in
reserve; it being understood that the candle 'doups'
became the perquisite of the man himself. . . . Before
being told off to their respective beats, a number of the men
exercised their lungs in calling the hours, to show how
rapidly they had acquired proficiency in this important part
of the watchman's functions. . . . At the commencement
we had no fire brigade, that department being specially
under the charge of the magistrates. Neither had we any
separate scavenging squad. The watchmen were engaged
to do the duty of scavengers, on two days of the week, and
for two hours each day. In the summer mornings they
were relieved at four o'clock, but instead of going to bed
they plied the broom till six. In the winter mornings they
knocked off at six, when they immediately went to bed for
a comfortable sleep, and with renovated strength they commenced their sweeping operations at twelve. . . . The
squad was superintended by one of the officers, who appeared
on duty in a short blue coat with a red neck. This jacket
was manufactured out of the uniform coat of last year,
which had been turned, and had the tails rumped off.

"In these early times the officers and watchmen assumed
a discretion in the performance of their duty which would
look rather queer at the present day. It was nothing uncommon then for a watchman to take a man to the office,
and lock him up for a few hours, and then let him out again,
without any charge being entered or any record kept of the
proceedings.

"Each watchman had a wooden box, called a sentry-box,
for resting in when he felt fatigued, or when the weather
was cold and rainy. The wild youths of the town used
often to lock Dogberry in his nest altogether, and sometimes
they even tumbled the box over on its face, in which position the poor fellow lay till relieved by his fellow-watchmen.
. . . There was no regulation to prevent all the watchmen
in the city being in their boxes at one and the same time;

and it was well known that many a snooze they took in these retreats, while the city took care of itself." The police, however, had soon the effect of driving the desperadoes beyond the city bounds. In self-defence the Gorbals Police Act was passed in 1808, the Calton in 1819, and the Anderston in 1824. For a long time Calton continued to be very lawless. The policemen used to go two by two, armed with cutlasses, which they were not slow to use. In a fight with a determined gang of resurrectionists, one of the body-snatchers had an arm cut off. Whether he was able to sell it to the doctors for purposes of anatomy or not, history does not inform us, but his brotherhood withdrew their patronage from the Glasgow kirkyards from. the date of the amputation.

THEATRES IN GLASGOW.

THERE was no theatre in Glasgow till after the middle of the last century. Stage representations had been performed in booths or other temporary premises, but no place worthy of the name of a theatre was erected till 1764. The building was situated in a garden on the north side of the road leading to Anderston, very nearly opposite to the head of Jamaica Street, at that time the farthest west street in the city. There was no Union Street in these days. This new theatre had a checkered experience for sixteen years, but was ultimately put out of existence by fire. While many rejoiced at its destruction, it was no *feu de joie* to the poor actors, who lost their all. The second theatre was built in Dunlop Street, and opened in January 1782 by Mr Jackson, the manager of the first theatre. It was a very small affair, and, as recorded by Cleland, was only capable of accommodating one hundred persons. This was the only theatre in the city till 1802, when some of the leading citizens joined together for the formation of a company, with a capital sufficient for the erection of a building worthy of what was even then considered the great city of Glasgow. The shares in the company were £25 each. This new theatre extinguished the Dunlop Street one. It was built in Queen Street, at a cost of nearly £20,000, and was " unequalled by any provincial theatre in the kingdom." The area of the building, as an old map of Glasgow shows, was 170 feet by 80

feet.   This speculation resulted in failure.   All the original
capital was lost, together with large sums laid out by different lessees, who did their best to keep afloat "the sinking
ship," but all to no purpose.   It was sold for £5,000 in
order to meet pressing claims, and, as a finale, on Saturday
the 10th of January 1829, it was burned to the ground.   No
lives were lost.   Edmund Kean, the eminent tragedian, had
played in it at £100 a night.

David Roberts, R.A., in his autobiography, says :—" In
1819 I commenced my career as principal scene painter in
the Theatre Royal, Glasgow.   This theatre was immense in
its size and appointments—in magnitude exceeding Drury
Lane and Covent Garden.   The stock scenery had been
painted by Alexander Naismyth" (the friend of Robert
Burns, and father of James Naismyth, who invented the
steam hammer).   " It consisted of a series of pictures far
surpassing anything of the kind I had ever seen.   These
included chambers, palaces, streets, landscapes, and forest
scenery.   One, I remember particularly, was the outside of
a Norman castle, and another of a cottage, charmingly
painted, and of which I have a sketch.   But the act scene,
which was a view on the Clyde, looking toward the
Highland mountains, with Dumbarton Castle in the middle
distance, was such a combination of magnificent scenery, so
wonderfully painted, that it excited universal admiration.
These productions I studied incessantly, and on them my
style, if I have any, was originally founded."

Anderson, the Wizard of the North, had a theatre built
behind the space of ground where the Sir William Collins
Fountain stands, opposite the Jail.   It was a brick building,
but was very handsome inside.   It only endured two seasons,
and was burned after the pantomime in a few minutes.

Sims Reeves' first performance in Glasgow was at
Anderson's, in the " Bohemian Girl," on 25th August 1845
(see *Glasgow Dramatic Review*, 27th August 1845).

At the same time as Anderson's, there was also a wooden
theatre, the Adelphi.   Here David Prince Miller brought
before the public Macready, G. Brookes, and other eminent
actors.   It was burned one forenoon about 1848.   The
greatest theatre disaster was at the Royal in Dunlop Street,
when, on 17th February 1849, sixty-five persons were
smothered on the stairs.

NEWSPAPERS IN GLASGOW.

THE first newspaper in Scotland was printed for Cromwell's soldiers at Leith in 1653. It was called *Mercurius Politicus*, and was a reprint of the English *Mercury*. In 1662 the *Caledonian Mercury* was commenced in Edinburgh. The first newspaper published in Glasgow appeared on November 14, 1715,—the *Glasgow Courant*, price three halfpence, or to regular customers one penny.

After the abolition of the Stamp Act, the first regular daily newspaper in Scotland was started in Glasgow. In 1847 Mr Allison, a Lanarkshire iron merchant, with a hopeful disposition and a long purse, began the *North British Mail*. The first office was in Dunlop Street, and Mr George Troup was the editor, but after two years the proprietor · had to give up the enterprise, having lost all his money. Two Dublin Scotchmen, Messrs Gunn & Cameron, then purchased the concern, and it continues to this day to be the organ of advanced Radicalism in the west of Scotland. During its early years Mr W. Anderson, author of " The Scottish Nation," was sub-editor.

The columns of the *Citizen* were enriched by the contributions of Hew Macdonald, the " Rambler." Mr Mackenzie, of the *Reformer's Gazette*, was another journalist of some notoriety. " Familiarly known as ' Peter,' he affected to be a man of the people, willing to go to the stake if needful on their behalf, but he never attained that honour."

The *Glasgow Herald* was started in 1782. It was a very small affair then, and was entitled the *Advertiser*, appearing twice a week. John Mennons, its publisher, fell under the suspicion of treason during the reign of terror in 1793. In 1802 it became the *Herald and Advertiser*. The latter part of the title was dropped three years later. Mr Samuel Hunter joined the company on 10th June 1803 as partner and conductor, and it was he who made the paper a prosperous commercial undertaking. His father was minister of the parish of Stoneykirk, Wigtownshire, where he was born on 19th March 1769. Educated for the medical profession, he served in Ireland as a surgeon, and subsequently as captain of the North Lothian Fencibles, taking part in the suppression of the rebellion of 1798. He was a man of wit, kindly nature, strong good sense, and unbending integrity. With the exception of a brief eclipse during the Reform Bill of 1831 and 1832, he was always popular with the people. He became a magistrate, and colonel of the Glasgow Highland Volunteers.

A venerable citizen (ninety-two years of age), under date 1st January 1869, contributed the following :—" With regard to the *Herald* office, I can recollect that about 1809 or 1810 it was on the north side of Bell Street. Young Dr William Dunlop was then a partner with Mr Hunter, and very well I recollect a fire breaking out in their premises one evening. We had great difficulty in obtaining water, but the fire was notwithstanding overcome. Dr Dunlop was very active, and got access to the roof of the house by going into a garret for the purpose of throwing buckets of water on the fire. Next day, he told his friend Samuel that while he was on the roof he lost his hold, and was sliding down, but was fortunately saved by a rhone, otherwise he would have been killed. 'Ay,' replied Samuel, 'I daresay; thae rhones kep a heap o' trash.'"

Mr Hunter was not only a man of wit but of weight,—eighteen stones. His salary as editor is said to have never exceeded £100 a year. On coming first to Glasgow he had joined a calendering business, and lost largely by the venture. It took many years of his savings in the *Herald* to pay off the liabilities then incurred.

Robert Wardlaw, a brother of the famous divine, was engaged on the staff of the *Herald* as reader. He died suddenly in 1839. On Mr Hunter's resignation, Mr George Outram, advocate, was appointed editor, at the same time being assumed as a partner. He was of a retiring disposition, but great ability, and his poetical writings are now known to a large circle. He died on 16th September 1856.

The *Glasgow Herald* held its centenary in 1882, when many interesting and memorable speeches were made. The following verses were published in connection. The beginning of the poem compares the work of the writing and printing of the newspaper to a shipwright building and launching paper boats. It goes on :—

"A hundred years ago,
The *Herald* craft first felt the sea breeze blow !

A hundred years ago ! as in a dream,
Our ships have floated down the human stream.

Through all that time, to every airt unfurled,
Their sails have ringed the waters of the world.
Where'er a Scottish foot has pressed the earth
And left the royal stamp of work and worth,
There has our craft been hailed with smiles and tears,
Through the long sea-toil of a hundred years.
And ever at the sight some Scot has blest
His dear old native city of the West,
Has jumped on board, and grasped with eager hand
The welcome traveller from his cherished land ;
Made merry with the new-wed folk he knew—
Danced with the blushing bride, and kissed her too ;
Dandled the new-born weans—for every trip
Some mother's darling sails in ilka ship ;
Paused with a saddened heart and drooping head
At the white face of some old comrade dead ;
Listened, with greedy ear and brightening face,
To all the gossip of the dear old place ;
And felt, despite a thousand miles of foam,
That once again his spirit was at home !

A hundred years ago ! as in a dream,
All things have changed along the human stream !
The thousand roaring wheels of traffic pass
Where the maids spread the linen on the grass ;
The mighty ocean-liners, outward bound,
Heave o'er the spot where windmill sails went round ;
The haystacks of the Trongait, where are they ?
Where the green meadows which produced the hay ?
Who were the last fond lovers (who can tell ?)
That kissed beneath the alders at Arn's Well ?
Oh ! quaint Arcadian city, which appears
In the bright vista of a hundred years !
The ancient merchant in his scarlet cloak,
Great wig, and silver buckles, if he woke
From his archaic slumber, would he know
Th' Havannah of a century ago ?

In that brave year of seventeen eighty-two
The stars looked out of smokeless heavens, and knew
The city by its nine dim lamps. At dawn
The glimmering vapours from the Bens were drawn,
And Lomond with a cheerful face looked down
Through the clear morning on the thriving town.
Gay stomachers and hoops, swords, cloaks, and wigs,
Moved in Sautmercat and the Candleriggs.
The city's worthiest kept the city's peace ;
Worshipful bailies served in the police.
Two postmen bore, a century ago,
The news of loss and gain, of joy and woe ;
Twice nine divines instructed men to live,
And preached the hopes that Faith alone can give ;

Sixteen physicians, when Death tapped the door,
Opened it wide !—sixty could do no more.

A hundred years ago ! as in a dream,
For ever and ever flows the human stream,
And all things change and pass ; but evermore
The constant shipwright stands upon the shore,
Launching his paper navies to the sea.
Bright as the past years may the future be !
May *Herald* sails, to every airt unfurled,
Still carry Glasgow round about the world !"

———

THE FOUNDRY BOYS.

FOR some years prior to 1865 various efforts had been made by philanthropic citizens for the social and moral improvement of the young lads and apprentices employed in the foundries and workshops of the city. It was found that in the streets and lanes where these lads spent their early years they were hedged around by evil influences and many temptations. In the vicious atmosphere in which they lived, lying and swearing were esteemed clever accomplishments; in their young minds the seeds of grosser vices were too readily sown, and in the absence of any educative or reforming influence these took deep root. Some of the lads while still too young for work attended Sabbath schools ; but whenever they entered the workshops and wrought at the same benches with their fathers and elder brothers, Sabbath school attendance became—in their eyes — a humiliation, and was usually discarded with the playthings of boyhood. Between the parents—some of whom attended church—and the little children —some of whom attended Sabbath schools—they formed an intermediate class, who were found lounging away their Sundays and leisure hours at close mouths or street corners, or outrivalling their elder associates in drunkenness and vice. The reclamation of these lads was a task of the greatest difficulty, requiring tact, skill, and patient endurance ; and it was the subject of earnest solicitude to their employers, who saw in them the coming generation of artisans. Amongst those who engaged in this arduous work was a young Glasgow mill-girl named Mary Ann Clough. In 1860 she got the use of a room below the factory where she was employed, and commenced a little meeting for "Working Boys." She brought to the work a sympathetic disposition, great kindness of heart, much experience in the homes of the working classes, and a pure high-toned Christian spirit that enriched her character and increased her influence. She succeeded beyond expectation, and the number of "Mary Ann's Boys"—as those attending her meeting were sneeringly termed by their fellow-workmen—rapidly increased. But in 1862, Mary Ann, on account of failing health, emigrated to Australia, and for a time the work which she had so well begun was allowed to languish. In May 1865 an attempt to revive it was made by a number of zealous working men. In addition to conducting a meeting for the lads on Sabbath afternoons, they opened educational classes for them during the week; and though their meritorious efforts and self-denying labours for a time met with considerable success, the attendance at these classes latterly declined, and the discipline became relaxed. At this crisis a meeting was held of those who were interested in the work, and as a result there was instituted on 21st November 1865 the Glasgow Foundry Boys' Religious Society.

The new organisation commenced operations by issuing a pamphlet setting forth the object of its formation. As there stated, it was the religious, educational, and social improvement of the neglected lads employed in the workshops and foundries of the city. This end it sought to accomplish by uniting, as parts of one system, religious classes and meetings during the Sabbath,—with educational classes, literary, musical, and social meetings, and banking and other provident facilities, during the week.

Evening meetings were made as attractive as possible, and were designed both to act as useful feeders and adjuncts to the Sabbath meetings, and to be in themselves forces for mental and moral improvement; but though their importance was fully recognised it was never exaggerated, but was always made subordinate to the religious department of the Society's work. This was the centre round which all the other agencies were ranged, and towards which they all converged. From the first, attendance at the religious meetings on Sabbath was made an essential condition of membership of the Society; and, on the other hand, it was as far as possible restricted to those who did not attend any other place of worship.

For a year or two after the Society was formed, working lads only were admitted to its meetings. Soon, however, they sought permission to bring their sisters and younger brothers along with them, and thus the Society was gradually led to include these also within the scope of its work.

Beginning in 1865, with 14 regular workers, 2 Sabbath forenoon meetings, and an average attendance of 100 lads, the Society has grown and extended, until to-day (1887) it has over 2,300 workers on the roll; it has 86 branch meetings scattered over the city—stretching from Possil Park to Crossmyloof, and from Rutherglen and Camlachie to Partick and Whiteinch; and it has over 22,000 lads and girls on its roll, with an average attendance of over 14,000 at the forenoon meetings. Further, stimulated by its success and emulating its example, Christian workers have started organisations in Edinburgh, Paisley, Greenock, and Dundee, and many other towns in Scotland; and during 1885 a former member of the Society successfully began a similar institution in Cape Town.

These outward manifestations of success are very gratifying to those who are engaged in carrying on the work, but they are trivial in comparison with those indications of mental improvement and spiritual reformation which are shown by many of the lads and girls attending the Society's meetings.

The circulating library scheme, instituted in 1884, has proved itself a success, 376 volumes have been divided into ten lots, and the branch meetings receive the use of one of ten sets for three months at a nominal charge, at the end of that period exchanging it for another lot.

Healthy recreation and innocent enjoyment are absolutely necessary to the development of a harmonious well-proportioned disposition, and to growing lads and girls entertainments and wholesome amusements are simply indispensable. It is the aim of the Social Reform Department to supply this want, to link together religion and recreation, while preserving to each its proper sphere. At the same time the attractions and advantages of the total abstinence movement are put prominently before the young people. One of the most arduous undertakings of this department is the Fair Week Excursion. By its means 824 senior lads and girls were last year enabled to exchange the grimy dust and ceaseless din of the city's foundries and factories for the music of the rippling waters on the seashore, and for invigorating walks amidst the enchanting scenery of the Western Highlands. For nearly a week they were enabled to revel in the unfamiliar sights of hills whose sides were clad with heather, fields carpeted with daisies, and glens and corries rich in wild ferns and summer flowers. And when they returned to the city, sun-burned faces and brighter eyes told of the renewed health which they had received during their brief and much-prized holiday.

CLINKS OF THE BELLS.

In 1569 it was "statute and ordanit be ye magistrats and council yat ye pynt of wine be sauld na darrer yan 18 pennys ye pynt."

.   .   .   .

4th July 1570.—"At ten hours at night there was ane earthquake in the city of Glasgow, and lastit but ane short space ; but it causit the inhabitants of the said city to be in great terror and fear."

.   .   .   .

The burgh records of Glasgow, as published by the Maitland Club, of about 1574, contain some curious passages. The quarrels, flytings, and acts of personal violence form by far the most conspicuous entries. Men strike women, women clapperclaw each other, and even the dignitaries of the town are assailed on the streets and in their council house. Whingers (swords) and pistols are frequently used in these conflicts, and sometimes with dire effects.

.   .   .   .

9th April 1574.—"Alexander Curry and Marion Smith, spouses, are found in the wrang for troublance done by them to Margaret Hunter, in casting down of two pair of sheets, tramping them in the gutter, and striking of the said Margaret." Surety is given that Alexander and Marion shall in future abstain from striking each other ; and " gif they flyte, to be *brankit*,"—*i.e.*, an iron bridle, with a tongue turned back into the mouth, put on.

Glasgow, 1574. — Every booth-halder (shopkeeper) is required to have in readiness within the booth " ane halbert, jack, and steel bonnet, for eschewing of sic inconveniences as may happen, conform to the auld statute made there-anent."

During the terrible rebellion in Ireland of 1641, many of the Scottish and English Protestants fled to Scotland for safety. In February 1642, the Council votes a sum from the city funds for behoof of the refugees. This not proving sufficient, on the 5th March the Corporation " ordainis ane proclamation to be sent throw the toun, to desyre all those quha will give or contribut any supplie to the distressed people that com from Ireland, that they cum upon Weddnes-day next, at the ringing of the bells,"—St Mungo's bells.

The plague had raged in 1350, 1380, and 1381 in Glas-gow with great severity. It visited the city again in 1645, just after the battle of Kilsyth.

On 17th July 1652 a great fire broke out and raged for several days in High Street, Trongait, Saltmarket, and Gal-lowgait. Colonels Blackmore and Overton, in a letter to Cromwell, state the damage as £100,000. He set on foot a subscription to relieve the consequent distress.

" A fire-engyne for slockening of fyre" was got from Edin-burgh in 1652.

From 1636 till 1700 certain families seem to have been supreme in the Town Council, namely, the Campbells, Bells, and Walkinshaws ; and among them the lands belonging to the city were pretty handsomely parcelled out. To the Campbells the Blythswood portion fell ; to the Bells the northern quarter—Cowcaddens, &c.; and to the Walkinshaws the lands of Barrowfield and Camlachie.

Sir Patrick Bell was provost when the Town-house and Tolbooth with its stately steeple were built in 1636. He died of the plague in London in 1640.

" His son, Sir John Bell, caused build the Guild-hall and

its steeple in the Briggait in 1659." The great fire occurred during his period of office.

1st October 1657.—A supplication was this day given in to the Town Council of Glasgow by one Robert Marshall, showing that he was willing, if permitted, to exercise the calling of a house-painter in the city. The Council, having had it represented to them that there was "but ane the like within this burgh, and not ane other in all the west of Scotland," gave Robert permission to wash and paint houses to any who pleased to employ him. The magistrates had a little before this time induced a printer to come from Edinburgh and settle amongst them. He does not seem to have succeeded, for in May 1660 they gave him fifty merks "to help to transport his guids and flitting to Edinburgh again." A few months afterwards Robert Sanders was encouraged to set up a printing-office in Glasgow, with a pension of £40 a year, "he to print gratis anything that the toun shall employ him to print." In 1660 they caused a plasterer to be sent for from Perth, "to come here for plastering of Hutcheson's Hospital."—*Memorabilia of Glasgow.*

Soon after Cromwell's death there is notice of a Glasgow pirate, who is represented as lying at the mouth of the Clyde, with seven guns, robbing all travellers going and returning from Glasgow to Ireland. He took seven vessels in a week, and General Monk writes to the Admiralty Commissioners his hope that they will "clap him up in some secure place." *

During the humiliating reign of Charles II., several Glasgow vessels having been seized by the Dutch, some merchants of Glasgow fitted out a privateer to cruise against the enemy. She was named the "Lion," and was a vessel of 60 tons burthen, had a crew of sixty, and carried six months' provisions, besides the following furniture :—5 guns, 32 muskets, 12 half pikes, 18 poleaxes, 30 swords, and 3 barrels of gunpowder. M'Ure gives her name as the "George," commanded by Captain Robert M'Allan, and the date of the letter of marque 23rd June 1665, and adds that several

---

* Calendar of State Papers, Domestic Series, 1659-60.

prizes were brought into Port-Glasgow. The ship may have changed her name before going into the new sphere of action.

⁘

In 1677 a malicious apprentice blacksmith, having been beat by his master, set the workshop on fire. This was at the head of the Saltmarket. The clock in the Tolbooth was destroyed, and great damage done. The populace broke open the prison doors, and enabled those in confinement, who were chiefly Covenanters, to make their escape.

⁘

In 1710 the townsmen of Glasgow made a harbour at Port-Glasgow, twenty miles down the river, to be a port of their own. In 1718 the first Glasgow vessel crossed the Atlantic. In the same year James Duncan, bookseller, introduced the art of typemaking in Glasgow.

⁘

About 1742 coal was sold in Glasgow at 1s. the cart of 10 cwt. In 1776 the price had risen to 3s. · The total quantity of coal consumed and exported at Glasgow at that date appears to have been 181,800 carts (see page 166).

⁘

About 1750 no street lamps were lit on Sabbath evenings, and the inhabitants were prevented by the authorities from walking on the streets during the day.

⁘

In 1755 Joseph Knight, a negro slave, was set at liberty in Glasgow. His master strove to have it declared that he was his slave, but came off second best in the legislation that ensued.

⁘

1777.—Until this year there were no flagged pavements in the city, and all the sewers were open except those under the piazzas.

⁘

1777.—At this time, besides the Kirk of Scotland, there were the following denominations in Glasgow, each having one place of worship :—Episcopal, Anti-burgher, Methodist, Glassite, Relief, Seceders, Independent, Anabaptist, &c.

⁘

From 1777 and until 1832, Glasgow, Rutherglen, Renfrew,

and Dumbarton had only one representative in Parliament amongst them.

. . . . . .

1782 was the year of the great flood. On the 12th March the Clyde rose twenty feet above its ordinary level. The Briggait was several feet under water, but was not so deeply immersed as the famous stone with "He River 12 Ma" seems to indicate. Some waggish mason is supposed to have built it away up at its present height as a joke. The house at the corner of Briggait and Saltmarket had a slice cut away when the latter street was straightened at the beginning of the century. The stone in question then made its extraordinary ascent of two stories. The flood was bad enough. Great trees were carried down the river; one young woman and many cattle were drowned. The village of Gorbals was a complete island.

. . . .

1782.—In this year the first umbrella seen in Glasgow was brought from Paris by Dr Jamieson.

. . . .

1783.—Glasgow Chamber of Commerce founded.

. . . . . .

1783.—David Dale and George M'Intosh brought M. Papillon, a Frenchman, to settle in Glasgow to introduce the Turkey-red dyeing of cotton yarns.

. . . .

There seems to have been a need of a Mr Plimsoll even in the old days, for on 19th May 1784, two Greenock ship-owners were found guilty at Edinburgh of having caused the sinking of ships, in order to defraud the underwriters. On the 28th July 1784 they were placed in the pillory at the Cross of Glasgow, where they were pelted by the mob with missiles of all kinds, after which they were banished from the country.

. . . . . .

On 7th July 1788 the first London mail coach pulled up at the Saracen's Head. From that day till 15th February 1848, when the Caledonian Railway was opened, the London mail ran Sunday and Saturday, summer and winter, fair weather and foul. In 1789 the journey was accomplished in sixty-six hours; in 1836 the speed was quickened, so that the up run was made in forty-six hours, and the northward journey in forty-two hours. Road travelling had then reached a perfection that the world had never seen before and will never see again. In posting it was impossible to keep up the pace, and though the mails scarcely beat some of the crack coaches in speed, they beat them all in punctuality. The Gallowgait shopkeepers could set their watches by the London mail as she passed their doors after a four hundred mile run.

On 18th November 1795, the Clyde rose again nearly as high, after a storm of wind, rain, and snow. A boy was drowned, and the new bridge at the foot of the Saltmarket was swept away.

On 18th August 1808, after a thunderstorm, there was another rising of the Clyde.

In 1797 Lord George Gordon came to Glasgow, and entertained a hundred anti-Roman Catholic friends in the Black Bull. He then went to Anderston, and returned by a torchlight demonstration to his hotel. There was only one Catholic chapel in Glasgow then.

The streets of Glasgow were first lit with gas in 1818. Before then oil lamps were in use, which on windy nights were often all blown out and the town left in darkness.

MODERN CLINKS.

During the American War many fortunes were made in Glasgow by blockade runners conveying stores to the Confederates and bringing out cotton. One successful run was looked upon as a great prize. As speed was the chief desideratum, an impetus was given to the building of very fast vessels.

Glasgow gave a generous helping hand to the patriots of Hungary and Italy in their struggles to attain their freedom, and no society of sympathisers in Britain or anywhere else were so prompt in supporting the various movements on the Continent as the Glasgow friends. As cash is the sinews of war, not once nor twice a rising that promised to be national proved abortive for want of funds, but the city of Glasgow always fulfilled her part of the bargain with promptness, as Garibaldi testified with gratitude ; and this quickhandedness in whatever she does is characteristic of the city.   No doubt it has been derived from the training of the people in mercantile habits, where rapid decision so often is necessary.

.   .   .   .

The enterprise and energy of Glasgow commercial travellers is proverbial.   In a country village on one occasion, the question of the moon's being inhabited was under discussion, when a worthy old woman, who kept a small shop, emphatically settled the question—" Na, na, there's nae inhabitants in the mune, or the Glesgy traivlers wid have found it out lang ere now."

————

Our book is finished, but how many Glasgow stories have been left untold, how many songs unsung !   In listening to the chimes of long ago, an attentive ear has caught the sound of many an interesting episode in the history of the town that it has been beyond our power to reproduce here.   And St Mungo's Bells have not stopped.   They still ring out strong and clear, with as true a Scottish accent as in the days of auld lang syne.

INDEX.

www.ingramcontent.com/pod-product-compliance
Lightning Source LLC
Chambersburg PA
CBHW030818020726
47499CB00006B/1974